How To Get Away with Scandal

Caroline Linden

PROLOGUE

The first time Evangeline was widowed, it was a relief.

She hadn't wanted to marry Viscount Cunningham; she hadn't even known him. He had been her father's choice—and very nearly her father's age—in a vain attempt to rein in Evangeline's "wild and ungovernable" nature, as Sir Robert Bennet had disapprovingly termed it. Her transgressions had ranged from sneaking a ride on her horse in her brother's old breeches to allowing a barrister's son to kiss her, rather passionately. Her mother had wept from the shame of it. Evangeline had also cried, and promised to reform, but to no avail. She'd been barely seventeen years old, and had met Cunningham exactly twice, when her father marched her down the aisle of the church to become his viscountess.

The best thing that could be said of their marriage was that it was blessedly short. They were horribly mismatched. Evangeline, young and outgoing, liked dancing, masquerade balls, and theater, the more outrageous the better. Cunningham preferred fishing at his Scottish estate, drowsing by the fire over a good book, and maligning the French with his cronies at his club. Within a year, neither wanted anything to do with the other.

One evening, four years after they wed, Cunningham went to bed early after dinner, complaining of indigestion. He never woke. A fatal attack of bilious dyspepsia, the doctor informed her the next morning.

Evangeline hadn't been there. Always cross when unwell, Cunningham had told her to leave him be, and she had been at a masquerade, drinking champagne with other gentlemen and a woman she suspected was a courtesan. It had been marvelous.

"And now you'll have to wear black," said her friend Fanny, Lady Woodville. Fanny was a dozen years older, and a widow with a substantial fortune. She had no children and her late husband's title had gone to a distant cousin, who had no interest in her; she was as free and independent as a woman could be. She was dashing and opinionated and Evangeline admired her greatly.

"Of course I will." She plucked listlessly at the black crepe they were attaching to bonnets. Cunningham would have wanted a decent mourning, and Evangeline felt remorseful enough not to deny him that.

"What a pity you look marvelous in black," remarked Fanny.

Evangeline pursed her lips to keep from smiling. "You shouldn't say that to a widow."

"I imagine a host of gentlemen will say it soon enough." Fanny leaned toward her and lowered her voice. "It's not as though you killed him."

"Of course not!" Evangeline hissed back, glancing fearfully at the closed door. "But neither am I . . ."

"Sorry he's dead?" supplied her friend when she hesitated.

"Heartbroken." Evangeline gave her a guilty look. "I feel as though the prison cell has been unlocked."

Fanny smiled in understanding. "It has been, my dear. And a world of consolation awaits."

The second time Evangeline was widowed was more upsetting.

She observed a proper mourning for Cunningham but then decided she was due a little freedom . . . and pleasure. The Earl of Courtenay—Court, he begged her to call him—was tall and fit, handsome and charming. He was only thirty-one, which seemed vital and young after Cunningham, and he pursued her with a very flattering abandon.

She never meant to *marry* Court. It was only an affair, to savor the sort of pleasures she had heard of, but never experienced with Cunningham. Court was ardent, romantic, and terribly good in bed, and she was careful to be discreet.

But not discreet enough. When her father called on her unexpectedly one day and discovered the two of them in a highly compromising position, he threatened to call out Court. Once again, over her furious protests, Evangeline was unwillingly married to a man she didn't love.

It was even worse than the first time. Court lost interest in her almost as soon as the ink was dry in the parish register. It turned out his favorite sport was chasing young widows and married ladies, and he didn't mean to give it up. Nothing Evangeline did deterred him: not pleading, not seductive attire, not the sight of her flirting with other men. By the end of the third year, Evangeline had realized it was hopeless, and had resigned herself to another empty marriage.

It came to an end the night Viscount Ambrose returned home early and discovered Court in bed with his young bride. Ambrose shot him—not in a duel, which would have been shameful enough but was widely accepted as the proper way to settle the issue between gentlemen—but right there in the bedchamber, while Lady Ambrose shrieked in the background. Then he'd had his servants dump Court, bleeding and naked, on the front steps of their house. Court had died, wrapped in a tablecloth, on his own dining table.

The scandal had been immense.

"This time you're truly free, don't you see?" was Fanny's consoling advice after the funeral.

Evangeline's father had died the previous year. After forcing Court to marry her, he'd never lifted a finger to prevent her husband from making a mockery of their marriage. Men were allowed all the wickedness, while women bore all the shame.

"Yes, *free*," she said bitterly. "Free to be called the Black Widow in every drawing room in London. Two husbands dead before their times! Young or old, no man is safe!"

Fanny waved that away. "Rubbish. You're still young and beautiful. You've got a handsome fortune. Enjoy it all."

Perhaps, Evangeline reflected, that was the only thing she could do. Scandal couldn't hurt her, not now. She'd grown a tough shell over the years, as people whispered that she was a foolish, flighty young bride, then a wanton widow just waiting to cause a scandal, and finally a scorned, shrewish wife who'd trapped an earl into marriage only to drive him into another woman's arms. If everyone already thought her wicked and immoral, she hardly had a reputation to protect.

And that meant . . . freedom. She could do whatever she wanted now—and not do anything she *didn't* want to do— such as marry again.

Evangeline vowed to herself that she would never make that mistake again.

No man was worth it.

CHAPTER 1

1812
London

She was going to be late.

It was her own fault, of course. She hadn't really wanted to come. While not exactly shunned, she was hardly a darling of society, and it was a bit of a mystery to her why she'd been invited to the Allens' benefit ball.

"Because Henry Allen made a wager at White's that he can raise more money from *his* benefit ball than Lady Cartwright can from hers," was Fanny's explanation.

"He must have wagered very dear, if he's willing to go to such lengths to win," Evangeline retorted.

"He always has done," observed Fanny. "No head for gambling, that one. Still," she went on, "you might as well go. It's for a good cause, after all, and I shall be there." When

Evangeline still hesitated, she added, "And it will give Beatrice Allen the start of her life, to see you walk through her door again."

"The invitation was in her handwriting," said Evangeline sourly.

Once upon a time, she had considered Lady Allen a friend. After Court's ignominious death, though, Beatrice had ceased responding to her letters. Evangeline had always suspected that was as much Lord Allen's doing as Beatrice's own wish, but it still stung. Allen had been one of Court's closest friends, and Evangeline knew he had been well aware of her husband's predilections. She suspected Allen shared them, and had probably recoiled from the scandal as a threat to his own affairs.

Beatrice, perhaps, had dropped her friendship to avoid having to consider her own husband's tastes.

Fanny smiled in victory. "Then she must truly want you to come, my dear."

So Evangeline gave in—or rather, fell for Fanny's manipulations yet again. And now she would be even later than could be called fashionable, as the carriage crawled in fits and starts along the street toward the well-lit house with footmen on the steps. Twice she nearly told the coachman to turn around and take her home, or on to Fanny's house, where she regularly spent the night to avoid the long drive to Chelsea. But still she dithered, until the last side street had been crossed and there was no alternative but to stop in front of the Allens', screw up her courage, and go inside.

"Lady Allen," she cried warmly, clasping fingertips with the hostess. "How delightful to see you again."

Beatrice Allen faltered a moment before she assumed a smile that was both simpering and stiff. "And you, Lady Courtenay."

"I was so delighted to receive your invitation," she went on, unable to resist a little vengeance. "Such a worthy cause! How very noble of you and Lord Allen to take it up. Those poor, *dear* children deserve every bit of your support." Beatrice's eyes flashed murder. "And ours, of course—we fortunate members of society who can afford to provide for them," Evangeline added lightly.

Lately, Lord Allen had decided he was a philanthropist and patron of sundry impressive causes. He'd named this event a "benefit ball," with the noble (somewhat ostentatiously so) goal of raising funds for the Foundling Hospital. Allen had probably contributed a few bastard children himself to such homes, and Evangeline had to admit the irony was partly what had persuaded her to come.

"Yes," said Beatrice Allen, her face and her tone wooden. "Of course. We are so pleased you accepted."

You hoped I wouldn't have the nerve, thought Evangeline as she tipped her head graciously.

Well. Enough of that ancient history, water so far under the bridge that it had reached the ocean.

Evangeline knew she'd been invited for her wealth, not for her company. Tonight, she decided she would not care. Defiantly she smiled and nodded at a passing matron who was goggling at her. There would be dancing, a singer, and several prominent guests of honor making short speeches about their work, and then an appeal for funds. She'd come to enjoy herself, no matter why she'd been invited.

"At last!" Fanny reached for her hands and pressed them as Evangeline joined her. "Thank God you've come. I thought I might perish of boredom."

She smiled at her friend. "You are never bored."

Fanny rolled her eyes. "Beatrice wanted that opera singer—do you know the one I mean? The Italian woman?" She waved one hand impatiently at Evangeline's blank look. "Quite scandalous, I believe. Allen refused to have her. He's such a tedious fellow." She lifted a glass of champagne from a passing tray and raised it in salute.

"So there's not to be a singer?" Evangeline also took a glass. She adored champagne. It was one of the few unadulterated pleasures of these events.

"No, only musicians. Lord Allen invited several speakers." Her expression said everything about that. "It will be a miracle if I survive the evening without dozing off."

"Hush," said Evangeline with a laugh. "We mustn't slight the speakers before they even begin."

"You're far more patient than I," murmured the other woman. "Although one of the honored guests is rather handsome. When he speaks, I shall be very attentive."

"Oh?" Evangeline flicked open her fan. "Which one?"

"An explorer. He's to speak of his journeys in Africa tonight. Or the Arctic. I'm not sure, and it doesn't matter."

Now that would interest Evangeline. She looked around in real hope. "How fascinating. Who is he?"

"His name is Campion," said Fanny. "Swiss, and extremely handsome, did I mention it?"

"Twice, as a matter of fact," Evangeline replied.

Fanny grinned. "Let us beg an introduction."

Evangeline laughed and agreed.

Arm in arm, they made their way through the crowd. Fanny had embraced her reputation as an eccentric, knowing the vast Woodville fortune made her a highly favored eccentric. Tonight she wore peacock feathers in her turban and a gown of spangled green silk that blazed brightly in the candlelight. Evangeline aspired to be so dashing.

Lord Allen appeared in front of them. "Lady Woodville! How do you do?"

"Very well, sir, although I was anticipating the soprano, and I hear you refused to have her." She turned away from his suddenly pinched face to scan the room. "Where are our guests of honor?"

"Mr. Cambridge, the geologist, is with Lady Allen," said their host, recovering his poise. "And Lord Michael Layne, the famed astronomer, is just by the windows there."

"I've no interest in geology or astronomy," she told him bluntly, even as he raised one hand as if to lead her to meet either man. "Where is the explorer?"

"Ah, Richard Campion!" Lord Allen rocked on his heels, looking pleased with himself. "The king has just bestowed a knighthood upon him."

Fanny raised her brows. "Excellent! Allow me to present Lady Courtenay to *Sir* Richard, then. She's been longing to make his acquaintance—quite fascinated with the Nile, don't you know."

Discomfort flitted over Allen's face as he was finally forced to speak to Evangeline. "Lady Courtenay. How good of you to come."

"Thank you, sir." She smiled, ignoring his strained

expression. "I hope we shall do a great deal of good tonight for the children's home."

"What? Oh yes, yes." He cleared his throat. "I see Campion now, Lady Woodville. If you'll pardon me, I shall bring him to make your acquaintance." He gave a quick bow and shot off through the crowd.

"Do you think he'll come near us again tonight?" asked Evangeline in amusement.

Fanny snorted. "He wants two hundred pounds from me tonight. He'd better come near, and bring that explorer with him, if he intends to collect it."

"I know you'll give it anyway, for the children's sake," said Evangeline.

Her friend gazed at her in affront. "Of course I will. But there's no reason I can't make Allen work for it, is there? It was his decision to throw a party instead of simply asking for subscriptions." She went back to studying the room. "Besides, he's too young for me, but I do believe you will like him."

"Lord Allen?" Evangeline shuddered. *"Never."*

"No, the explorer!" Fanny tapped her arm with her fan. "Mark my words, he's a fine one."

"I've no need of a man, thank you." This was an old conversation between them.

"Need! Who said anything about *need*?" Fanny scoffed. "I speak of *wanting* a man."

"It sounds to me as though you want him for yourself."

"Don't be ridiculous! I'm far too old for him." Fanny's keen gaze swept up and down Evangeline. "But you're not."

Fanny was only twelve years older than Evangeline, but

sometimes she took an excessive delight in imagining various romances and love affairs for her. "I feel twenty years older just hearing you say that," she said tartly.

"At least you don't look it. Here he comes." Fanny arranged her face into a welcoming expression as Lord Allen approached, a tall, sandy-haired man barely visible behind him. Evangeline finished her champagne and glanced around for a servant or table where she could dispose of the glass. It was advisable to consume more wine, rather than less, before speaking with members of the ton, but it was always so awkward navigating introductions and conversation while holding a glass. A footman whisked up beside her and she gave him the glass with a grateful look.

"Lady Woodville, Lady Courtenay, allow me to present to you Sir Richard Campion," Lord Allen was saying.

Evangeline was smiling, her hand already extended, when she looked into Campion's face.

Oh Lord, she thought with a sinking heart.

"My lady." Campion gazed back at her with crystal blue eyes. Tall, lanky, handsome as sin, and Evangeline felt the heat of his smile deep in her bones.

"Sir." She ducked her flushed face as she curtsied.

"He has come to regale us with stories of his adventures into the dark heart of Africa." Lord Allen pushed out his chest proudly. "I expect you've seen all manner of beasts and savages, eh, Campion?"

"Yes." He flashed a distracted smile at his host before his gaze veered back to Evangeline, like a compass needle seeking north.

Still scrambling for composure, Evangeline put up her chin. "Savages! Of what sort?"

Campion seemed startled. "Oh—some of the tribes treat each other quite brutally, ma'am. They are fierce warriors."

Evangeline thought she'd take some of the dragons of the ton over any warrior, any day, for fierceness. God above knew they'd shredded *her* to pieces.

"Savages," drawled Fanny, sounding disappointed. "How novel. Do explorers ever encounter anything else? Are there no civilized, gentle, or even kind peoples in the greater world?"

"I daresay not," Evangeline cut in as Lord Allen's face turned a shade of puce. "Do the Africans cut off their peoples' heads with guillotines, as the French do? Or make public spectacles of hanging them, as the English prefer?" She tipped her head to one side and tapped one finger to her lips as both men stared at her in dumbfounded silence. "It would take some doing to surpass the brutality of our own land, I imagine."

Lord Allen seemed to be choking. "Yes, well, that is a very harsh view, Lady Courtenay. I beg your pardon, my ladies, but I must introduce Sir Richard to our other guests." He forced a laugh. "He's much in demand, you know!"

"Of course we know," said Fanny tartly. "That's why you invited him—to lure in the rest of us."

Evangeline was fighting hard not to laugh at the men's expressions, Lord Allen offended, Campion thoroughly nonplussed. She smiled at them. "That is quite true! And see how splendidly it has succeeded. Go forth and encourage people to donate generously, Sir Richard, for the children's home."

"I—" His disconcerted gaze jumped to Fanny, then back to Evangeline. "Naturally I will, madam." His words were faintly clipped with an accent she hadn't noticed before.

Because you could barely hear him over your own racketing pulse, ninny.

"Right, right!" Lord Allen shuffled sideways, as if he would break into a run at any moment. "This way, Campion." And he all but dragged the explorer away.

Fanny watched them go. "The man was tongue-tied— almost an idiot. It seems unlikely his speech will be exciting." She turned to Evangeline. "Hopefully he recovers his wits when he's not staring at you."

She snapped open her fan and tried to chase the blush from her face. She could still feel her blood throbbing recklessly. "I've been rendering people speechless for years. Why should he be any different?" She gave a tiny huff. "Allen likely put a flea in his ear about wicked women. He must have thought he'd encountered one in the wild tonight."

Fanny snorted. "If so, I think he'd like to make a closer study of the species. I may be old, my dear, but I am not blind."

"You are not old," Evangeline returned, "merely a busybody."

Her friend laughed. "That's a privilege of age. I never felt at liberty to speak my mind until I reached the age of forty."

"And then it all came spilling out without subtlety or discretion." She pointed her fan at her friend. "Do not start plotting to throw me together with Richard Campion."

"Plotting." Fanny snorted again. "As if I need to! He'll do that himself, mark my words."

Evangeline said nothing. The last man who had looked at her with such open interest, and elicited such a response in her, had been Court. Fortunately for her, this time she knew better than to fall for it.

The speakers surpassed Fanny's dour predictions. Mr. Cambridge, the geologist, spoke with enthusiasm and energy about his studies. Lord Michael meandered a bit, talking rather a lot about the ancient Greeks and their study of the heavens, but Sir Richard lived up even to Fanny's hopes, portraying himself as a modern Gulliver, visiting foreign lands where he was both humbled and honored, and speaking with a genuine reverence for all he'd seen.

"I never knew ordinary rocks could be so enervating," said Fanny as the crowd applauded at the end. "But that Campion fellow was worth every farthing, even before he dances with you."

Evangeline choked on a sip of champagne. "*Fanny.*"

"Don't scold me," murmured Fanny, her gaze fixed over Evangeline's left shoulder. "I'm only giving you warning."

Evangeline turned around and came face to face with the explorer, just as Fanny had said.

"Lady Courtenay." He bowed. "I hope you remember me."

"Of course." She smiled brightly—too brightly, probably. "It's not even been two hours since we met."

"Indeed?" He smiled back. Her heart took an unwanted leap at the sight. His eyes crinkled and an endearing little dimple appeared in one cheek. He was, as Fanny had said, very handsome. Devastatingly so, to be honest. "It seemed much longer to me."

"That must be a sad judgment on the company present."

"Not at all." His smile dimmed a degree, but his eyes never wavered from her. "It is entirely due to you."

The nerve he had. She found it both alarming and exhilarating. "How so?"

"I could not stop thinking of what you said earlier. You were the only person to encourage me to solicit donations for the children. I entreated everyone with whom I spoke to make a generous donation to the cause—a foundling home, is it not?"

"Well done, sir," she said in mild surprise. "The children deserve it."

"Thank you for reminding me of them," he went on. "It added greatly to my satisfaction with the evening to think of the unfortunate children who may be helped as a result of my speech. I confess that I do not always attend closely to the deeper purpose behind these evenings."

Not many people did. There were some genuine patrons of charitable causes, but Evangeline would have guessed that most of the guests tonight had come for the entertainment. They would donate fifty pounds for the benefit of the children, and then spend several times that at the wine merchant or the modiste.

"May I beg the pleasure of your hand in the next dance?" asked Sir Richard.

Evangeline looked at his extended hand, in its pristine glove. Fanny, the traitor, had managed to melt into the crowd and leave her alone with the man. "I don't think that would be wise, sir."

"No?" He lowered his voice. "Are you a dangerous creature?"

"Why, yes!" She pursed her lips in irritation, even though she'd meant to smile and laugh it off. "I am. I thought Lord Allen would have warned you."

"I have scaled Mont Blanc and sailed around the Cape of Good Hope." His dimple reappeared. "I am not afraid of a beautiful woman."

She hesitated. Merciful God, he was attractive. He met her gaze so directly. His eyes were such a startling blue because his face was tanned. His hair was not blond, but brown, bleached by the sun. At his collar, where it curled, she could see the darker color. Most London gentlemen were as pale as the ladies.

This man was not a Londoner, though. He had climbed mountains and sailed oceans and ventured deep into uncharted territories.

If Fanny were right about him . . .

Perhaps she might not mind being studied more closely for one evening.

"Once," she said, placing her hand in his.

"Only once?" He led her to join the formation of couples. Evangeline caught the startled glances of the fellow guests and dancers.

"We are not acquainted, sir."

The smile he gave in reply was nothing short of wicked. "We shall become so, while dancing."

She sighed and tried to look unmoved by his flirting even

as it made her heart speed up. It had been a long time since a man flirted with her like this.

With some effort she concentrated on the dance. It was a long country dance, where all the couples took their turns going up and down the set, which gave her plenty of opportunity to see the shocked expressions around her. Evangeline had stopped caring what the matrons of society thought of her, but it still irked her that they couldn't even allow her this one, eminently ordinary and respectable, dance without openly displaying their horror. She told herself it must be envy, because Sir Richard was without doubt the most gorgeously virile man in the entire room.

Perhaps the entire country.

"What brought you to England?" she asked when the dance brought them together for a few moments.

"My sister," he replied. "She married an Englishman and begged me to visit her here. She wished me to meet my young nephews."

"How very devoted."

He grinned. "She encourages me to attend events like this. It is her hope that I will become attached to English society and not wish to leave."

"Don't you wish to leave?" She smiled as she said it. "Of course you do. An explorer won't discover much of interest in England."

He gave her a searing look. "I would not say that."

The dance sent them separate ways. Evangeline caught Fanny smiling smugly at her, and it took real effort to keep from glaring back at her friend. She went through the motions of the dance, newly aware of the curdling glances sent her way by every other woman in the set. That wasn't right. She hadn't done anything remotely scandalous tonight.

When she was back by her partner's side, she tried to talk of mundane things. "Your presentation was well-received," she told him.

"Was it?" He smiled faintly. "It seems my travels are the most interesting thing about me." He lifted one shoulder in an almost Gallic shrug.

I doubt very much that's true. Evangeline's pace slowed as her interest grew. "You must know they are fascinating, especially to the British who have felt penned in by wars these last several years."

"Then they should go where the wars are not. Do you find my travels fascinating?"

"Yes," she said before she could remember to be more sophisticated and disinterested. "Very."

He touched her arm, even though the dance didn't require it, and she felt it like the hot burn of a candle flame, passing too near her skin. "I would be very pleased to tell you more about them."

She should be wary. He was wildness and temptation and sin, his fingertips barely brushing the skin above her glove and setting off the most ferocious want she'd felt in years, which unsettled her. She was a woman of two-and-forty now, not a headstrong girl seeking adventure or a young widow yearning for passion. She saw Campion's flirting for what it was, recognized the desire in his focused gaze, and that should have protected her against all of it.

It did not.

She had been tarred by scandal before, sometimes for things she had done, but largely for things she had not done; she had tossed her head and declared she didn't care, but the gossip and stares had left their mark. Tonight, it felt as though the part of her that had been weighed down by all that had finally reached the breaking point.

"Indeed," she murmured, letting her fingers slide through his as she released his hand. "I believe I would like that."

The dance was ending; they made their bow and curtsy and Sir Richard offered his arm to escort her from the floor. "May I call on you?" he rasped, ducking his head slightly until his lips almost brushed her ear. Evangeline shivered; he wasn't much taller than she, just enough that if she turned her head and raised her chin, her lips would meet his.

She could barely think; her skin prickled and her breath seemed to sear her throat dry. "Yes," she said. "Good evening, sir." She slipped free to hurry to Fanny's side, reaching for her fan.

Fanny glanced at her, then looked closer. "My dear, are you ill?"

"Yes." Evangeline seized a glass off a passing footman's tray and gulped down the champagne, hoping it would cool the fever sizzling inside her. "I feel a fit of madness coming on."

Keenly Fanny peered past her. "Heavens above," she said, sounding pleased. "He has aroused your interest."

Aroused was a terrible word to use now. Evangeline gave her friend a dark look.

Fanny turned fully toward her and took her hand. "My

dear, you have spent your whole adult life as a resentful wife or an unhappy widow," she said quietly. "You are not dead. You deserve to enjoy yourself."

Evangeline hesitated. "But I made such a mistake with—"

"This is a different man."

"And it ended so very badly with—"

"Break it off with Campion before he can break it off with you," replied Fanny, who knew all her history with men, as well as all her fears and worries. "The man is leaving England within the week," she added gently. "He won't be here to cause a scene or become a nuisance. Really, he is quite perfect for your needs."

She was having a hard time arguing with that. "I don't dare," she whispered.

Fanny, the old busybody, understood again. "Take him to my house. Your usual room is always kept ready for you." She released Evangeline with a final squeeze. "And Brumley will throw the man out, forcibly if necessary, if he causes any trouble."

Evangeline's mouth was dry. Could she really do this? Without thinking, she glanced toward the man in question, and found his vivid blue gaze fixed on her.

Fanny waved one hand. "You may thank me later." And she strolled away without a backward glance.

Evangeline felt as if every candle in the room was shining on her, highlighting the sinful desire warming her blood. Taking a strange man home to bed him, with no thought of anything else! Other women had done it, but she'd never been this brazen herself. She had always let the men pursue her; even Court had had to woo her for a month before she gave in to his seduction.

Sir Richard hadn't even tried to seduce her. She felt his desire like the heat of a red-hot stove, but all he'd actually asked was to call on her . . .

Strangely, that calmed her. He hadn't pushed her—nor would he. This time, *she* would be in charge. This time she would set the rules, and this time she would not get burned by the affair. She was a widow; she was her own mistress; and she hadn't had a lover in over a year. She wanted Richard Campion with an intensity that both unsettled her and thrilled her—and he was leaving London, virtually on the morrow. From his speech, she knew his journeys lasted for years at a time, plenty of time for him to forget one wicked widow in London. There was no risk of consequences.

She turned on her heel and looked his way. He hadn't moved since she left him, and as if he'd heard a summons, he came straight to her, winding efficiently through the crowd.

"Perhaps," she said to him, "you would care to pay your call on me tonight." Her heart thudded as she gazed at him. "Perhaps . . . now."

His breath caught. His throat worked. "Now," he repeated.

Feeling like a different—wilder, reckless, lust-crazed—person, Evangeline nodded. "My carriage is outside. Will you come?"

Color rose in his face. "Now?" he asked again in a guttural tone fraught with meaning.

She nodded, meeting his eyes squarely.

"Yes," he said. "I will."

Chapter 2

Evangeline, familiar with the Allen house, slipped out the servants' entrance and made her way to her carriage. She had nearly ten minutes to ponder the madness of what she was doing, feel a sense that she should stop it, and finally revolve back to her initial plan before Campion tapped at the window where she had hung a handkerchief to alert him.

The footman had barely closed the door on them before Sir Richard had her hand in his, his fingers dancing up her wrist as he unbuttoned the glove. He peeled it off as she seized the lapel of his coat and pulled him toward her.

"This is madness," he whispered as his bare hand wrapped around her neck, turning her face up to his.

"A most delicious madness," she agreed, before his lips were on hers, his arm around her waist, pulling her across the carriage into his lap as if she were the merest slip of a girl. Evangeline felt delirious as he pushed up her skirts.

"Where are we going?" he asked. She was straddling him

on the narrow seat, her arms around his neck, his hand on her bottom, his mouth on her breast.

"A friend's home," she said breathlessly. "There's plenty of time to make your escape . . ."

"Escape?" He raised his head. Even in the dim light of the single lamp, she could see the blue of his eyes. He pushed one hand up her thigh, his palm hot. "I have no wish to escape any moment you will grant me."

His accent had grown stronger, his words tighter clipped. With her skirts up around her thighs, Evangeline could feel how aroused he was—nearly as much as she was, she realized with a shudder.

"In that case," she whispered, winding his sandy hair around her fingers until she could tug his head back. "You will be mine until morning." She bent her head and sucked at the skin of his neck, gratified by the tremor that went through him.

When the carriage reached Fanny's home, she recovered herself in time to step down from the carriage calmly, grateful for the darkness that hid her flush. She was a frequent guest at Fanny's home, staying over so often she had a regular room. Brumley, the Woodville butler, barely blinked when he opened the door and beheld them.

"Good evening, Brumley," she said, holding her head high.

"Good evening, my lady," he replied, taking her wrap, then Sir Richard's coat and hat. The explorer appeared a bit wary now, waiting for her. "May I bring you anything?"

Evangeline smoothed her hands down her skirt. Goodness, what should she do? She had no idea how seductions were managed. She had always been the one pursued, never the pursuer. "Brandy, if you please."

The butler bowed and she headed for Fanny's elegant drawing room. Brumley was taking this all very much in stride, and she wondered how many times Fanny had lent friends her home for secret assignations.

Sir Richard followed, closing the door behind him, but when Evangeline faced him she could see that his mind, at least, had cooled and resumed some sensibility.

"Where—?" he began, but she stopped him, pressing her fingers to his lips.

"This is my friend's home," she said. "I am a frequent guest. There is nothing amiss."

He eyed her, his pulse throbbing rapidly but his gaze alert. "No? You have done this often?"

She gave a nervous little laugh. "No, never." She fingered the lower button of his waistcoat. "But I want it tonight. I want *you* tonight."

He blinked a few times. "My lady . . ."

"My name is Evangeline," she whispered, sliding the button loose and letting her fingers graze his stomach—flat, firm, the muscle leaping at her touch.

"Evangeline," he breathed, his hands brushing her shoulders, only to jerk away as the door opened.

"Brandy, my lady," said Brumley blandly, setting down his tray without meeting anyone's eyes. "Will there be anything else?"

"Thank you, no," she managed to say. "Good night, Brumley."

"Good night, madam," he replied, backing out of the room and closing the door.

For a moment the silence seemed deafening, then Sir Richard strode to the table and poured two healthy measures. "Santé," he said, handing her one.

Evangeline raised the glass and bolted down the brandy in one go. Warm and rich, it melted away the faint hesitation that had crept in, and steadied her nerves. She was a mature, adult woman, an independent widow. Fanny was right; she deserved some pleasures.

She faced her companion. Lord above, he was gorgeous, his sun-bleached hair falling to his collar, his body tall and lean and hard, his blue gaze fixed on her. "Am I too forward?"

He paused. "No."

She put down her glass and laid her hand on his waistcoat. "I brought you here to make love to you."

His chest expanded under her palm. "Why not to your own house?"

She gave him a slight smile, tipping her head to one side. "It's too far away."

"Gott im Himmel," he breathed, and cupped her face, pulling her to him, and she kissed him with the sort of reckless daring she hadn't felt in years—decades.

His mouth was hot, demanding—overwhelming. For all her singed reputation, Evangeline hadn't been quite as wicked as many people thought. It took only a few minutes for her to feel swept away and out of control. His hands were in her hair now, sending the dark locks loose down her back. She forced his jacket open and shuddered at the flex of his muscles under his linen shirt. He ran his hands down her back and pressed her to him and she moaned at the feel of his body against hers, hard and ready.

"Not here," he rasped, his lips on her ear. "Where—?"

Feeling drunk, she nodded. She grabbed a lamp and took his hand and led him, hurrying through the hall and up the stairs and into the room she usually stayed in when she visited Fanny. Thankfully they met no other servants, and she dragged him inside and closed the door. There was no fire, but it was a warm evening and she felt no chill at all as she set the lamp on the desk and stripped off her remaining glove.

Sir Richard turned her around, pushing her up against the door, holding her there with his own body. Evangeline's bones seemed to wilt as she felt him surrounding her.

He coiled her half-undone hair around one hand and tugged, but as soon as she turned her head his hold eased. He brushed his lips against the nape of her neck, and exhaled a long, hungry sigh that sent tremors through her. She tried to turn but he stopped her; his hand replaced his mouth, his palm on her nape and his fingers around her throat. Evangeline went still, her heart banging so hard inside her chest she was incapable of moving.

Holding her there, he leisurely began working on the buttons at the back of her bodice. It was a fairly small bodice, but he took his time. As he opened each button he stroked her skin, sometimes stooping to lick her, all of which made her vibrate with anticipation.

"Pull it down," he whispered as he tugged loose the ties.

Clumsily she worked the dress down her arms, letting the dark red silk drift to the floor.

"Again," he ordered, untying the petticoat.

She did, feeling the cool air on the backs of her bare legs. Her chemise was short, barely to the top of her thighs. She gasped and went up onto her toes as his hands slid down and cupped her bottom, squeezing firmly.

"Get on the bed," he growled, stepping back.

She took a steadying breath. This was what she wanted . . . almost exactly. She straightened from her pose—splayed against the door, arms and legs soft—and stepped out of the puddle of her garments. Self-consciously she tugged her chemise down, over her round hips and plump thighs. It had been a while since a man saw her naked . . .

If he doesn't like what he sees, better to learn it now, she told herself. She put back her shoulders and turned to face him, chin up and hands clenched at her sides.

He was staring at her with smoldering eyes. His gaze moved down, lingering on her breasts, then down. Then back up, and down once more. The concentrated lust on his face was undeniable, and her confidence—and her own desire—roared back.

Deliberately she plucked the remaining pins from her hair, shaking her head to let the dark locks fall. If she had one vanity, it was her hair, beautifully thick with just enough curl to be fashionable and still richly dark, despite a few gray hairs. The fierce, focused look on his face was ample reward.

Feeling unspeakably desirable and marginally more in control, she strolled to the bed, letting her hips roll, feeling the heat of his attention. She lay back on the mattress, propping herself up on her elbows and watching him.

"Now you take off your clothes," she said. And she set the heels of her ivory satin slippers on the edge of the bed and let her legs fall open.

Sir Richard prowled toward her, peeling off his jacket as he came. With maddening deliberation he undid the buttons of his waistcoat and stripped it off. It took him an eternity to undo his cuffs and unknot his cravat.

"Faster," she demanded in a whisper.

He raised one brow. "You might help."

Her chin came up. She slid to the edge of the bed and reached for the buttons on his breeches. As she unfastened them and shoved the fabric down, he pulled the shirt over his head and stood before her, bare-chested, eyes glowing with lust, breeches clinging to his hips. She met his gaze directly, boldly, almost challengingly, as she cupped his ballocks in both hands and lowered her head, looking away only as she closed her lips around the head of his erection.

His chest expanded with a sharp hiss, and his fingers tangled in her hair. He was pulsing with heat in her mouth, and she ran her tongue along the crest. With a muffled curse, he shoved her backward, sending her sprawling on the bed.

He leaned over her, and she lifted one foot to his chest to stay him. "Everything off," she said softly.

He flipped off her shoe and ran his hand reverently down her calf, still in her white silk stocking. She gave a little push, even though his touch had sent a white-hot jolt of lust through her.

This time he obeyed with some speed. His clothing

would be in a terrible state; his breeches were inside out, she was sure she'd heard ripping when he pulled off one stocking, and everything was crumpled on the floor. Then he stood there for her inspection, arms raised. "Like so, madam?"

Evangeline almost moaned with desire. Good Lord, he was a handsome man, and perfectly made, save for an inch-wide scar that ran just above his hip. He was lean but solid, his shoulders just the right width. His skin was as sun-bronzed as his hair, all the way down his lean hips. She pictured him swimming naked off some tropical shore. "Yes," she whispered. "Like that."

She caught a flash of feral smile, and then he was above her, his hands on her, then his mouth, then his weight. It made her gasp, to have a man like this again, and then *he* made her gasp, with his leisurely, relentless exploration of her body and how to make it sing.

He brought her to climax twice before he hooked her leg over his arm and slid inside her to take his own pleasure, riding her with hard, long thrusts that scrambled what was left of her brain. When he finally growled in his own release, her face was wet with tears from her unprecedented third ecstasy. Not even Court, who'd been a skillful and passionate lover—before their wedding, at least—had played her this well.

"Merciful God in heaven," she gasped faintly.

He turned his head to press his lips to the inside of her knee where it curled around his neck. Evangeline hadn't even known her body could still bend the ways he'd made it do. She hoped she could walk in the morning. "Ja, God is very good to us, is he not?" He uncoiled her from around him and held her close, full length, and kissed her. "You are spectacular."

She laughed. "I must say the same to you!" On impulse she kissed him back, much harder. "Never have I benefited so much from one of Lord Allen's parties!"

"Nor I." He grinned lazily. "Who cares for a journey through Moscow when there are such wonders to be found in London?"

"I daresay you won't think of it once you are besieged by the daughters of Russian Cossacks," she replied in amusement.

He snorted softly. His hand was around her breast, just cupping it lovingly while his thumb stroked her nipple, and Evangeline thought she could become addicted to that simple pleasure alone. "I have no longer any desire to go to them. Not when you are here."

She laughed. "Nonsense," she said with a contented sigh. "You spoke so eagerly of it! I am astonished you haven't already left."

"No." He kissed her shoulder, his mouth lingering. "I never want to leave this bed, let alone London. I am your conquest."

A small chill went through her. She only wanted one night of pleasure from him—and oh my, had she ever got it. It had never occurred to her that he might want more.

Of course, a man said many things he didn't mean when he was naked and still slick with sweat from making love. In the morning, they would both pretend he'd never said them.

"Nonsense." She adopted a brisk tone. "I don't need any

flowery seduction. This is enough." She gave a small laugh. "More than I expected, even! Of course you will go on your expedition, just as I will go on with my own life." She twisted in his arms to press a kiss to his jaw. "And this night shall be a treasured memory for me," she whispered with a smile, tracing the edge of his jaw with one fingertip. "As I hope it will be for you."

He looked at her for a long moment. "This night only?"

She put her hand on his cheek. "Darling," she said in surprise. "Of course."

The thin line between his brows deepened into a frown. "No. I do not understand. Why?"

She blinked. "Why? Why *not*? What else can you possibly want?"

"This." His hand moved down her side to caress her hip. "You. Again and again. Do you not want me?"

"Well, I won't deny that," she admitted, unconsciously pressing into his hand. "But this is really all it can be, don't you see?"

"No, I don't see." He sat up, looking more puzzled than angry. "Have you no interest in me other than lovemaking? You listened most attentively to my presentation and invited me to call. Was it a pretense?"

"No, of course not," she protested, blushing a little. "I find your adventures fascinating." She paused. "I find *you* fascinating. But it's tempting fate to spoil this . . . this one beautiful thing we shared."

He stared at the lamp for a minute, the light gilding his sharply cut features with gold. Then he glanced at her, his expression easing. "I see. You do not trust me. That is understandable. You do not know me." He rolled back over her, brushing the hair from her face tenderly. "I will prove myself to you," he murmured. "I will be your friend as well as your lover. You will see."

"Oh my," she burst out a little uncomfortably even as her stomach leapt at the feel of him atop her again. "That's not what I was trying to say . . ."

"No, no." He smiled. "I will call on you. I will bring my journals and tell you about my journeys down the Nile, through Tripoli, into the Alps, and about Switzerland, my home. I will show you my sketches and tell my stories. I will sip all the tea and eat all the dry biscuits, and we will talk for hours."

"Oh my," she said in surprise. "Have you really been all those places?"

He smiled. "Yes. Since I was ten years old, I have been driven to explore—first the area around my home, then farther and farther away. It is a thrill beyond compare to see the glorious variety of people and creatures around the world."

"I can only imagine." That was true. Cunningham had dragged her away to Scotland, but not to Edinburgh or even Glasgow; he'd taken her to his old and drafty fishing lodge. Court had never stirred from London. But she'd read about such places in books and magazines—stories likely written by people like him, she realized—and they sounded amazing.

He had been running one finger along her collarbone, and now he pressed a kiss to her jaw. "I will listen to you as well. You intrigue me. I want to learn everything about you."

Court had said such rubbish, when he wanted to get

under her skirts. It was a little unnerving that Sir Richard said it *after* he'd achieved that, but no less reliable.

"Goodness," she said with a forced laugh, still striving to brush off the whole thing. "Of course you don't."

"I do," he said calmly. "I know you are a widow, with no husband to make jealous. I know you are beautiful and sensuous, and also independent and clever and good-hearted."

"I—what?" She was disconcerted by his words.

He nodded. "Allen told me you are a widow. Naturally I asked him, because I was fascinated by you the moment we met. The rest, I saw for myself."

Good Lord. Allen would have told him she was scandalous and evil, a wanton widow with a large fortune, courtesy of two prematurely dead husbands. Suddenly Evangeline wondered if Allen had encouraged Sir Richard to seduce her, with an eye on getting her to financially support his travels. She wouldn't put it past that man.

Again she made herself laugh. "Don't be silly. I'm much too old to fascinate you! How old can you even be?"

"Two and thirty," he said, jarringly. He was ten years her junior. *An entire decade.* She'd been married before he was out of short pants.

She didn't want to hear more. She didn't want to argue, or talk at all. With a sudden motion, she pushed him over and sat atop him, straddling his hips. "I must take advantage of such rash, impetuous youth."

"I—I accept," he gasped as she took him firmly in hand. He was already swelling again, growing hard and ready.

This was all she wanted from him, she told herself as she

moved above him, reveling in the touch of his hands on her skin, in the concentrated desire in his face, in the exquisite pleasure he wrung from her body. This time she made love to him until he could barely speak, holding down his arms and staving off her own climax until he was thrashing beneath her, begging to touch her in a jangle of English and German. When she relented, he returned the torture until she gasped in release.

He pulled her into his embrace and mumbled something against her shoulder as he fell asleep. Evangeline gave in to temptation and rested against him for a while, savoring his close embrace, his body warm against hers and his hair soft against her cheek.

But when she heard a distant clock strike three in the morning, and his breathing was slow and deep, she slipped out of bed and left, determined to end things her way.

CHAPTER 3

Richard Campion awoke in an unfamiliar bed surrounded by an unfamiliar perfume. It took him only a moment to remember whose it was and how he'd got there. He rolled over and buried his face in a pillow, inhaling deeply. *Evangeline.* Even her name hinted at the almost-religious fervor she'd stoked in him.

Never in his life had he been so struck by a woman. She was tall—perhaps that was it? She'd looked him straight in the eye when she invited him to come with her, right then, walking out of Lord Allen's ball where he was a guest of honor. And he'd done it: gone without a single thought for his host or the guests who were waiting to speak to him or even for his companions, who had presumably stayed at the ball and wondered at his disappearance.

But no; it was not just Evangeline's stature. She was beautiful. Magnificent. Mischievous dark eyes that sparkled with some private amusement. Dark hair that looked darker still against her bare skin when it fell to her waist. Lush, generous curves that made him want her the moment he laid eyes on her. A full, soft mouth that mesmerized him whether she was telling him to take off his clothes or whispering that she was too old for him.

He had been in London for over three months now. How had he never met her before last night? Every other ball his sister Clemency had begged him to attend had been dull and ordinary. If he had known England contained a woman like her, he would have given in to his sister's pleading and gone to parties much sooner.

He bounded out of bed and threw open the drapes so he could find his clothes. He had to see her again—although first he had to find her. He shook his head at himself; he had slept much too late, and too deeply, if he hadn't heard her rise. She must be downstairs at breakfast.

All thought of his impending journey to the steppes vanished from his brain. All desire to see the yaks and yurts of Mongolia was gone. He had the clarity of a man who had just seen a holy vision and meant to devote his life to worshipping it.

There was a tap on the door when he'd got his clothes turned right side out and back on. "Ja!" he barked, buttoning his breeches. "Come!"

The man who had admitted them the previous evening came in, a tray in his hands. "Good morning, sir. I've brought coffee, tea, and the morning papers, if you care for them." He set it down on the dressing table.

"No, I don't," he said as he pulled on his waistcoat, which looked as though a wagon had run over it. Karl would be appalled, as it was his one fine suit of clothing. "Where is

Lady . . ." He blanked on her title for a moment; *Evangeline,* was all he could think. "Lady Courtenay?"

"She has left, sir, but she bade me make you at ease. She expresses her regret that she cannot see you off and wishes you a safe and rewarding journey."

He froze, hands on his buttons. "Gone? When did she leave?" It was still early. His sister, Clemency, rarely rose before noon the day after a ball. And Evangeline had spent half the night making energetic and uninhibited love. He'd heard the clocks chime two in the morning.

"Yes, sir." The butler poured a cup of coffee, expression serene and unreadable. "Is there anything else I can bring you?"

"Yes," he said. "Her direction."

Sunlight gleamed off the man's spectacles. "I'm very sorry, sir, I do not have that information."

Very well. He could find it elsewhere. "Is my host awake? I wish to pay my respects."

"Alas, Her Ladyship is unable to see you. She extends her apologies and also wishes you a safe journey."

Annoyed, Richard drank the coffee as he yanked on his stockings. Lord Allen would tell him. Allen had already told him about her, and the man disliked her enough to tattle even more.

But he was wrong about that. At the Allen house, the butler reluctantly roused Lord Allen only after Richard insisted, but it was all for naught.

"Lady Courtenay?" Allen groused. "What can you want with her?"

"Her direction."

Allen eyed him sideways. "Stay away from that woman. Man to man, she's a siren, luring you to your doom."

Richard frowned. "Rot."

Allen lowered his voice. "Mind you, I don't blame a fellow for wanting to ride her once or twice. Those bubbies are magnificent . . ." He cupped his hands suggestively in front of his chest, then dropped them and grew stern. "But her late husband was a friend of mine, and he told such tales of her shrewishness and demands . . . Keep your distance, I strongly advise you."

Richard glared at him.

Allen seemed to think he'd been persuasive. His tone softened. "I like you, Campion. First-rate adventuring, and a damned sight more exciting than a London Season. I tell you this for your own sake. Consider Lady Courtenay like one of those savage beasts you met on the African savannah— splendid to behold, but wild and untamable, and liable to kill any man who gets near enough to catch her." He yawned and scratched his belly. "And your ship leaves within days! Your man was telling me about the tides and the North Sea, and we can't have you missing it over any woman, let alone that one! I've a mind to come to the docks and see you off myself."

"I want to see her before I leave," Richard repeated.

Allen's cheer faded. "Campion," he said, almost sternly. "The woman buried two husbands, good men both."

Every widow had buried at least one husband, by definition. "Why is that a mark against her? Did she kill them?"

Allen's face turned red. "I—I never said that!"

Richard nodded. "Then I see no scandal. Men die all the time."

"She's a termagant!"

"I have faced hungry lionesses in Africa. I am not afraid of a lone Englishwoman."

Allen stared at him. "Then you're a damned fool," he said, wrapping his dressing gown around him. "And I'll not contribute to it. Go to Mongolia. See the Huns. They'll be more hospitable than she will be. I'm telling you now, she's not worth the trouble. You'd do well to get this strange taste for trouble out of your mouth." He stalked from the room without another word.

Steaming, Richard went home. When he reached his lodgings, Gerhard was railing at the porter who had already taken much of their baggage to the docks, including apparently a box of navigational instruments Gerhard wished to keep by him. Karl, his manservant, did protest when he saw Richard's evening clothes, crumpled and abused, but even he was distracted. He helped Richard into fresh garments and bundled away the evening clothes; they would not be going on the journey, but into storage.

Gerhard quit his argument with the porter when Richard said he was going out on an errand. "What errand? I have completed everything that needs doing. We wait only upon the tide now. Are you going for food? I also am hungry."

"No. I have to do something," he said, putting on his hat. "A personal matter."

Gerhard had been his friend since both were small boys.

He ran after Richard. "You go to see Mrs. Murray, to bid her farewell?"

"No." His sister had declared that she would come to see him off at the docks, and neither her husband nor Richard had been able to dissuade her. He didn't need to go see her.

"Who, then?"

Richard hesitate. "A woman."

Gerhard's ears pricked up. "Who? One of the wealthy ladies who has sponsored our journey? Perhaps I should see her, too."

"She is not a sponsor."

"Ah. Then she is a lover. Which one did you choose? The blonde lady from the theater?"

Richard frowned. He barely remembered the woman who had invited him to her home, murmuring that her husband was in Wales for the month. He never accepted those invitations. Gerhard thought that was a bit prudish of him, but Richard wanted no part of a jealous husband. "No."

Gerhard kept up his protests and questions, dogging his heels and blustering about the tides and schedules until Richard managed to outpace him. He had an excellent sense of direction and retraced his steps to the house where he had spent the previous night in erotic bliss, but the same butler who had poured his coffee that morning said the lady of the house was not at home. The man remained obstinately ignorant of Lady Courtenay's direction as well.

He turned away in bitter disappointment. Whom could he ask? Not his sister. Allen had refused. He didn't know many people in London, and certainly none well enough for him to confide his very deep, very personal interest in Lady Courtenay.

Grudgingly, he returned to his lodgings. He sent Karl to ask at the post office, but the man returned with no information. She did not have a house in London, it seemed.

His trip through the North Sea and the Baltic into Russia and the far eastern provinces had been planned over the previous eight months. Most of the funding for it came from people like Lord Allen, who wanted to stand on the dock and wave them off and boast of their connection to the brave explorers. Gerhard was rumbling about nailing him into a cask and shipping him to Copenhagen. All his belongings had been either put into storage or packed for the journey. Beleaguered and thwarted on all sides, Richard boarded the ship.

He was coming back to London, in a year and a half—two years at the most—and he would not forget Evangeline.

CHAPTER 4

1816
London

"We must find you a house."

Richard Campion raised his coffee cup and sipped, gaze fixed determinedly on the window. A cart full of chickens was rumbling past, squawking loudly, as if they knew they were on their way to imminent death at the market.

He sympathized.

"A good house," Clemency went on. His sister had been on this theme for a fortnight, and he'd begun tensing up every time she opened her mouth. Her prodding was like the stick of a needle, a minor irritant at first but now it had raised a welt that burned and irritated. "Something near us."

But not too near, Richard thought.

He ought to regret thinking that, but he could not. He'd come back to England for Clemency, after the French invasion of Russia had scrambled all his travel plans and prolonged the journey from a planned year and a half into nearly four. When Clemency's letter had finally reached him in Urga, it was already a month old, and its tearstained message had made him head west at once. Clemency's husband, Daniel, had died of a sudden illness, and she begged Richard to return to England to help her untangle his affairs.

He had returned expecting to find his sister prostrate with grief; instead, he found her still grieving, but no longer prostrate, and bent on getting him to stay. He was beginning to wish he'd remained among the yaks.

"Such a lot of trouble to go to," he said aloud, "taking a house when I am not certain I shall stay here more than a few weeks."

"No!" Her brows drew together, and she turned to the other man at the table. "Gerhard, you must persuade him to stay."

Richard shot his friend a look that warned him not to join the battle. Gerhard turned mournful eyes toward Clemency. "How can I, if he is idiot enough to wish to leave?"

"You can," she cried, reaching to put her hand atop his. "You are so dear to both of us—even if Richard will not admit it—and I know you will think of something. You have never disappointed me, Gerhard, never."

He fairly glowed under her regard. "I hope to never! I will try to talk sense into him."

Richard shook his head and went back to watching the bustling street outside. It was the touch on the hand that did it, he knew. Gerhard had been pining over Clemency since she turned sixteen, but the great oaf had been too cowardly ever to say anything to her. Instead he'd become a loyal puppy, grateful for any scrap of her attention.

Clem, oblivious creature, had never noticed he was madly in love with her. She'd married a dashing Englishman who'd come to visit their father in Zürich during one of the lulls in the wars, and Gerhard had never recovered.

"I don't like this city," Richard said. He could feel both of them plotting their attacks, Clemency because she never liked to be thwarted and Gerhard because she had touched his hand and thrown fuel on the smoldering embers of his dreams. Richard hoped he was never so pitiable over a woman.

"Something in Paddington," suggested Clemency. "Lady Ardle was telling me about the most delightful picnic she went to in Paddington. It was quite rustic."

Great God. Clem's idea of rustic meant stone cottages and landscaped parks, within a convenient hour's drive of a town with a proper number of fashionable shops. If he took a house there, his sister would bring parties to picnic on his grounds.

"I can send word to an estate agent to help locate such a place," offered Gerhard, who was gazing at Clem raptly.

"Not Paddington," said Richard shortly. "Somewhere out of town, or I won't go." He realized he'd have to view a place or two. Nothing else would satisfy Clemency, and despite her desire to dictate his life, Richard *was* fond of her.

She was eight years younger than he, and he had spoiled her as a child. Before their father died, he had impressed upon Richard that it was now his duty to look after Clemency. Since she'd been newly, and happily, married to Daniel Murray at the time, Richard had thought this would mean an occasional visit, gifts for her children, and regular letters from wherever he roamed.

Papa ought to have given that speech to Gerhard, who already thought Clemency a veritable goddess he would die to protect. Now Richard might have to take a house in London, of all places, or bear not only his sister's tearful disappointment but the lashes of guilt from his late father's spirit as well.

"Greenwich, then, or Richmond," Clemency forged onward. Richard lifted one shoulder noncommittally, and she gave a happy chirp of delight. "Gerhard, do find an estate agent."

"I will do it today," he promised her. Richard gave him a sour look and Gerhard only grinned back, like an idiot. If Gerhard had to choose between pleasing Clemency and anything else, he'd please Clemency no matter the cost.

"Verräter," he said.

"Ja, natürlich," agreed Gerhard. Richard could call him any bad name under the sun, not just a traitor, and Clemency's smile would wash it all away for Gerhard.

"Don't do that, Richard, you know I don't remember my German," Clemency reproached him. "What did you say to him?"

"I urged him not to delay." He leaned forward and set down his coffee cup. "Since we've clearly exhausted your hospitality here and you are eager for us to be gone from your home." Gerhard had come along to England as a matter of course—it was difficult to dissuade him from anything involving Clemency, let alone a widowed Clemency—and the two of them had been here ever since, in her house in Clarges Street.

"What?" She blinked at him. "Oh no! I'm so glad to have you here—do *not* think I long to be rid of you, Gerhard," she added, reaching to not just touch, but clasp his hand this time. "Never. You will always be welcome in my home."

Gerhard melted under her imploring gaze like butter on a stove. "I would never do anything that displeases you, Mrs. Murray."

She gave him a wide, grateful smile. Richard idly thought that if he stabbed his table knife into Gerhard's thigh under the table, his friend would neither notice nor care. He might even be pleased, for then Clemency would fuss over him and hold his hand and stroke his face.

The door opened and two boys burst in, chasing each other with wooden swords in hand and shouting at the top of their lungs. Clemency shot to her feet. "Gabriel! Rafael! Stop that at once!"

"He destroyed my fort!" cried Rafael, swiping at his brother.

"I did not! You kicked it over, because you're a clumsy ox!" Gabriel ducked and twisted around his mother's chair, evading her reach.

"Liar!"

"Idiot!"

Richard watched his sister's face turn red, then pale, and

her mouth began to quiver. He put out one arm and caught his nephew as Rafael ran by him. Gerhard snared Gabriel on his side of the table, and both boys went quiet, breathing hard and glaring at each other.

"Who built the fort?" Richard asked.

"I did, sir." Rafael seemed to wilt in his hold. "Of blocks. It was this high." He held out one hand at his waist.

"That is excellent building," Richard told him. He turned to his other nephew, now sitting on Gerhard's lap. Gabriel was two years younger than Rafael, but was just as tall and bigger, with his father's fair hair and energetic nature. Rafael was the cleverer of the two, dark like his mother and more sensitive than his boisterous brother. "Gabriel, what did you do?"

"Nothing, sir," muttered the boy.

"Really?" asked Gerhard mildly, and Gabriel flushed.

"I only tried to add a turret. But Rafe got angry and charged at me, and the whole side of it collapsed. It was not my fault!"

"It wasn't your building to change!" cried Rafael. "Build your own!"

"You used all the blocks!"

"Stop," said Richard firmly, and the boys fell silent. "Gabriel, would you like Rafael to interfere with your activities?"

The boy's lower lip came out. "No, sir."

"Rafael, was it worth destroying your entire building merely to stop him from adding something?"

The boy in his arm blinked away tears. "No, sir."

"Gabriel, you will put away all the blocks by yourself,

and you may not use them for three days. Rafael, you will compose a letter to your mother apologizing for such disruptive behavior. Do you not see she is upset by this fighting, which has not solved anything?"

"Yes, sir," they mumbled.

He released Rafael. "Go."

Gabriel climbed off Gerhard's lap and the two of them picked up their swords and left. Rafael paused by Clemency's chair. "Sorry, Mama," he whispered.

She bit her lip and put her arms around him, kissing his cheek and smoothing his hair. Gabriel got his hug in turn. When the door had closed behind the boys, she turned to Richard. "This is why I need you to stay in England, close to me. They need a man's guidance."

"They need to be outside, not penned up in a schoolroom in the city," he replied. "Find a house for yourself in the country, where they can climb trees and swim in a pond and get dirty and tired as boys should."

She flushed. "I would lose them in the country. They would never come home."

"Besides, I will not be here if I take a house of my own." Richard glanced slyly at Gerhard. "Perhaps they need a new father."

Gerhard's face went pink even as he glared murder at Richard. Clemency sat upright in astonishment. "What?"

"Someone to build towers with them and show them how to swing their wooden swords. Someone who will be kind to them and teach them how to behave like gentlemen." Richard watched his sister blush. Gerhard sat in stubborn silence, but he deserved to be tweaked. Perhaps if he thought

Clemency was looking to marry again, he would untie his tongue and finally say something to her. It never failed to amaze Richard that his friend, so fearless on the side of a mountain, so unflappable on the deck of a ship in the middle of a storm, grew starry-eyed and stupid under Clemency's sparkling smile.

"Let me know when your estate agent has found something acceptable," he said, rising from the table. With any luck, he would be able to locate and secure passage on a ship back to the Continent, or perhaps to South America, before that happened. "Hercule, come," he said, and his dog scrambled up from where he'd been lying by the hearth.

"What would be acceptable to you?" she protested as he went to the door.

"In the country. Out of view of other houses. On top of a hill. With plenty of trees." *That ought to occupy her for a good while,* he thought, and made his escape, Hercule at his heels.

Chapter 5

It took her nearly a month, but Clemency called his bluff.

He went to view the first house purely to put a stop to her pleading. It was a rather grand manor house, the sort of house that required a lady, several children, and a full staff to feel like a home. Richard pointed out that there were precious few trees on the manicured grounds of the place, and his sister rolled her eyes at him.

The second house was more like an old castle, with drafty halls and winding staircases and suspicious stains on the flagstone floors. Even Clemency agreed it was *too* rustic.

The third house was too close to London—he could see the city from the sitting room windows, he pointed out to Clemency, which quite spoilt his decree that he didn't want to see any neighbors. Clemency scowled and told him not to be a hermit, which made Richard laugh.

The fourth house was possibly the worst of the lot. The roof was swaybacked, there was no library, and the dining room's narrow windows faced north, giving it a dreary air even on a hot sunny day.

"This house does not reflect well on England as a country," he said to his sister.

"You're being impossible," she told him crossly.

"I would be more at home in Zürich," he replied. "I like the houses there."

"No! I will keep looking. There will be a house to suit you somewhere near London." She stormed out, leaving Gerhard gazing at Richard with censure.

"Why are you determined to find fault with every house she presents? She is making a great effort to satisfy your demands."

"You did all the work," Richard pointed out. Gerhard had become Clemency's personal manservant since they returned.

"For her," explained his friend patiently. "She wants you to stay. Do you feel the pull of the mountains so strongly that you can deny your only family?"

Restlessly he paced to the window and gazed out. "It is that I feel no pull *here* other than Clemency and her children."

"You are famous here." This, Gerhard knew, was a tender subject, and Richard scowled at him for raising it. Several years ago, some lord had got hold of one of the travel memoirs Richard had written—his trips down the Nile into Africa, with its vast savannas and deserts, and his subsequent encounters with the native peoples and creatures—and raved about them to everyone of his acquaintance. Soon his accounts of scaling mountains in the Alps had also become famous. To indulge Clemency, he had attended some parties and given a few speeches about his adventures, and as a result he'd become a minor celebrated figure in London.

This delighted his sister. Richard knew she was scheming to get him invited to parties again, to speak about his recent travels into Mongolia. She had hinted that he ought to go on a speaking tour of England. Richard would much prefer to sail back to the other side of the world and be slaughtered by Mongol tribesmen.

"What is wrong with this house?" Gerhard asked when Richard said nothing. "It is miles from London."

"Barely four."

Gerhard raised one shoulder. "That is miles. It is in the country, as you asked. The grounds are wooded and the house sits on a hill." He squinted at the window. "And I cannot see any neighboring buildings at all."

"The trees obscure them. Wait until winter when the leaves have fallen."

"Regardless, this house fits your requirements. Did you lie to Mrs. Murray?"

"No," he grumbled.

"Take a walk. See if the grounds suit Hercule." Gerhard looked at the dog, sitting obediently in the doorway. "He would be glad to be away from town."

That was true. There was no place for a dog like Hercule in London, who would be more at home herding sheep in the Berner Alpen foothills. Richard had acquired him from a farmer outside Bern, on his journey west to England.

Hercule looked at him, his tail beginning to wag in appeal.

Richard sighed. "Very well. I will take a short walk."

"And when you come back, try to think of your sister," Gerhard added. "She will be most distressed if you leave. She needs you."

Richard raised his brows. "Then perhaps you should console her, Gerhard. Hercule, come." He walked out with his dog before his friend could reply—or punch him in the face.

The day was splendidly bright and sunny, very warm. He peeled off his jacket as he left the neglected garden around the house and followed a path down the hill into the trees. The estate agent had pointed out the hedgerow-lined lane that bounded the property, and indicated that the grounds covered three acres west of it.

It was cooler in the trees, but he still tugged at his cravat, wishing he could strip off more clothing. Gerhard's words rumbled around in his mind like boulders in an avalanche. Was he right about Clemency? Did she need him? Richard had always thought not; Clem had always seemed to know what she wanted, and had a plan to get it. Witness Daniel Murray, her late husband. It had taken only two months from the night they were introduced to the day Murray asked for her hand. Murray was dead now, but Clemency, while still grieving, was recovering her spirits.

But her boys . . . They were almost eight and ten, and would be taller than their mother in a few years. Gabriel especially looked more and more like his father, and Richard acknowledged that might it be striking Clemency in the heart. She had loved Murray.

He exhaled. He'd told her to get them a new father. He'd

meant it to tweak Gerhard, but it surely hurt his sister. He didn't want to do that. She was the only close family he had left, and he loved her.

Would it harm him to spend another year or two in England, helping raise his nephews? No, he admitted. It might even be his duty, as he had no wife or children of his own and Murray's family kept largely to their estates in Scotland and had shown little interest in the boys. Perhaps Gerhard was correct, ulterior motive notwithstanding.

Hercule ambled on ahead. He was not fast, but he was thorough, sniffing carefully under every bush and tree. Richard watched the big dog explore and did not miss the wagging tail. Hercule was a young dog, and he was happy out here, away from the narrow streets filled with carriages and carts and yapping spaniels.

A splash up ahead caught his attention. Another splash, and then another. A pond, he guessed. Just the thing on a hot day. He imagined taking off his boots and stockings and cooling his feet, and his steps sped up as Hercule loped ahead of him. This property grew more appealing with a pond.

By the time Richard came in sight of the water, glittering like a mirror in the clearing, his brain was just putting together the rhythm of the splashing to deduce that the pond was occupied not by ducks or fish, but by a person. Perversely annoyed, he strode forward. Someone was trespassing.

The woods ran up to within a few feet of the water's edge, enclosing the modest pond in a ring of leafy privacy. It made an ideal swimming spot. Richard paused there, watching. The pale arms of the trespasser languidly emerged from the water to stroke lazily along. The glare off the water's surface was blinding, but he narrowed his gaze and made out a dark head, and the flash of a foot.

The swimmer turned toward the shore, swam a few more strokes, and stood up.

He should turn away. He should close his eyes, or make a discreet sound of warning. He did neither. If a crocodile had bitten him at that moment, he couldn't have made a sound.

The woman wore a shift, but it was soaking wet and absolutely transparent. It clung to her lush, generous breasts, rosy nipples visibly taut. As she sloshed toward the edge of the water, the shift shaped itself to a neat waist, full round hips, long legs with a mesmerizing shadow at the top of her thighs. She was running her hands over her head, slicking back her long dark hair, and as he watched, tongue-tied and mesmerized, she turned her face up to the sun, a smile of pure joy on her lips, and recognition hit him like a bolt of lightning to the head.

It was Evangeline. Lady Courtenay.

Chapter 6

He must have made a noise, for her head whipped around toward him.

For a moment neither moved. A drop of water fell from her eyelashes and slid down her cheek, over her jaw, and he watched it as if in a trance. Once, he had put his mouth there, where that droplet slid.

"Oh dear." She cleared her throat. "How mortifying."

That was not the word that came to his mind.

"A gentleman would turn his back," she added in mild reproof.

"I—" He could barely remember how to form words. "I've an order to view this house," he said stupidly, motioning behind him with one arm, even more stupidly.

Pink colored her face, but she smiled. "And here I am, trespassing upon your future property! I do apologize. It shan't happen again."

Richard just stared like an imbecile. It was difficult to think, with his mind fogged by lust and a renewed feeling of the frustration and fascination of four years ago, but he was slowly realizing that, while he knew exactly who she was, she did not recognize him."

At his prolonged silence and frankly rude staring, she gave a small sigh and walked out of the water. She bent over to pick up something from the ground, and his knees almost gave way at the view of her magnificent bottom through the translucent shift. Then she swirled a blue dressing gown around herself, and his brain finally lurched into order again. Belatedly, he turned, until he could just barely see her from the corner of his eye.

"You live nearby," he said.

"Oh dear." She sighed in chagrin. "Let's not make this more awkward than it already is, sir."

"No need for awkwardness." It was hard to form a thought. He kept thinking of her breasts. And her hips. And the way she had once rolled him over and ridden him until he thought he would die of the pleasure of it. He dared a peek over his shoulder just as she knotted the sash of her dressing gown.

"No?" She arched one dark brow as she put on her shoes. "You look stunned speechless, I'm afraid. I do apologize again."

"It was my fault," he managed to say. "I did not expect anyone here. When I heard splashing, I thought it must be a boy shirking his chores—"

She looked at him, still wearing that contrite expression. "Very reasonable. I succumbed to temptation—the heat, the sun . . . Alas." Another wry smile. "It shan't happen again, sir. You have my word."

"Wait," he said, scrambling for sense. She turned away and started toward the trees. "Evangeline!"

She flinched, glancing back in shock.

He reined himself in. He was behaving like a madman; no wonder she was alarmed. He put back his shoulders and gave a brief bow. "Forgive me, Lady Courtenay."

Then, finally, recognition flared in her face. For a moment she stared, her eyes wide, and then she gasped, saying something under her breath that he didn't catch, before turning and hurrying into the trees, lost to his sight within minutes.

Richard reached out and gripped a nearby sapling until the bark bit into his palm. Blessed Mother of God. He was dazzled, shocked, and aroused in equal measure. Hercule nudged his other hand and he almost leapt out of his skin.

"Right," he said, realizing he was breathing hard. "Come, Hercule. We must return to the house."

He had only somewhat recovered by the time the house came into view. Gerhard was waiting in the garden, arms folded impatiently.

"Where have you been? Mrs. Murray became fatigued in the heat."

"What?" Richard shook his head. "Where is she now?"

"Inside." Gerhard followed as he strode back into the house. "You took forever. She is resigned that you will reject it. I told her you do not like this place, and perhaps that is rational. It is small and dark and unappealing. But she is trying to please you. Be gentle when you tell her. You may not care about her hopes and feelings, but I do."

"Be quiet, Gerhard." Richard opened the door of the small, ugly morning room.

Clemency's head popped up from the wingback chair she was sitting in, a fan clutched in her hand. "There you are!"

"Are you well, Clem?" Distracted, he nodded at her, then walked out of the room, looked around the hall, then went back into the sitting room. "Where is the estate agent?"

"Here, sir." Mr. Fields hustled in behind him, flushed. Gerhard must have fetched him, for his friend was close at the man's heels.

"Good." Richard put out his hand, and instinctively the agent clasped it. "I'm taking this house. Send the lease at once."

Chapter 7

Evangeline had never been particularly demure or modest, but walking out of the pond nearly naked in front of a strange man was a new experience, even for her.

She gave herself a firm scolding as she hurried home. She ought not to have gone to the pond in the first place. It was not on her property, and she could have no idea who might be wandering the grounds.

She ought to have paid more attention to her surroundings as she swam, instead of floating lazily along, reveling in the supposed solitude and cool water.

She ought to have worn a proper bathing costume instead of stripping down to her shift.

She ought to have remembered a comb. Her hair was sure to be a nightmare by the time she reached home.

She sighed. She ought to have recognized that man at once and drowned herself in the deep end of the pond.

What a pity he had to recognize *her*. Surely he'd seen sights far more memorable in the four years since that one night. She was astonished that he remembered her name—and just as astonished by the thrill that pulsed inside her when he said it. *Evangeline.* Rough and desperate with longing, the way it sounded in her mind when she allowed herself to think of her wild night of sin, when she'd seduced the famous explorer.

She pulled the dressing gown tighter around her and nearly leapt over the stile at the crumbling stone wall. The wall wasn't quite the boundary between Humberton Hall and her own property, but she told herself to think of it as such from now on. Humberton Hall had stood empty for months. The locals called it Tumbledown Hall, which probably explained why.

With a small sigh of regret, she looked back at the overgrown path that led to the pond. She did not have a pond of her own, and she would miss it on days like this. Even if he didn't take the house, she'd never be able to swim there again without imagining him stepping out of the trees and looking at her as if they'd ravished each other the previous night, rather than on a cool April night four years ago.

Solly was waiting for her by the bathhouse, settled on a bench in the sun with her sewing. There was another thing she ought to have done—brought her maid with her, for modesty's sake. Evangeline almost laughed at herself on that thought. After a lifetime of bucking convention on that score, she was hardly likely to change now, not even if ten men should catch her swimming naked in the pond.

"Did you have a pleasant swim?" asked Solly as she approached.

"The water was quite refreshing." She wouldn't say

anything about the man, and hopefully he would do the same for her. She opened the door of the bathhouse and stripped off her dressing gown again, and the shift as well this time.

"I thought you would be longer." Solly shook out the lengths of toweling that had been warming in the sun.

Evangeline thought of what might have happened if she'd stayed longer at the pond and stepped right into the plunge bath.

The frigid water took her breath away. Teeth chattering, she dunked her head twice, running her fingers through her hair to rid it of any leaves. Usually she loved the sudden shock of the plunge bath, where the icy water left her heart racing, her skin tingling, and her mind clear.

But not today. Today, nothing seemed likely to erase the image of Richard Campion, staring at her with desire in his eyes.

A fortnight later, Richard was installed in his new house, which he had learned bore the pretentious name of Humberton Hall. He'd heard someone in the solicitor's office whisper that it was a wreck. No matter. He didn't care if every chimney smoked, the roof leaked, and the whole place was haunted. Now that he'd found Evangeline, he wasn't about to lose sight of her again.

She had to live nearby. She'd walked to that pond in a dressing gown. Sure enough, a few casual queries to Mr. Fields, the estate agent, cleared it up. Lady Courtenay owned a comfortable manor house called Wyndham House two miles from Humberton Hall. In fact, the two estates bordered each other. The agent was more anxious to tell him about the other local gentry, and Richard was forced to listen to it all, because Clemency was there and delighted by his apparent interest in his new home.

"Just think, you can now hold your own salons," she enthused. "And dinner parties!"

"I hardly think so."

She waved it away. "I will be your hostess, naturally. Leave it all to me, Richard, I will only invite the best people!"

"That is what I fear," he said, and she laughed.

Clemency, Richard had to admit, was very happy. He overheard her and Gerhard, a few times, puzzling over why he'd chosen this particular house, with its small rooms and poor light and hideous wallpaper, but she'd spoken not a word of doubt to him. She simply unleashed a small army of servants and tradespeople on the place to repair and paint and polish everything, and then somehow filled it with furniture, whence he knew not where. She found a Viennese woman called Frau Loretz to keep house for him, and a marvelous chef who'd spent a decade in the Piedmont. Richard supposed she feared that any delay or inconvenience would give him time to change his mind and wriggle out of the lease, but he did not enlighten his sister.

The first fine day, he told Clemency he was taking a walk to explore his new grounds, and set out to find Wyndham House, leaving Hercule shut up in the parlor. He discarded the idea of trying to follow the path from the pond, not knowing where on Lady Courtenay's property it might lead him. He intended to walk up the front drive, very respectably, and call on the lady. The way he'd intended to do years ago.

Along the way he took the opportunity to gather a bouquet of wildflowers. Not only did it conceal his motives from Clemency, it felt spontaneous, almost romantic. Even if he did have to tramp through more than one field in search of a pleasing variety of flowers.

Eventually he came upon the winding drive, leading to a comfortable manor tucked out of view of the road, surrounded by trees and a garden that rambled out of its confines. He studied the facade and decided it looked almost Viennese, with the baroque window surrounds. Wisteria climbed one side of the house. It gave the air of a dreamy retreat, as if the owner wished to hide away. Instinctively he liked it.

He strode up the drive, suddenly a little nervous. They hadn't really conversed at the pond, and it occurred to him only as he came near the house that he didn't know if anything he'd learned about her four years ago was still true. Was she still unmarried? Was she still unattached? Was she still attracted to him? He'd been gone for four years, and while he'd thought of her a great deal, perhaps she had forgotten him.

Well. Too late now. Fortunately he was accustomed to making his way along one step at a time, with no certainty where the next step would land. At least this time there was no icy crevasse yawning in front of him.

The front door of the house stood open to admit the

breeze. He rapped the knocker, twice, then cautiously stepped inside when the echo had died away and no one responded.

It was a wide hall, clear of furnishings and fuss. The floor was worn stone, the walls a bright yellow. Another door stood open opposite to let the breeze blow through, leading into the rustic garden he could see beyond it. As he hesitated, a woman walked in that door, striding toward him, her attention on the small dog trotting at her feet. He must have made a sound, for her head came up and she stopped.

"Oh, dear," said Lady Courtenay in surprise.

He bobbed his head, transfixed yet again. She was fully clothed today—in *trousers*, that clung to her hips and thighs and were tucked into tall riding boots such as a man would wear. Her fitted jacket was a traditional woman's riding coat, but the flare at the waist only emphasized the swell of her hips. He remembered vividly how lush those curves looked, draped in soaking wet muslin . . . and how they felt, bare under his hands.

"Yet again you have caught me unawares, sir," she said with a rueful sigh. Her dog, a little ball of orange fluff, gave a sharp yap, but sat at a look from his mistress.

"I apologize," he managed to say, never less sorry for anything in his life.

She smiled wryly. "I shouldn't be surprised. You appear to have a talent for it." She looked down at herself in some chagrin. "I was just returning from my morning ride. I didn't hear your horse."

Richard had to clear his throat to speak. "I walked."

"Of course," she said, coloring slightly. She was remembering how they had last met, he knew it.

"As you may have surmised, I have taken the lease of Humberton Hall, and wished to introduce myself to the neighborhood." He gave a short bow and extended the bouquet he'd picked. "It is my great pleasure to make your acquaintance again, Lady Courtenay."

Something odd flitted over her face as she took the flowers. Surprised, wistful, perhaps even regretful—it was gone before he could decipher it. "Thank you, sir," she said, then paused. "Won't you come in? I've already sent for tea."

The Pomeranian followed at her heels into the drawing room. Richard had always preferred large dogs, like Hercule, but he had to admit this little one was charming as he bounded obediently onto a cushion obviously meant for him next to the sofa. Lady Courtenay arranged the flowers in a vase on the mantel, then seated herself on the sofa. Richard chose a chair opposite, where he had the best view of her.

"So." She gave him a polite smile. "You've taken Humberton Hall. Are you pleased with it?"

"The house is a bit dreary, but that will be remedied soon enough. I like the situation very much."

"The locals call it Tumbledown Hall," she went on. "Is it? I've not seen it in a few years."

He smiled. "Tumbledown? It is not so bad. Perhaps you will return my call and see for yourself."

She gave him a sharp look, but a maid brought in a tray with tea, and that provided a few minutes of distraction as she poured for both of them and offered a slice of cake, which he declined.

"How quiet you must find this rustic corner of the world, after all you've seen."

He shook his head. "I find it very beautiful here."

"And yet you were away from it for so long."

"Ah, yes." He sipped his tea. "I left in the year Twelve, and expected to return within a year and a half. Bonaparte, unfortunately, did not respect this plan, and his . . . misadventures in Russia caused great turmoil. I was forced to travel ever eastward, returning by a southern route that took far longer than expected."

"It's no concern of mine what you decided to do!" She looked startled by the vehemence of her own statement and took a hasty sip of tea. "Of course, I am relieved you were unharmed by the wars."

"On the contrary," he said, pleased. "I am gratified that you noted my extended absence. I thought of you nearly every day of it."

She didn't look at him. Her eyes moved over the windows, the fireplace, the chandelier, the carpet. The dog came and sniffed at her skirt, but she didn't seem to notice until the Pomeranian gave a little bark, and Lady Courtenay started so violently, she spilled tea into her saucer.

"Goodness. Louis, behave," she scolded the dog, whose ears drooped before he went back to his cushion.

Richard said nothing as she appeared to wage some internal battle, taking a deep breath but then not speaking, turning her cup around on the saucer before setting it down, clasping and unclasping her hands. Finally, she seemed to reach a decision, and turned toward him.

"Sir Richard," she began, "there is something I must address. You may have formed a . . . a false opinion of me."

"Oh?" He also put aside his cup. "If so, I most heartily apologize."

"No." She gave an aggravated little shake of her head. "It was my fault. When we first met, years ago, I behaved . . . very unlike myself. It was scandalous, and presumptuous, and not at all my usual manner. I understand why you might think otherwise, after our . . . second meeting, a fortnight ago. I had no thought of seeing anyone at the pond, I assure you."

He nodded soberly. "I see. You believe I have come here today anticipating that you will once again invite me into your bed."

She closed her eyes as a deep, mortified blush stained her cheeks.

He sat forward. "If that is the case, allow me to put your fears to rest. I have no such thought. I came here today purely to make your acquaintance—in full, this time. Yes, I was . . . charmed by you four years ago." *Bewitched, more like.* "And I was elated to discover you lived so near the house I expected to take."

Now her face was bright red. "I apologize profoundly—"

"There is nothing to forgive," he replied.

"I solemnly promise never to trespass on your property again."

He smiled. "But I have come to invite you expressly to do so. You must make free of my pond as often as you desire."

"Then it would not be trespassing," she pointed out.

"And then *you* would not continue to beg my pardon, and we would all be much happier."

Finally she laughed, although she choked it back at once. Richard grinned. He liked her laugh, perhaps even more than he had four years ago. She sat back and regarded him more thoughtfully, a trace of smile still curving her lips. "You're persistent, aren't you?"

"One must be, to scale the Little Matterhorn or sail through a typhoon."

"Have you really?" she asked with interest, then gave a tiny shake of her head. "I am trying to say, you must think me very uninhibited, then and now. And despite how I have behaved, then and now, I am not. Not really. If I were to swim in your pond regularly, people would discover it. They would whisper about it. They would impute all manner of shocking and inappropriate behavior to both of us, but especially to me, and I don't wish for that to happen."

"How would people discover it, if they have not thus far?"

Again she looked aggravated. "Your staff! Gardeners and groundskeepers and bailiffs will roam over the property and pass right by that pond. Some of them may even wish to swim in it, too, very likely on the same hot days I would choose."

He shook his head. "It is not so large a property that I require a bailiff or a groundskeeper to oversee it. I suppose I must have a gardener, but he shall tend only the area near the house. I give my word that the pond will remain private and undisturbed for your use."

"That's ridiculous!" she burst out. "It is *your* pond. You must be able to use it as much as you desire."

"My desire is that you use it."

Her eyes narrowed. "And perhaps *you'll* be the one roaming over the property, covertly watching for any trespassing neighbors swimming naked in the pond?"

He raised his brows. "Naked? I intended to stay away, for your privacy, but if there will be *naked* swimming—"

"Oh, stop," she exclaimed, trying to fight back another smile. "Stop teasing!"

Richard sobered at once. "I will." He hesitated. "But in return, I beg you to think less badly of me. You fear I came here because I am only interested in something illicit and sinful. I am not." He leaned toward her. "I am interested in *you*."

"That's much the same thing," she said under her breath. "Why?"

He had the sense his entire future hung on this answer; if he said the wrong thing, she would always view him with suspicion and doubt. And he did not want that—not at all. "I cannot fully explain it," he said honestly. "I said earlier that I thought of you, and I did. On cold nights in Mongolia, and hot nights in Delhi. I never forgot how you urged me to remember the children in the foundling home, and how my actions could benefit them, nor how you said I could call on you to speak of my adventures. I wished to do so, before, and then after, but there seemed to be a conspiracy to prevent me doing so. I . . . found that maddening." He spread his hands in a gesture of helpless frustration. "You made me laugh. I wanted to speak to you again." He paused, trying to think how to describe it. "It was like being caught in a small avalanche, where the only way to survive is to allow yourself to be borne along, even though you cannot control your flight."

She stared at him, then reached for her tea again. "That sounds thrilling. At least until the ending, when you are buried by snow and freeze to death."

He laughed. "Not always. And I am not afraid. May I call on you again?"

After several minutes, a faint smile touched her lips. "Yes, Sir Richard. You may."

CHAPTER 8

"Sir Richard Campion has returned to London," was Evangeline's greeting when Fanny came to tea two days later.

"At long last! Yes, I know." Fanny helped herself to one of Cook's tiny cakes with a frosted violet on top.

"You knew!" Evangeline stared at her old friend. "And you didn't say a word to me?"

Fanny raised her brows as she chewed the petit four. "You said you never wanted to see him again. You said you'd had your fun with him and that was that, the urge was sated, the itch was scratched. You told me to order Brumley not to reveal anything about you at all if he should happen to ask—which he did, by the by, more than once. I took your word that you were done with him."

"I am! I was!"

"Then what does it matter if he's in London or Paris, or wandering the streets of Kolkata for that matter?"

Evangeline chewed her lip in discontent. "It *doesn't* matter. It took me by surprise, is all."

"I know how you feel. I was quite shocked by the way Mr. Brummel fled the country. Sneaking out of his box at Covent Garden, during the curtain call! The gossips may never recover. At least he did not leave a poor, abused wife to be dunned by his creditors, as Lord Byron did." She sipped her tea. "How did you hear of Campion's return?"

Evangeline frowned into her tea. "I didn't wish to see him again because I didn't want . . . an entanglement."

"Of course." Fanny took another little cake, this one with a sugar-encrusted rose petal on top. "And having discovered he is once more nearby and available, you have reconsidered becoming entangled with him?"

"No," she said at once.

"I see," said Fanny in the tone that indicated she had noticed Evangeline was avoiding her questions.

Wise woman.

With a huff, Evangeline set down her teacup. "I discovered his return when he came upon me bathing in his pond."

Fanny's brows went up again, higher this time. "Indeed!"

"I didn't know it was *his* pond," hissed Evangeline. "At the time, it was no one's pond!"

Enlightenment dawned on Fanny's face, and—curse her —a little smile crossed her lips. More of a smirk, actually. "Ah, I see. The little pond not far from here? The one you regularly go swim in? And if it is now *his* pond, that suggests he has taken that ramshackle old manor across the hill? Which means he is your *neighbor?*" Evangeline had nodded in grim silence at each query and now her friend looked vastly amused. She took another cake. "Is he as handsome as he was four years ago?"

"No." Evangeline threw herself back into the cushions and blew out an enormous sigh. "Even more so."

"Oh my," murmured Fanny.

"He came to call on me," Evangeline continued, staring up at the ceiling. "Strolled up to the front door with a bouquet in hand and bowed like a gentleman."

"Promising," said Fanny in approval.

"Then he sat right where you are sitting and said he wanted to make my acquaintance properly this time," she raged on. "He said he had thought of me *every day* he was gone. What unspeakable cheek! He was gone for four years!"

"Oh *my*," murmured Fanny.

"Then he invited me to swim in his pond any time I liked. How is a woman to respond to that sort of thing?"

Fanny pursed her lips. "By fetching a towel?"

"Fanny! Can you imagine the scandal if people knew? Merely that he said that to me?" Evangeline glowered at her. "And I've been so good!"

"You've been so bored," corrected Fanny.

Evangeline sighed, deflating like a burst ballon. That was true. "I'm doomed! Everything I do leads to scandal."

"Would that we all experienced such doom as being pursued by a handsome, exciting man," said Fanny wryly. "So he only came here to pursue a new affair?"

She picked at her skirt. "He says not."

Fanny nodded sagely. "He was crude and lascivious, urging you to swim naked in his pond so he might discover you more often?"

Against her will, Evangeline smiled. "No."

"He brought flowers. I presume he drank some tea. He's even more handsome than he was four years ago. He wants to know you as you really are." Fanny gave her a look. "If I were you, I would restrain myself from descending into a melancholy of despair over this tragic state of affairs."

Evangeline sat up. "No. You would seduce him again."

Fanny smirked again. "Well, if it had been a while since a man warmed my sheets, and an appealing potential lover presented himself, willing and eager, not to mention proven capable of satisfying any and all of my desires . . . I would be well within reason to do so."

Fanny knew she hadn't had a lover since Allen's ball. She did not know that no lover Evangeline had ever had had been half as appealing as Richard Campion, because Evangeline had not wanted to admit that fact. She had tried to erase him from her mind; she'd flirted with a number of gentlemen, thinking she would discover that Campion wasn't so special after all. She'd been certain that, sooner or later, a new man would make her forget about piercing blue eyes staring deep into her soul as he whispered that he wanted to be her friend as well as her lover, and that she would find equal pleasure in his arms.

It hadn't worked. Every other man had let her down in one way or another, some dramatically and some quietly. She'd eventually given up. She wasn't sure she could even remember them all. But the memory of her one night with Sir Richard still sent a little tremor through her.

"I won't do it," she declared. "I *am* done with him. It was only one night, and trying for more can only ruin the memory of how perfect that night was. I should forget it, and forget him, and find a new man who can please me just as well as he did."

Fanny regarded her for a few moments in silence. "Perfect?"

Evangeline flushed. "It was . . . fairly magnificent." *He* was magnificent, she thought to herself. Likely still was.

Her friend shook her head, brow wrinkled in pity. "My dear, if you can find another such man in Britain, I suggest you set a trap and devote every waking hour to luring him into it. They are surpassingly rare."

Evangeline glared at her. "Where is the solace and comfort you are supposed to be offering? I pour out my heart to you and receive this in turn."

Fanny laughed. "When you are so stubbornly refusing to admit that you still want him, and adamantly insisting you will not accept what he is offering, no matter how desperately you want it, you do not need solace, my dear. You need someone to tell you to stop being a fool."

When the cakes were gone and Fanny had left, Evangeline wandered restlessly through the house. Had that night truly been perfect? Save for the fact that she hadn't woken in his arms to experience another just like it? She replayed the memories in her mind and found no flaw, nothing that left her dissatisfied, except his declaration that he wanted more.

That *had* given her a start. She hadn't been in the habit of seducing men, having always been the one seduced, but it had never occurred to her that the man she seduced would want more than a few nights of mutual pleasure. It certainly wasn't common among Englishmen, who were pleased to seduce a woman and equally pleased to be spared the burden of supporting a mistress.

Well, perhaps a few nights of pleasure *was* all Sir Richard had meant. He was a young man, far younger than she—Evangeline had not forgotten that important fact—and to him, an affair of a few weeks' time might be an eternity. Perhaps that was all he'd intended: to call on her, amuse her with his stories, make her climax three times a night, and then drift away on some new adventure. Really, what was so wrong with that?

Evangeline began to calm down as she thought about it. It was slightly mad to assume she would end up facing marriage to every man she bedded. She knew it wasn't true; she'd had other lovers, and none of them had ever come close to falling to one knee. Just as Sir Richard had gone on his planned travels, no matter what he said in the flush of passion.

She was being silly. A hearty man such as Richard Campion wouldn't even want marriage to a woman as old as herself. She had money, it was true, but she wasn't old enough that she was likely to die soon and leave a wealthy widower. She was too old to have children, perhaps even unable, after two childless marriages. She had always been strong-willed and independent, and if the thought of ordering her about ever crossed Sir Richard's mind, he would soon discover how fruitless that was.

No, he'd only wanted someone to gaze at him adoringly as he spoke about himself, like most men. Even if she could admit that he *was* a fascinating topic. And they did suit each other very well in bed, although so had she and Court, in the beginning. That hadn't lasted, and there was little reason to think it would last with Sir Richard, either.

Which suited her perfectly, as Fanny had pointed out.

Yes. She was safe from him. Surely, as Fanny said, there was no real danger in allowing herself a few weeks of private pleasure. Campion was an explorer. No doubt he would make it all very easy for her and leave the country again in three or four months.

Very well, she decided, aware that she was breaking her own rule on thin justification. Let the man come to call on her. Let him talk to her, and make her laugh, and perhaps even seduce her. It would only be a few weeks.

No man was irresistible.

CHAPTER 9

"Louis!" Evangeline put her hands on her hips and huffed in irritation as she surveyed the garden. "Louis!"

The little dog did not come. He had been in the house an hour ago, snuffling for any dropped crumbs from the breakfast table, and now he was nowhere to be seen. She'd looked through the entire house, especially the kitchens, and not heard a bark or the tap of his tiny paws on the floor. She called one more time, then went back inside.

"Is he not there?" Solly sat in the morning room, where the light was best, re-attaching the trimmings that had been torn from a bonnet the last time Evangeline wore it.

"No. He must have wandered off again." She took down her pelisse from the hook beside the garden door. "I'll have to go find him."

"He always comes home on his own, sooner or later," remarked Solly in her offhand way.

"It looks like rain, and I don't want to have to bathe him, if he comes back with his fur full of mud."

Solly just looked at her. She'd been doing that a fair amount since Sir Richard Campion's unexpected visit the other morning, when Evangeline had thrown all good sense out the window and received him. Which led to the even greater thrill of hearing him profess that he was intrigued by her.

He wanted to *know* her.

Also, he kissed like a man who could make her forget every good intention she'd ever had in life. She'd not forgotten that, either.

Solly had been with her four years ago, when she'd returned home after her night with him. Solly had eyed her —disheveled, wearing her horribly crumpled gown of the previous evening, but glowing with sated bliss—and simply shaken her head. How Solly knew Sir Richard was the source of the glow, Evangeline had no idea. Unless she'd been glowing like that after taking tea with the man? Perish that thought.

Regardless, she was *not* walking out in hopes of meeting Sir Richard. She was thinking only of her dog. "He can't have gone far. He was here less than an hour ago."

"And the rain will be here soon."

"Then I shall walk briskly." She buttoned the pelisse and took down Louis's lead.

"I'll prepare a hot bath for when you return, soaking wet and freezing cold," said the other woman.

"That will be lovely, thank you." She swept out of the house before Solly could say anything else.

Wind rustled the trees around her as she strode through the garden. Lovely and wild, it was her favorite thing about Wyndham House. It sprawled around the side, more cottage garden than formal parterre, and it soothed her just to step into it.

Wyndham House had been her escape from the horrid, spiteful whispers after Court's death. His heir, a nephew, had ordered her from the Courtenay house in London a few days after the hasty funeral, and Evangeline had been only too happy to go, just as she'd been only too happy to quit Cunningham's house. The one good turn her father had done was insist on a large widow's portion, which had allowed her to buy her own house for the first time in her life. Here she was mistress and master, lord and commander. She liked it. That was another reason she would never marry again.

The house sat nestled into the edge of a copse, hidden from the road. Not far from the end of the garden ran the path into the woods, the one she had followed to the secluded pond. A faint roll of distant thunder sounded, but the sky was still mottled with patches of blue. She hesitated only a moment, then took the path toward Humberton Hall.

Louis had roamed every inch of her property; there was nothing there to intrigue him. Besides, the paths that went northward were overgrown. Louis could scramble under the brush, but she could not.

Humberton Hall was tidier than she remembered. The garden had been severely cut back, the garden paths had been raked, and now one could see all the windows, which were much cleaner than they'd been the last time she was here. *When was that?* Evangeline wondered as she climbed the rise. Three years or more. Old Lady Elmore, who'd had it then, had fancied herself a grande dame and something of an eccentric, and she'd made a point of inviting Evangeline to one of her dinner parties.

She'd never been invited back. Evangeline supposed arguing that women deserved the right to vote had been a bit *too* eccentric for Lady Elmore.

The path led around the side of the house, past the windows of the dining room. Evangeline smiled, remembering Sir Richard calling it dreary. She meant to go to the front door, like a proper caller, but a familiar bark stopped her.

She stopped. Regardless of the threatening skies, the windows stood open, emitting the smell of freshly cooked bacon. She heard a clink of silver on china, and a faint murmur of voice. Another bark sounded.

"I say, there," she called. "Sir Richard!"

A moment later he appeared at the window, coffee cup in hand. "Good morning, Lady Courtenay." He bowed, not looking surprised at all.

"I do beg your pardon for disturbing you," she said, "but I'm missing my dog. Have you seen him, by any chance?"

He grinned. "Ah. The fluffy ginger fellow with an ungovernable passion for bacon?"

"Yes," she said wryly. She'd been fairly certain Louis was here the moment she'd caught the scent. "I take it he has invaded your house and forced his acquaintance upon you."

"My door was open," he replied, "and I was pleased to make his acquaintance. Won't you join us?"

As if she had much choice, if she wanted to retrieve her wayward dog. Still, Evangeline had already untied her bonnet, and her heart skipped a beat as she followed his gestured invitation to come through the garden to the terrace door.

Inside, the dining room was not as dreary as she remembered. Sir Richard had removed most of the furniture, she realized, along with the draperies, so the room felt bigger and brighter even on this gray day. And it was painted a pale blue, not the deep red of Lady Elmore's day.

"Lady Courtenay, allow me to present my friend and companion in travel, Gerhard von Rieger. Gerhard, this is Lady Courtenay, my new neighbor."

She curtsied to the other man in the room, a very large fair-haired fellow who surveyed her with interest. "A pleasure, sir."

"A very great pleasure, my lady."

Sir Richard pulled out a chair from the round table in the center of the room. "Won't you join us? I have rung for tea."

"Oh no," she tried to say. "I've only come to fetch my incorrigible dog."

At her voice, Louis trotted around the table and gave a sharp little yip. He came over to sniff her hand, but dodged when she tried to slip the lead over his head. He ran back around the table.

"He has been establishing his dominance over Hercule,"

said Sir Richard, his hands still on the back of the chair he'd pulled out.

"Hercule?"

He smiled. "My dog."

Louis yapped again and Evangeline took a few steps into the room. Louis was climbing over the largest dog she had ever seen, a mountain of black and brown and white fur, who seemed to be tolerating Louis with great patience.

"He is from the mountains near Zürich," explained Sir Richard. A gray-haired older woman carried in a tray with a steaming teapot, which she set on the sideboard. "Danke, Frau Loretz." Her host got a cup himself and began pouring. "He has taken to your dog—Louis?"

"Prince Louis the Only, my pampered little despot of a canine." Evangeline watched her pet sniff at the big dog's chin before giving it a delicate lick. The larger dog returned the lick, nearly tumbling Louis over. "Have you been feeding him bacon?" She glanced over in time to see a guilty look flash across Sir Richard's face, and an amused expression on Mr. Rieger's. She sighed in exaggerated despair. "He will never go home with me now. Take good care of him, sir, he is yours from this day forward."

"Nonsense." Sir Richard carried the cup to the table and set it in front of the chair he'd pulled out. "His affections are only distracted and will swiftly revert the moment I have no more bacon."

She laughed, and finally gave in and took the seat, setting her bonnet aside. The smile Sir Richard gave her was downright sinful. He would tempt her into so much trouble, if she weren't careful. Not that she minded much about her reputation anymore, but her appetite for being the focus of scandal had faded over the years.

She sipped her tea, startled—in a good way—to realize it was the same type she favored. She eyed her host over the rim of the cup. Could it be chance? He was drinking coffee, as was the other gentleman, who was watching her with unnerving interest.

"My favorite kind of tea," she said lightly. "What a coincidence we favor the same brew."

Sir Richard's smile deepened, his eyes merry. "Indeed, madam. The very happiest coincidence."

It wasn't coincidence. He'd remembered what tea she served him and now he had the same in his own house, ready to serve to her, when she came to see him. As if he'd known she would.

Yes, Evangeline thought, *I am definitely doomed.*

Richard's heart was thumping, and his skin prickled all over. From the moment the little orange dog had come sniffing around his terrace, obviously enticed by the sizzling rashers of bacon Frau Loretz had just brought out, his senses had sharpened to the clarity that he found when facing a river boiling in full flood or a near-vertical wall of rock. Fate was leading her back to him, in the form of a hungry Pomeranian.

Which was not to say he hadn't played a supporting role. He'd opened the doors wide. He'd set the plate of bacon near them. He'd dropped a few pieces of meat on the flagstones, in case the dog should prove shy, and had to order Hercule back to his place by the hearth to ensure the proper party was ensnared.

Gerhard had begun to laugh when the little dog trotted boldly into the room, his nose in the air and his puffy tail wagging. "Now you are setting lures for dogs?"

"This dog is destined to be a particular friend of mine," said Richard, his gaze trained on the small animal. "He is our neighbor."

Gerhard's brows went up. "Oho! I take it he is the reason you took this house."

Richard sipped his coffee. "Nonsense. I had not met him then. This house satisfied all my requirements. You told me so yourself when we came to view it."

"Yet still you hated it, until you went for a walk and saw the grounds."

"I considered your counsel carefully during that walk. I took the house to please Clemency."

Gerhard scoffed. "I have known you too long to be treated with this level of contempt! You despised the house and you did not care if that grieved your sister. Something happened on that walk to change your mind, and I wager this impudent little fellow is part of it."

"Nonsense." Richard extended his hand with a shred of bacon. The little orange dog walked right up to him and stood on his back paws to nip the meat from his palm.

"No? Then shall I chase him away?"

"Don't be rude, Gerhard. He is our guest." Richard watched with quiet satisfaction as the Pomeranian advanced on Hercule. The big dog put his head down on the floor, but his tail gave a few friendly thumps. "Hercule has better manners than you."

For the next half hour, Richard endured his friend's teasing while refusing to reveal anything. He had to quell one bout of throat-rumbling from the two dogs, but a fresh plate of bacon resolved the matter amicably. By the time Richard heard footsteps and a familiar voice calling from the garden, Hercule was allowing the Pomeranian to walk all over him.

When Lady Courtenay came inside to see her dog at ease in his home, Richard mentally ticked that item off his internal campaign plan. *Demonstrate respectability. Befriend her dog.* When she sipped her tea, he saw her pleased surprise with satisfaction. *Entertain her hospitably.*

"You dog is a marvelous little fellow," Gerhard told her.

She laughed. "Fearless in the pursuit of bacon! Wolves could not keep him away, could they, Louis?" The Pomeranian had come around the table to sniff her skirt again.

"No wonder he has taken fondly to Richard." Gerhard shot a gleaming glance his way. "Adventurers recognize each other."

"Are you also an explorer, Mr. Rieger?"

Pleased, Gerhard nodded. "I am why Richard sits here today, alive and well."

Richard sighed as Lady Courtenay turned an impish look on him. "Oh?"

"I have saved him from the depths of the sea, many times. I have plucked him from the brink of a deadly crevasse on a glacier. I have fought off tigers who wished to eat him, a

Mongol warrior who wished to gut him, an elephant who would have crushed him to dust beneath its giant feet, a Cossack who—"

"Lies," said Richard, now smiling. "Don't believe a word of it, Lady Courtenay."

"It sounds like a ripping good tale," she retorted in delight.

"Of course you may listen to Gerhard's tale. I only warn you not to believe in it as truth."

Gerhard shook his head. "After I have risked my life to save your ungrateful person!"

Richard raised his coffee cup in salute. Lady Courtenay laughed. The sound caused a ripple of pleasure inside him. The dog might be a charming little fellow, but she was the most magnificent creature he had ever met.

"But here, I am interrupting your breakfast," she said, rising from her chair. "And it looks like rain. Thank you for caring for my wayward dog, but I must get home before the rain comes."

Richard walked to the window and looked out. "It looks very threatening. You are most welcome to stay until the sky clears."

She smiled. "I am an Englishwoman, sir. A little rain is nothing to me."

He was not put off. "Allow me to walk you home. I have no carriage as yet, but I do have a sturdy umbrella."

"That is very kind, but unnecessary."

"I insist. For Prince Louis's sake, if not your own. He could be carried away by the wind." Without waiting for her reply, he strode from the room.

Behind him, through the door he'd left open, he overheard her ask Gerhard, "Is he always like that?"

"Quick to assess the surroundings? Prone to make decisions for everyone around him? Yes, indeed." Gerhard was enjoying himself immensely, thought Richard as he shrugged on his coat and snatched his hat and umbrella from the hall. But then his friend added, rather graciously, "And also, it infuriates me to admit, most often correct in his judgment. It has saved both our lives several times."

When he reentered the room, Evangeline had put on her bonnet again and was peering out the windows at the darkening sky, her brow creased in concern. Thunder rumbled overhead.

Ignoring Gerhard's gloating look, Richard tugged his broad-brimmed hat lower on his head. Evangeline stooped to pick up her pet, and Gerhard fluttered his eyelashes at Richard behind her back.

"We shall have to hurry," she said, tucking the dog under her arm.

Richard turned his back to Gerhard before stepping outside and opening his umbrella. "Shall we?"

Evangeline's smile looked a trifle forced, but she nodded once, firmly and decisively. "Yes."

Chapter 10

He was only a few inches taller than she and made no protest at the brisk pace she set. Their elbows collided a few times until Richard slid his arm beneath hers, to support Louis. The little dog was heavier than he looked, and Evangeline was absurdly touched by this gesture. Louis also seemed to approve, as he began licking Sir Richard's fingers.

They made it as far as the pond before the first patter of raindrops struck. Evangeline started to hurry, but he slowed. "Do you wish to turn back?"

She looked at him in surprise. "Of course not!"

He met her eyes, then gave a firm nod. His arm around hers tightened, holding her nearer, and they continued. The trees sheltered them fairly well, even as the rain grew steadier, but when they reached the end of the winding path toward her garden, the skies opened.

She gasped, clutching Louis with both arms. Richard's arm went around her waist, the umbrella over their head doing a poor job of protecting them from the downpour. They had still to cross the meadow, climb the slope, and make their way through the garden, which was already bowed down under the thundering rain.

By the time they reached the glass doors of the conservatory at the back of the house, they were nearly running, and thoroughly drenched. "There you are, my friend," said Richard, wrenching open the French door and depositing Louis inside. The dog, who had been tucked into Evangeline's pelisse and sheltered between them, was barely damp. Louis gave himself a shake and trotted off.

Richard gave her a wild grin, reckless and alive with excitement. "I told you we would be wet!"

She laughed, but it faded quickly. He shoved aside his sodden hat to run one hand through his hair. The rambling wisteria had climbed to the roof here and sheltered them from the worst of the deluge, but raindrops ran down his temples, across his lean cheeks, over his wild, reckless mouth.

She put her hand on his chest. Even through the wet layers of wool and linen she could feel the steady thump of his heart. He went still, his gaze sharpened, and then he took her hand. Reverently he tugged off her glove, brushing his lips over her knuckles, then over the pulse in her wrist. Evangeline gulped back a sigh of want. Still holding her hand as gently as he might hold a newborn kitten, he moved her fingers across his cheek, his eyes drifting closed and something like rapture in his expression.

She kissed him.

He tasted of coffee and cinnamon, and he kissed her back tenderly. It was lovely, but Evangeline wasn't after tender reverence; she wanted the forceful hungry lover who had devoured her four years ago, whose touch she had never forgotten. She caught his shoulders in both hands and pushed him back against the stone wall. Raindrops dislodged from the wisteria showered down on them, but she didn't care. She shoved her hands under his jacket, reacquainting herself with the feel of his body, as his hands cupped her jaw and angled her face for a deeper, devastating kiss.

When she came up for air, his arm was around her waist, her fingers were tangled in his wet hair, and both were breathing heavily. For a moment they stared at each other, and Evangeline knew it was her last chance. Step away, go into the house, and never see him again; or fling herself into the abyss.

"I have two conditions," she began in a low voice. "This must be an affair between equals. Neither of us will have the keeping of the other, nor exclusive right to the other's company or affections."

His eyes darkened, but all he said was, "I understand."

"And the moment either one of us wishes to end it, it will end—calmly, rationally, with no outburst of recrimination or dismay from either. We will both walk away, irrevocably."

This time he hesitated. Evangeline realized she was clenching her teeth, and made herself take a breath. He was going to make it easy for her, rejecting her conditions . . .

"I agree," he said, his voice dark and low. He raised her hand to his lips and murmured against her knuckles, "To anything you demand. You may have me any way you want me, whenever you want me, for as long as you want me."

Oh God. Her knees went weak as he pressed his mouth to her wrist and traced his tongue over her racing pulse.

"Good," she managed to say. "I want you now."

He smiled darkly, as if he knew very well that she was all but burning with lust, and he wrapped one hand around the nape of her neck, the other arm around her waist, and guided her backwards through the open door into the conservatory.

His kiss was hot and demanding this time. Her hat came off, followed by her pelisse, as his hands roved over her possessively. "Take down your hair," he growled, his lips skimming the side of her throat.

She took a deep, shuddering breath, and said, "In my house, I command."

Lightning seemed to flash in his eyes. His hands dropped away from her, and he stepped back. "I await your orders, madam."

"Take off your coat."

He shrugged it off and let it fall.

"And boots."

Never taking his gaze from her, he sat on the edge of a nearby chaise longue and pulled off his boots. He rose again and waited.

"The waistcoat," she whispered. Without looking away, he began undoing the buttons.

Evangeline watched for a moment, mesmerized by the way his piercing gaze stayed fixed on her, then realized he was actually going to undress all the way. She darted past him, around the potted palms, to quietly close the door that led to the corridor back into the house and turn the lock. Louis was long gone, no doubt being fussed over by Solly. The rain drummed down without respite on the slate roof above, streaking the tall windows that overlooked her flooded garden. On sunny days, this room was filled with light, but today it felt quiet and isolated.

She returned to her spot before him, where he waited, waistcoat on the cold tile of the floor. She gazed right into his eyes as she pulled loose his cravat. He inhaled as she undid it.

"Do you object?" she asked softly, stripping the cravat away.

"No."

She glanced at his hands, flexing at his side. "Good. Take off your shirt."

As he opened the collar and pulled the shirt free of his trousers, she undid a button at the front of her bodice, then another. His eyes focused there, and he went still as she let her gown droop open and caressed the top of her breast.

"The shirt," she whispered, and he whipped it off and flung it aside. Unbidden, he undid his trousers and stepped out of his remaining garments to stand before her, naked as a babe, but very, very aroused.

Her poise faltered. He stood as tall and bold as if he were fully clothed. God help her, he was just as beautiful naked as she remembered. No wonder her vow to avoid him had fallen by the wayside so quickly. She closed her eyes for a moment. She'd never had *that* much discipline.

"What now?" he asked quietly.

"Ah . . ." She couldn't get enough of the sight of him. "Kiss me."

"Very good, madam." He closed the distance between them in one step. He took both her hands, kissed each one, then clasped them both in his left hand and raised them above her head. His right hand traced down her throat, toward her partially bared breast. "If you wish me to stop," he breathed, his lips almost on hers, "you have but to say."

She was trembling. "*Don't* stop . . ."

He pressed light, tantalizing kisses over her face and neck while leisurely undoing the rest of her gown with one hand. When the front sagged open, he forced down the front of her stays until her breast was free. She arched into his palm, unabashedly rubbing against him as he fondled her.

"Exquisite," he murmured, rolling the nipple between his fingers.

"Show me," she gasped, writhing. He was *naked,* pressed against her, and she was rapidly regretting taking control. He was obviously paying her back with this relentless, patient, torture.

He bent and took her nipple into his mouth, sucking hard until she moaned. His tongue stroked over her flesh, up, under, over.

"Hold," he whispered, drawing her hands down and pressed them into fabric. Her skirt, she realized in a daze, which he had rucked up without her even noticing. Clumsily she gripped the fabric, and his hand slid neatly between her thighs, stroking right up to the slit in her pantalets.

"There," he murmured, his fingers sliding through the wet folds, teasing her. "Here." He curved two fingers inside her and did something that made her surge onto her toes and give a high-pitched gasp. "Tell me what you want," he whispered, his lips against her ear.

"That," she sobbed. *"More."*

"What else?" His thumb was circling, stroking, and her legs were shaking. A tear ran down her cheek.

With terrific effort she forced herself to focus, to look him in the eye. "Take me."

A shudder went through him. "Like that?"

Hard, he meant; roughly, without delicacy or tenderness. She managed to nod. It had been four years since she'd had complete satisfaction. Only he had done that for her. She felt feral and wild with dammed-up desire.

He gripped her hand, hiking her skirts higher. His wicked fingers slipped out of her body and caught her knee, pulling it up around his hip. She almost lost her balance before he cupped his hands under her bottom, pulled her up onto her toes, and thrust into her.

"Oh God," she whimpered. He withdrew, and slid his hand back down her thigh to settle on her aching sex before he thrust home hard once again, pinning her against the wall behind her.

She let go of her skirt and put her hands on him, on hot, firm flesh, on muscles that tensed and flexed, and all the while he worked himself deeper into her body as his fingers sent her spiraling into a hard, abrupt climax.

She made an inarticulate noise of release. He bent his head, sucking at the skin at the side of her neck, then pulled back and lifted her, carrying her as if she were just a slip of a girl, to the chaise, where he set her down.

"That makes a good beginning," he said, his color high.

"What?" She could barely hear him over the pounding of her heart.

He laid her back and deftly rolled her skirts up around

her waist. He hadn't climaxed, she realized with a jolt, as he spread her legs apart, each off the side of the chaise, leaving her fully bared. "Now," he said in an ominous voice, "we reach the lovemaking."

Later, Evangeline would almost believe lightning must have struck her that day. Richard opened her bodice and applied himself to her breasts until she writhed. He didn't seem bothered by her clothing, or his lack of it, but worked his way steadily under it until every inch of her skin felt alive with nerves. The backs of her *knees* tingled. But every time she felt a climax approaching, he would shift and change, tormenting some new part of her body until she was ready to weep from frustration.

"Please," she begged at last. Her hair was down in a tangle around her face, her dress was falling off, and she was behaving like the most sinful wanton alive, and all she wanted was for him to hold her down and give her the release she craved.

"Over," he said, breathing hard. "On your knees."

Shaking, she turned over onto her hands and knees. His hands settled on her hips. "Look up," he said, his voice guttural and raspy.

Evangeline peered up through the disarray of her hair and realized that with the stormy sky outside so dark, they were reflected in the window of the conservatory. She was a dim shape on the chaise, her fine green dress hanging off her, but he was clearer, golden skin and lightning blue gaze, watching her.

He thrust into her. Evangeline gasped, her hands fisting on the cushions and her spine bowing. He pulled back, then drove home. She moaned. He slipped one hand beneath her, between her legs, and stroked her there as he began moving, slow and hard. She felt him take a firm grip on the folds of her dress, bunched up around her waist, and increase the tempo of his thrusts.

He didn't stop until she came apart, gasping and sobbing. Her elbows gave way and she collapsed onto her face. He moved twice more, then froze, pulling her dress so tightly she dimly heard the fabric rip, and then she felt him come, shuddering and whispering frantically in a foreign tongue.

A moment later he shifted his weight. With a soft thump, he collapsed onto his back on the floor beside the chaise where she still sprawled, on her face, legs spread wide, hair everywhere, feeling better than she ever had in her life.

"That," he said between gulping breaths, "was incredible."

She laughed, pulling herself to the edge of the chaise to peer down at him. "Your English is faulty," she murmured. "The correct word is incendiary."

Eyes closed, he smiled. "It was both. I am bereft of all languages at the moment."

God above, he was beautiful, stretched out naked on her floor. She reached down and trailed her fingers down his chest, through the golden-brown hair, and after a moment he put his hand over hers. Not to stop her exploration, but to simply press her palm to his breast, where she could feel the rapid thump of his heart.

She could so easily grow accustomed to this.

It was a dangerous thought.

Evangeline sat up, clutching her ruined clothing to her chest. "Come," she told him.

He opened his eyes but didn't move. "Where?"

She stood, and smiled down at him, holding out her hand. "With me."

Chapter 11

Feeling blissfully relaxed, Richard let her lead him out of the conservatory and down a path lined with paving stones. The rain has eased to a thin drizzle, not that he would have noticed if it were still pouring down. He would have let her lead him anywhere at that moment; if she'd demanded he sign over all his worldly property and take a vow of poverty, he would have done it. All that mattered was that she was here, still barely clothed, holding his hand.

He'd thrown his shirt back on, but left behind everything else—at her suggestion. She glanced mischievously over her shoulder, her dark eyes shining and her hair trailing in tousled locks down her back. "Guess what it is," she said as she led him, fingers loosely woven through his, toward a round stone building with high windows.

"A . . . folly?" He had to search for the name. Clemency had admired one on the grounds of the too-rustic home he had not taken—and thank God for that.

Evangeline laughed as she pushed open the wooden

door. "Of a sort!" She went inside and turned to watch his reaction.

Richard stopped in the doorway and regarded it with astonishment. He had indeed seen such a thing before, though not in England. Some previous owner of Wyndham House had been a Roman enthusiast, for he stood facing a full, if compact, Roman bathhouse. To his left, through a narrow stone doorway, he could see a circular plunge bath, which would be cold water. In front of him, through another doorway, was a larger pool, steam rising from the water's surface. "I have never seen a bath like this in England."

She grinned. "It's the reason I bought this house." She stripped off the last of her clothing, hanging it on pegs on the wall to his right.

"Very wisely so," he murmured, admiring her openly. She blushed, but didn't hide herself as she strolled toward the hot bath. Richard pulled the shirt over his head and tossed it toward the pegs, unwilling to take his eyes away from her, before following.

She moaned in pleasure as she lowered herself into the water, reclining on the submerged bench that ran around the pool. He stepped down into the water, hissing at the heat of it, and sank down opposite her.

Evangeline lay back and rested her head on the tiles. Her hair was beginning to curl around her face in the damp heat, giving her an unexpectedly impish look. Richard was charmed. He swirled his hands through the water, exhaling through his teeth as the heat began to seep into his bones. "This is amazing."

"I didn't build it," she said, her voice warm and easy. "Some prior owner had that brilliant thought. But oh, my, when I saw it . . . I had to have this house."

"I see why," he murmured. "This surpasses any pond."

She laughed. "It's a great deal of work to prepare a hot bath, but I do admit I revel in it."

"Who would not? I have not been this warm since . . . now that I think of it, never in England." He spread his arms along the edge of the bath.

She tipped her head to one side and gave him a wry look. "The water is warmed by coals shoveled into the space beneath the floor of this caldarium. When I set off this morning in search of Louis, my companion teased me that she would prepare it, expecting I would return soaked to the skin and half-dead of cold."

"Well," he said, "it is true you grew very wet."

A small, satisfied smile played across her lips. Her hair floated like a mermaid's in the water around her shoulders and breasts, as it had that day he discovered her swimming in the pond. She folded one arm behind her neck and put back her head, exposing her long, pale throat to him. "She said it to tweak me, setting out on such a forbidding day. But now I find I must thank her very sincerely."

Richard smiled. "I hope so. This is divine."

For a few moments they both half-floated in peaceful silence. There was a very dreamlike air about the whole thing, which Richard later blamed for what he said next. "I am not attempting to change the terms you proposed," he said, eyes still closed, "but may I ask how you chose them?"

He supposed some men would feel offended by her

demands. But the truth was, most affairs did not last; they hardly knew each other, aside from the irresistible attraction they both felt. She must have been treated badly by a past lover, a mistake Richard would do his very best not to repeat.

"Oh my." Amusement lurked in her voice. "It is a frightening and sordid tale. Surely you don't mean to ruin what has been, thus far, a day of unparalleled pleasure?"

Satisfaction surged through him at that. Yes, it had been.

Perhaps it was the aftermath of that unparalleled pleasure, or soaking in hot water, but something made her talkative. "I've had two marriages, which is more than enough for anyone," she told him. "Not only that, both were cruel disappointments." She gave a mock shudder. "I daresay it's very bad luck to marry me. I am doing the gentlemen a kindness."

For a moment he was shocked speechless. Disappointments he could understand, but bad luck? What had happened to her husbands? He would have to ask Clemency. "Perhaps the third time would be the charmed one," he suggested.

"Perhaps, but I'm not inclined to risk it." She gave an odd little huff of a laugh. "By rights, I ought to have had at least *one* decent marriage, to atone for the other. It seems terribly unfair for both of them to have been bad."

"A criminal injustice," he agreed lightly, since that seemed to be how she preferred to keep things.

She shook one finger in the air, splashing him a little. "Precisely!" Then she laughed. "But the criminal, if there were one, would be my own father."

He opened his eyes and stared at the ceiling for a

moment. It was arched and vaulted to a single point in the middle, as if to guide all the steam to one focus. "Not just bad luck, then?"

"Oh, no." She swept out one arm, sending a small wave of water into his chest. "This may shock you to learn, but I was wild as a girl. So very, very wild and ungovernable," she whispered with a coy smile.

He smiled, because she looked wild and playful as she said it and he loved that look. "Surely not. I refuse to believe it."

"No, it's true," she said, eyes twinkling. "Wild, incorrigible, reckless . . ." Her voice trailed off and for a moment the impishness faded and she looked sad. Then with a start she smiled again. "Naturally the only cure was a staid and respectable marriage, and my father knew just the man to moderate my high spirits. Cunningham was so much older than I—" She stopped short, then burst out laughing. "Old! I've just realized: he was the same age I am now!" She laughed harder.

Richard heaved a melodramatic sigh, trying to conceal his surprise. She must have been a girl. Such strange customs the English had. "Years of life do not make one steady and wise any more than youth makes one vibrant and wild."

"True," she agreed, her eyes still sparkling. Her foot slid up his shin. "See how wild and reckless I still am, inviting a stranger into my private bathhouse."

Richard took hold of her foot and pulled it firmly into his lap. "We are hardly strangers, I hope." Her face went blank in shock for a moment, but then he dug his thumbs into her sole, and she let out a breathy moan of delight.

"I always wondered if Cunningham ever wanted to do my father harm, for saddling him with me," she mused. "Not only did my spirits not moderate, I believe I drove him mad."

"I don't wonder."

"Oh, not in any good way. He might have genuinely wanted to murder me." Evangeline flexed her foot in his grasp, and he obligingly rededicated himself to her arch. "He expected I'd give him children, but not once was it even suspected."

Richard thought about that. "Did it distress you?"

"Lord, no! It was awful enough to be his wife. At least it was only my own person and happiness I had to preserve against him. He would have been a strict and distant father, dictating every facet of his heir's life, and I would have fought him fiercely to protect my child. Better for us all that no such child ever existed."

"Ah." He was quiet again for a moment, still rubbing her foot, propped on his thigh. "I do not blame you, then. It is difficult to mourn such men."

She clicked her tongue. "That's the thing, you see. I didn't mourn him. He was a respectable man, but when he died, I was so relieved to be free of him." She sent him another sideways glance. "See what a sinner you've taken up with."

He shrugged. "He ought to have lived a life that inspired more affection."

She blinked at him. "Oh my. I see you shan't be a good influence on me at all." But she said it in a tone that suggested deep approval of that fact.

"I have no desire to influence you to be anything you are

not." He returned her look with a heated one of his own. "I admire you precisely as you are now."

She arched her back, and his gaze dropped at once to her breasts, exposed above the steaming water. "*You're* a wild and reckless one, Sir Richard."

"Indeed. And we are only beginning to know each other." She laughed at that, and he grinned. "I have found that there are few accurate predictors of how wild, or staid, one may be. I have known hell-raisers who have achieved their seventieth year, and placid men still at university."

"So it's something immutable within us?"

He lifted one shoulder, slowly working his massage up her ankle. "No. A wild young man might settle down in his maturity—in fact, I believe this is the expected course, with wild young men. And a somber, respectable woman may reach a point where she no longer cares what anyone thinks of her, and casts off all inhibitions."

She raised her arms in the air with a smile, as if to say *Such as I*, and he laughed.

"I am pleased to see even an unsatisfactory marriage has not quelled your spirit," he told her.

Her smile faded. "Oh . . . perhaps not entirely."

Damn. He'd expected her to laugh, too. He said nothing and concentrated on rubbing her foot and ankle.

"My second husband was a scoundrel," she said after a long silence, startling him. "I didn't mean to marry him. It was . . . an accident."

His fingers paused. How on earth did one marry accidentally?

"I suppose I should tell you now, or someone else most

assuredly will," she went on. She put her head back again and stared up at the ceiling. "Cunningham was my father's choice, for my first husband, and when he died, I felt entitled to enjoy myself a bit. So I did. I carried on with all sorts of gentlemen, including the Earl of Courtenay, who pursued me so ardently . . ." She paused. "And I fell for it. I began an affair with him, and that outraged my father. He engineered another marriage by threatening to call out Courtenay for his 'vile seduction and despoiling of a decent widow,'" she finished in a mocking voice. "Courtenay wanted only an affair, not marriage. We were completely aligned on that matter, or so I thought, until my father threatened him with mention of pistols at dawn." She paused, clearly mastering herself and continuing in a lighter tone. "To my astonishment, *I* waged a fiercer protest than he did. Who would have guessed such a rogue would be an utter coward?"

"How could your father compel you?" Richard asked, not distracted. "You must have been of age."

"Six and twenty," she confirmed. "He had written the settlements of my marriage to Lord Cunningham in such a way that he had control over my property inherited from Cunningham, including my dowry funds. He could have left me penniless, if I disobeyed. My mother wept, begging me to atone for my sins. She completely took my father's side."

She fell silent and Richard realized with fury that she was fighting for composure, even after all these years. "Had you no one else? No ally to turn to, no friend to aid you?"

"My brother, George, was the one person who might have come to my aid, but he was newly married, with an infant son." She paused. "The birth was difficult for his wife.

He was distracted, and in truth, there was nothing he could have done. When George heard of it, he did corner Father in his study. The whole house could hear them shouting. My mother begged me to come away into the garden, but I listened at the door. It was *my* future they were arguing over. Father threatened to cut off his income, too, if he interfered."

Richard, scowling, reached for her other foot.

"You mustn't be severe on George," she went on, misunderstanding his silence. "Looking back, I suspect he knew far better than I how lascivious a rake Court was, and how dim the prospects of a contented marriage were. He tried to prevent it, but our father was implacable."

Thank God she'd had someone to argue for her, since her father seemed to have been an arrogant tyrant. "Are you still close with your brother?"

"Hmm?" She smiled, a touch wistfully. "We are still cordial, but after Court's death . . ." She swished her arms through the water. "Have you any siblings?"

Richard had to breathe deeply for a moment before replying. "A younger sister. She is responsible for my presence in England, as it happens. Her husband was an Englishman, and when he died suddenly last spring, I came with all haste to help her. She has two boys."

"Oh, the poor woman," cried Evangeline. "How dreadful." She leaned forward and squeezed his hand. "How good of you to come in her time of need."

"A good brother should do no less," he said with a smile. "I am very fond of her. It was she who insisted I needed a house of my own, and she who led me to view Humberton Hall."

Her brows arched. "So I am in her debt!"

He lifted one shoulder, a small smile playing on his face. "I hope you think so." He pulled her toward him, and she came into his arms so easily, so naturally he could have moaned from the rightness of it. "I know I will be eternally grateful to her."

She draped her arms around his neck and plowed her fingers into his damp hair. "Richard . . . I have to tell you about Court."

He heard the shift in her tone, but he didn't want to see her grow maudlin or sad. "I understand he is dead, and that is what I like most about him."

She smiled, but it was grim. "You should know now, because the instant anyone hears of . . . *this*, they will rush to tell you. Courtenay was an unrepentant, unreformed rake until the day he died, shot by his lover's jealous husband."

Richard couldn't hold back his jolt of astonishment.

"What aroused Court's passion was the chase, and perhaps the illicit nature of his dalliances. I was only one of the merry young widows he pursued. He had eight lovers that I knew of, but I suspect there were more in the nine years we were married." She didn't quite meet his shocked gaze, instead focusing on his shoulder. "His last lover was a newly married lady, and her husband came home unexpectedly one evening and discovered Court in her bed. The husband shot him, then and there."

"He died in another woman's bed?" he asked incredulously before he could stop himself.

Evangeline looked right at him and spoke dispassionately. "That would have been preferable. Lord Ambrose shot him in the stomach, then had his servants carry Court home, where they dumped him, naked and bleeding, on the front steps. They weren't quiet about it, either, and I vow every neighbor in the square saw him before our butler and footman could get him inside. It was the talk of London." She made a small, indifferent shrug. "It still is, at times."

"Good God," was all he could say.

"I was as horrified as anyone," she went on in the same cool, detached voice. "Not that he was dead, but that he'd gone so . . . dramatically. I did all that was proper. I wore mourning and left London to live quietly in the country. But none of that mattered. I was deemed a wicked widow."

"On what grounds?" He was outraged.

"I wore black in public, but not at home. I wore breeches to ride, as I'd done for years. Someone started rumors that I drank brandy, which I must confess appealed to me." She smiled faintly. "I began drinking it, and rather like it."

Richard shifted, settling her more securely in his lap. He felt a surge of renewed desire, but quashed it. She was baring her history to him, and that mattered more than the softness of her thighs atop his. "Surely these are not sufficient reasons to ostracize a woman, especially one who was blameless. Quite unlike the husband who was unfaithful, the woman he committed adultery with, and the man who killed him."

Evangeline clicked her tongue in reproof. "My dear Sir Richard, you have much to learn about London society! In every scandal there must be someone to vilify and blame. Court was dead, which greatly reduced the malicious pleasure in speaking ill of him. Ambrose, who shot him, is a man, and moreover a man with a prominent government position, so people were naturally quick to pardon him—for behaving as any betrayed husband might, you know. And Lady Ambrose, who knew her husband was a jealous man but carried on with Court and likely others, was still Ambrose's wife, young and beautiful and fashionable. While I"—she raised her shoulders—"was not."

"You were not beautiful?" He slid his hands around her hips in appreciation. "I refuse to believe that."

"I was *forward*," she told him, with a wry smile. "Almost eccentric. A twice-widowed woman is always irresistible to the gossips, and there I was, riding in breeches and sipping brandy. Far more entertaining to whisper about all my *shocking* behavior, which must have positively *driven* Court to adultery."

He swallowed another argument, because nothing to do with Courtenay interested him. "Do you worry *this* will also cause you torment?"

He meant them; him; this affair, which was already going so splendidly. Finally her expression eased, and she laughed, turning to straddle him. His abdomen tightened, and her smile grew intimate. "Torment? No. After all this time, I don't care what they say about me. And if I am to be called a wicked widow . . ." She slid her hands down his chest. "I may as well act the part."

This woman. She would wreck him. He inhaled unsteadily as her hand went lower still. "This is not wickedness."

She pushed one hand through his wet hair, grasping and yanking his head backward. Richard closed his eyes and inhaled deeply as she bent her head to his throat. "I want it to be wicked," she whispered fiercely. "Wild, intemperate, and unrestrained." And she bit the taut muscle at the side of his neck.

He gasped, so aroused he could hardly speak. "That is not wicked. Wicked would be . . . by force . . ." She had his ballocks in her hand now. "Or in violation of God's law," he croaked. "Meant to harm or betray, instead of only meant to bring pleasure." His hips lifted of their own volition, and she laughed. It sent a surge of ecstasy through him, and he used it to gather her into his arms and lurched forward, carrying them both back across the pool until she was once more on her original ledge, her legs still around him as he loomed over her. "I pledge my word that I will only bring you pleasure."

She ran her hands over his shoulders, down his arms. "Pleasure is your only object?"

"Yes." He kissed her. "But not merely the physical pleasure of lovemaking. The pleasure of your company. A connection with a kindred soul. Even, perhaps, love."

He regretted that last, impulsive bit as her expression froze. But then he kissed her again, and after a moment's hesitation, she kissed him back, sweet and tender. He made love to her again, first slowly and languidly in the steam and heat, and then wildly, passionately, not caring who heard them.

"Good heavens," she gasped weakly, as his fingers dug into her hips, holding her against him in the pool. The water barely came up to their waists now, after their exertions. "Solly will give me such a look when she sees the bathhouse . . ."

"I will clean it myself if you wish," he said over his hammering pulse. "Only grant me a few minutes' respite . . ."

She nestled against him, one arm around his shoulders, plucking at his wet hair again. "Richard . . . don't fall in love with me."

He pulled back to look at her in surprise. "What?"

She smiled. "This marvelous, lovely connection we've got is too pleasurable to sully with talk of love."

His brow wrinkled. "Love does not sully."

"You dear, sweet man," she said in amusement, stroking his cheek. "Love makes people do stupid things, things they regret, like *marry*." She made a face. "Not that I expected you were about to ask, but I don't want any misunderstandings." She paused as his expression didn't ease, and ran one finger over his forehead to smooth it. "Marriage was nothing but misery for me," she murmured. "I shan't make that mistake again."

"Ah," he said, finally grasping her point. "I understand. I would never wish you to do something miserable to you."

Evangeline let out her breath in obvious relief. "Thank you for walking me home."

Richard grinned. "And I thank Prince Louis for leading you to my door."

CHAPTER 12

C lemency was at his house when Richard finally strolled up the path from the pond.

"Where have you been?" she chided. "The rain stopped ages ago."

"Ah, Clemency. I did not expect you." Richard walked past her, tossing his hat in the general direction of the table in the hall. His coat he dropped on a nearby chair. One of the servants Clemency had hired would take care of it—or not, he didn't really care. He felt exceptionally well, in top form, and nothing could shake his good humor.

His sister followed him into the drawing room. "Did you forget? I brought the boys, as we agreed. You promised to show them how to tie knots."

"Did I?" Still smiling, he pulled the bell rope. "Where are they?"

She stared at him. "Gerhard took them riding, since you were away. Why are you in such good humor?"

"Should I not be?" He spread his arms wide and laughed.

"I cannot deny that I am." Frau Loretz entered in response to the bell, and he told her, "Something to eat, bitte. And a glass of wine." He glanced inquiringly at his sister, who shook her head, looking startled. "That will be all, Frau Loretz."

Clemency's brows went up as the housekeeper left. "What happened to you out in the rain?"

He came over and put his hands on her shoulders. "Thank you, Clem. You were correct and I was completely wrong about staying in England and about taking this house." He kissed her forehead. "In fact, I intend to buy this house."

She fairly goggled at him. "What?"

He released her and went to the window. The sky was still gray, but the rain had blown away and everything looked very green and lush. Down that hill lay the pond, and a mile beyond that lay Wyndham House. He couldn't see it, but he knew it was there—as was she. "Yes," he told his sister. "Immediately."

Her skirts rustled as she came to his side and peered out uncomprehendingly at the trees, then up at him. "Why?" she demanded, sounding almost alarmed. "What about it has changed? When we first saw this house, you despised everything about it! The light is terrible, it's old-fashioned, the rooms are small . . ."

He waved one hand. "I was wrong. You were right." He smiled at her expression. "I have admitted it twice now! What more can you want?"

A series of expressions flitted across her face: consternation, suspicion, bemusement, and finally determination. "I hope you take a lesson from that," she said stoutly. "I'm often right, and you might as well admit it more readily in the future."

"Of course."

Clemency folded her arms. "Is it a woman?"

He took a deep breath. He could not keep this secret. It was burning inside him like a fire scorching him from the inside out until he might combust if he didn't tell someone. He must speak of it, or be consumed by it. "A most remarkable woman."

"Who?" she demanded.

"The Countess Courtenay. *Evangeline.*" He said her name softly, reverently.

"Lady Court—?" Clemency's eyes went wide, and for a long moment she said nothing. Then she asked in astonishment, "How on earth did you meet her?"

He smiled a little, remembering. "At a benefit ball you urged me to attend."

She was shocked again. "A benefit ball? Those were all years ago! *When* did you meet her?"

He waved one hand. "It doesn't matter now. I met her, and Clemency . . . I like her. Very much."

Her eyes nearly popped from her face. She chewed her lip, then put her hand on his arm. "Richard . . . Of course I want you to be happy. But . . . Are you certain? She is . . ."

"What?" He waited patiently as his sister struggled to find words. "Notorious?" he finally offered.

"Yes! Scandalously so!" She exhaled in relief. "I've heard *gossip.*"

"Indeed. What does the gossip say about her?"

"Well—she's not respectable."

"How so?"

Clemency seemed to be racking her brains for an answer to that. "Her husband died in very shocking circumstances."

"That is about him, not about her. What were the circumstances?"

He knew he was making her uncomfortable, but he had known Clemency all her life. She did not like to be told things and would grow indignant if argued with. But if he simply asked patient questions, she would eventually come to see things in a rational light.

There was also a chance Evangeline had lied to him. Perhaps there was more to the story than she'd told him. There were two sides—if not more—to every tale, and Richard wasn't so drunk on infatuation that he dismissed any chance of it.

Her face was pink, but she finally whispered, "His mistress's husband *shot* him!"

"His mistress's husband?" Richard nodded. "So Courtenay was unfaithful to his wife and committed adultery with a married woman?"

She opened her mouth, then nodded.

"And what was Lady Courtenay's role in this affair?"

"I—Well—She . . ." Clemency frowned. "She didn't love her husband."

"How do you know?" Richard knew, because Evangeline had told him, but he doubted the scandalmongers knew—or cared.

"Their marriage was also scandalous," Clemency said,

not answering the question. "They say she seduced him and trapped him into marrying her!"

"That is a serious charge," he said gravely, even though it was nothing of the sort. Men routinely schemed to marry heiresses, just as ambitious women plotted to marry men of consequence. "But all it demonstrates is that it was not a love match."

She gave him a sharp look. She knew what he was doing. "Likely not."

"I see. You believe it is a woman's duty to resign herself to pleasing the man she marries, no matter how or why they were wed. Very well, let us consider love. Is it a tight rein on a man? If she had loved him, would he never have strayed? It says nothing of his affection for her, which seems more important in guiding his actions. How would you have felt if Daniel had been caught in a lover's bed?"

"Oh, I would have killed him," she cried, then put one hand over her mouth in alarm.

He shrugged. "Clearly Lady Courtenay did not murder her husband, if someone else did. Let us suppose, at worst, she was shrewish to him and drove him away?"

"Yes," she said at once. "They say she's very fast."

"I see," he said again, thinking of riding breeches and brandy-spiked tea. "How so? It must have been egregious indeed to send an otherwise faithful husband fleeing into the arms of another woman, who was also married."

"Richard!" She gave up with a cross sigh. "Perhaps she's not so black as she's painted. But she is still . . . Well, she is a great deal older than you."

He grinned. He hadn't thought so, and he'd seen the

lady without a stitch of clothing. "She is far from her dotage. And I am no boy to be taken advantage of, even were she a cunning seductress."

"But what if she is? The rumors don't end with her marriage, you know."

He rocked back on his heels. "Indeed. What are they?"

She pursed her lips. "It's indecent."

"You raised the subject," he pointed out.

She chewed her lip and looked around, then closed her eyes with a long-suffering expression and whispered, "She's had several lovers since."

Richard paused. That was not surprising, but he had not known. She hadn't told him. Of course, he himself had been one of those lovers, and he had hardly been disgusted by that. Well, there was much she did not know about him, too, and he planned to have plenty of time to learn everything about her. "I can only care about the future," he said. "I have not been chaste, either—"

"Oh, good heavens, I don't want to know about *that!*" His sister's face was scarlet. "Just—do be careful with her. I would hate for you to be entangled in scandal . . ."

"Scandal!" He grinned, relieved that that was her main worry. "My dear sister, I don't care what gossips say. Nor can I control it. I can only live my life as best suits me."

Clemency looked at him in mingled reproach and aston-ishment. "And she suits you?"

He couldn't stop smiling. "She does, Clem. Very much so." Impulsively he added, "Will you meet her?"

She blinked at him. "Meet her? I *have* met her . . ."

He shook his head, already planning the evening.

"Become acquainted. At dinner. Here. I shall have a dinner party, and you must be my hostess." He rang the bell for the housekeeper. "Do you think three days is enough time to plan it?"

"Three days!" Clemency goggled at him. "A dinner party? Here? You've only just taken up residence!"

"But you specifically promised me I could have dinner parties if I took this house. You have furnished it splendidly and found an excellent chef. What else am I supposed to do?" He smiled at his sister's thunderstruck expression. "Ah, come in, Frau Loretz. Would it be possible to have . . . shall we say eight for dinner in three days' time?"

The housekeeper's eyes darted to Clemency, but she nodded. "Ja."

He nodded. "Very good. Clemency, will you be my hostess and plan the menu?"

"Well—yes, if you are really determined to do this—"

"I am. I shall write the invitations."

And he walked out, whistling faintly, as his sister and his housekeeper stared after him.

CHAPTER 13

Evangeline fussed over her clothing as if she were a young lady about to attend her very first party.

"What is it, madam?" Solly finally asked in mild exasperation, after the second change of gown.

She put down the necklace in her hands—one of four spread across her dressing table—and sighed. "It's been so long since I went out."

Solly gave her a look. That was not true. She'd gone to the theater a week earlier with Fanny, and before that the opera.

"I don't know who else will be there," she defended herself. "I may not know anyone! In that sense, it's been a long time."

In fact, never had she been invited to dine at the home of a lover. Even thinking of it felt incredible. Did he not know that such things weren't done in England? Perhaps they *were* done in Switzerland.

"Lady Woodville will be there," Solly reminded her.

That was true. Fanny had sent her a note, somewhat startled to receive an invitation to dine with a man she'd only met once, in passing, several years ago. Since Fanny was perishing of curiosity about him, obviously she had accepted, and she would spend the night at Wyndham House afterward to save her the long drive back into London.

Of course, the invitation had come from Mrs. Clemency Murray, a respectable widow and Campion's sister. Her husband had been a viscount's younger son. Evangeline had seen her at the theater a few times; she was dark-haired and pretty, with the sort of delicate features and figure Evangeline had always envied. And Richard loved her.

But as a respectable widow, she'd not been in Evangeline's limited circle of free-spirited and scandalous people, with a few genuine radicals and even a true scoundrel or two thrown in for good measure. Evangeline supposed Mr. Rieger would be there, as he appeared to be a guest of Sir Richard's, but other than that, she was in the dark. Whom would Mrs. Murray invite? Dignified, respectable people like herself? Fashionable people like Lord and Lady Allen? She shuddered. Was it too late to send her regrets?

"It would be rude to send your regrets so late," remarked Solly, reading her thoughts. "Mrs. Murray will have planned the table already."

"I know," said Evangeline reluctantly.

"On the other hand," Solly went on, "if you wish to rebuff the man, there is no clearer way than staying home this evening. No doubt Lady Woodville would understand completely."

She braced her temples on her fingertips, resting her elbows on the dressing table. Solly was friendly with many of Fanny's staff, and had an ongoing flirtation with Fanny's forbidding coachman, Gaynes. Solly must know all about that night, years ago, when Evangeline had brought a famous explorer back to Fanny's house for a night of debauchery and then slipped out while he still slept in Fanny's guest chamber. Solly most certainly knew about the other day, when Evangeline had lounged for hours in the bathhouse with that same explorer, who just so happened to be their new neighbor, and left the whole bathhouse in wanton disorder.

Evangeline didn't think she had any secrets from Solly.

"Yes, it would be unpardonably rude. But I shouldn't do this," she moaned.

"No? Why not?" Solly picked up a discarded gown and began to smooth it back into order.

"*So* many reasons, Solly!"

The other woman sat down on the chaise nearby and regarded her with compassion. Few ladies would allow their maids such familiarity, but Solly was no ordinary maid. Born in Jamaica, Solly had run away from the plantation where she was raised by pretending to be a young man and getting herself hired on as a sailor on a trading ship. She wasn't discovered until a rope caught on her hand and mangled two of her fingers, which had to be amputated. She still maintained they gave her bad rum while the ship's doctor worked, which made her violently sick and betrayed her secret.

Evangeline had met her working at a London hat shop, where the tall, statuesque Solly had a keen eye and an infallible knack for hitting on precisely what a lady needed to hear to be overcome with desire for a particular bonnet. When Solly had remarked that Evangeline needed nothing so dramatic as the fussy plumes and wax cherries then in vogue, because she had dramatic coloring and height already, Evangeline had offered her a position on the spot. It had been barely a year since Court's shameful end, and she'd admired —and envied—Solly's proud carriage and forthright manner.

Solly had quickly become much more a companion than a maid. She, of all people, knew about Evangeline's doubts and fears. Evangeline had told her to always speak her mind, and Solly had never disappointed her. Cowed her a few times, and occasionally made her feel guilty, but never disappointed her.

"What are these reasons?" Solly asked gently now. "This is an eminently proper invitation. Mrs. Murray is very respectable. You have done nothing wrong in accepting it. Nor has he, as far as anyone knows."

"There is more to it than that."

"And will that color everything you do, for the rest of your life?"

Evangeline arched a brow at her. "One dinner party is hardly coloring the rest of my life."

Solly raised one shoulder. "Who knows which moments may be discovered, upon looking back, to have been important turning points along our path?"

Evangeline was fairly certain she had seen some stark turns in her path coming from a long way away. Too bad it hadn't helped her avoid them all. "Yes, one can only know for certain after the turn has been taken. What if this turn leads down a path I don't wish to travel?"

"Yes, indeed, this current path has brought you naught but joy and fulfillment," said Solly in the same calm, easy manner. "Who would dare to dream of veering off it?"

Solly would never be frightened by a dinner party. Evangeline began to feel silly and childish. "It's more a question of *which* turn to choose, when deciding to veer off."

Solly tilted her head and gave her a look. "Come, madam. There is only one direction worth veering toward."

That was true. To one side was a handsome man who seemed fascinated by her, who made her laugh and brought her absolute bliss in bed. To the other side . . . she didn't even know what was on the other side of her current path. Strict attendance at church, perhaps, and a dedication to self-righteous charitable causes. Obviously she would not be taking that path.

Could she be any more ostracized? Perhaps. Was it more painful than she could bear, after all these years of becoming hardened to it? Definitely not.

"You," she said to Solly, "have an uncanny way of telling me that I'm being a coward and a fool, without using either of those words. How do you do it?"

Solly grinned. "If a woman knew, at the moment she must make a decision, that it was a foolish decision, she would never make that choice. It is all hindsight that persuades us that it was foolish, or not, even when our own actions after the choice are far more likely to blame or to credit." She lifted her hands philosophically. "And many times, it is only doubt that persuades us we have erred. 'I should have done differently,' we tell ourselves, only because we don't know how things might have gone *had* we chosen differently."

Evangeline laughed. "Fair enough. Yet the charge of cowardice stands, I take it?"

Solly got to her feet. "Feeling cowardly is not a shame, or a sin. Only *acting* it."

"Would that I could send you tonight as my representative," she replied dryly.

The other woman chuckled. "I would find it no trial to share a table with the famous Richard Campion!" She heaved a sigh. "I shall content myself with beating Mr. Gaynes at chess, if he will deign to come inside and try his hand again."

"I have no doubt of that," said Evangeline wryly. Fanny reported with glee that Gaynes grew tight-lipped and crimson-cheeked whenever Solly was mentioned.

Her smile lingered as she stared at herself in the mirror. Yes, she was being a fool—but she was not a coward. Her butler tapped at the door to say that Lady Woodville had arrived. Evangeline gave herself a mental shake, clasped on her pearls, and went down to meet her friend.

"Ready to face the enemy?" Fanny said in amusement.

"Are you friend or foe tonight?" Evangeline shot back.

Fanny paused in the act of inspecting her gown. "Friend," she said. "And as a friend . . . are you really wearing that?"

Evangeline looked down at her burgundy gown, instantly flushed with doubt again. "What's wrong with it? I wore it to the opera two months ago, and you didn't bat an eye."

"You were not going to the opera with the purpose of driving a man wild with desire."

"I'm not going to dinner tonight with the purpose of driving a man wild with desire!"

Her friend raised a dubious brow. "Obviously not, more's the pity."

She exhaled slowly. The dress was fashionable—she was *trying* to follow society's expectations—but even she knew it didn't really suit her. She'd done away with most of the furbelows and ribbons on the skirt currently in vogue, but that did leave it very plain. The tiny bodice was not so tiny, to accommodate her generous bosom, and the sleeves that looked so dainty on others felt overly puffed and starched to her. But what else was she supposed to wear?

"If I change again, we'll be unpardonably late," she said irritably. "If Sir Richard is horrified by my gown, better to know now."

"Perhaps it will inspire him to thinking of nothing but removing it," replied Fanny. "I stand corrected—it is a stroke of genius."

Evangeline cast her eyes upward. "I should give the man the cut direct for inviting *you*, since you seem set on bedeviling me about everything."

Fanny laughed. "Oh, don't worry! I intend to do my best to charm him enough to be invited back, while also striking a frisson of fear in his soul." She laid one hand on Evangeline's arm. "If he should break your heart, my dear, you know I would be absolutely unsparing in my zeal to destroy him."

She had to laugh at that; Fanny meant it, even though she spoke lightly. She was the very best of friends. "Even when I despise you, I adore you. Let us hope Sir Richard has invited his hardiest friends."

AFTER THREE DISASTROUS ATTEMPTS, Richard had to let Karl tie his cravat. His man clicked his tongue over the mangled linen and brought a fresh length while Richard glared impatiently at the clock on the mantel.

"One moment, mein Herr," scolded Karl, his nimble fingers flying. He stepped back and eyed it critically. "Ja. All ready."

He took an unsteady breath, as nervous as a girl making her debut. He looked in the mirror and smoothed back a possible stray hair. "Ja. Yes, I think I will do."

Karl smiled briefly and bowed his head. "Good luck, sir."

Richard choked on a laugh and clapped his man on the shoulder. He would welcome all the luck he could find tonight. "Thank you."

He reached the front hall just as his sister came downstairs. "How beautiful you look," he told her.

Clemency smiled. She did look lovely, in a deep rose gown with her dark curls in elegant swoops of braids and ringlets. "Thank you, Richard." She inspected him. "You look quite splendid yourself. Karl has outdone himself."

"Indeed," said Gerhard, stepping out of the morning room. "And Richard has outdone himself by allowing Karl a free hand."

Normally Richard would have engaged in this banter and defended himself, but tonight he ignored it all, ducking into the morning room to have a look out the window for any approaching carriages. Evangeline had sent her acceptance, but until she walked through his door . . .

A carriage was approaching.

His footman swept open the door, and Richard went to meet his guests.

It was meant to be an intimate party, but he was still grateful that everyone else arrived first. Thomas Wayles-Faire was an artist who had roamed all over Europe in search of interesting scenes and people to paint. Hard on his heels came Lord Edward de Lacey and his wife, Francesca, whose artistic salons were a favorite of Clemency's. And then his waiting ears caught the sound of another carriage.

He went into the hall, ignoring Gerhard's faint smirk and his other guests, and then out the door, unable to conceal his impatience. When the footman opened the carriage door, he offered her his hand. Her face lit up as she took it, stepping down. For a moment he could only grin like a besotted boy.

"Good evening," she said warmly. "Lady Woodville, may I present to you Sir Richard Campion? Sir Richard, my dear friend, Lady Woodville."

"Enchantée, my lady." He tore his gaze off Evangeline to bow over the other woman's hand, while she eyed him knowingly through her gold-rimmed spectacles. She was older than Evangeline, with silver-gray hair fashionably styled, and her features were strong and intelligent. He bowed, liking her instinctively. "Welcome to my home. May I escort you?" He offered each an arm and then led them inside, feeling positively buoyant with satisfaction.

Chapter 14

The evening was everything Evangeline had hoped for, and virtually nothing she had feared.

Richard coming out to meet them set the tone. She heard Fanny's indrawn breath as he strode down the step and waited, with barely concealed impatience, for the carriage to halt.

"An eager man," Fanny murmured in approval.

Evangeline shot her another dark glare, but then Richard was opening the door and holding out his hand. Feeling as fluttery as a girl, she stepped down, hopeful the twilight hid how she must be blushing. This was ridiculous, she told herself; she was a mature, experienced woman, and she had no reason to be so thrilled by the way a man's face lit up when he looked at her.

But she *was* thrilled. Because it felt like ages since she'd seen him, not three days. And all her indecision about the evening blew away on the evening breeze when he tucked her hand about his arm and smiled at her.

The other guests were charming, and not as unknown to her as she had feared. Lord Edward de Lacey, who'd had some experience of scandal himself several years ago, was there with his wife, whom Evangeline knew slightly. Lady Edward, whose Christian name was Francesca, was a member of some artistic salon that Fanny also belonged to, and they chatted about art and artists.

Mr. Rieger was there, large and quiet but smiling at everyone. He inquired after Louis, and Evangeline regaled him with the tale of the cheese puffs Louis had stolen and eaten under the sofa, causing an uproar among the cook and maids.

Mrs. Murray was charming as hostess. She fluttered around the room, smiling and telling everyone how very glad she was they had come. The last member of the party, an artist called Thomas Wayles-Faire, was a gangly Scot prone to sweeping his elegant, long-fingered hands through the air as he spoke. Like Richard, it seemed Mr. Wayles-Faire was an explorer, or at least a traveler, and he was telling Lord Edward about Constantinople's churches.

"Thank you for inviting us," she said quietly to Richard. Everyone else seemed determined to leave them to each other, which was both disconcerting and gratifying. Was it that obvious that they only had eyes for each other? Or had Richard told everyone not to intrude on their moments?

"Thank you for accepting." Between them, hidden from view of the other guests, his fingers skimmed her wrist. "I wanted an excuse to see you again."

"You could have come to call," she replied lightly.

"People do it all the time, without the effort of arranging dinner for eight."

He smiled. "A call would last half an hour. Dinner will take three or four hours, at the least."

"That can be a good thing, or a very bad thing."

His fingers trailed up her arm toward her elbow. "It will be a good thing to me if I merely am permitted to gaze at you and listen to your voice." He lowered his voice even more as Evangeline fought off the urge to pull him into a private room for a few minutes, guests be damned. "I said I wanted to bring you nothing but pleasure. I hoped a dinner party would do that."

"Very likely," she said breathlessly. There were several people within ten feet of them, and she felt hot and flustered at the way he was touching her arm.

His smile deepened. "I sincerely hope so."

You already have, she thought helplessly. Why had she ever thought she could resist him?

He led her into dinner, Mr. Rieger following with Fanny. Mrs. Murray had placed Evangeline at Richard's right hand, which did not surprise her. From the other end of the table, Fanny sent her an arch look, her eyes flickering to Richard and then back to her. Evangeline pressed her lips together, to keep from giving the giddy smile she felt bubbling inside her, and tried to send her own message: *behave yourself*.

The other guests turned out to be a good mix for a dinner party. Lord Edward had been asking Wayles-Faire about his artistic travels, and he entertained them all through the soup and fish courses with tales of the lengths he had gone to in order to see the art he wished to study, from riding an ox up a mountain to dressing as a monk in order to visit one monastery.

"What do you make of the Museum bill, sir?" Fanny asked after a while.

"Oh my," murmured Francesca as the artist inhaled audibly.

"What Museum bill?" whispered Evangeline, finally distracted from Richard's profile beside her.

He leaned toward her. "The bill purchasing Lord Elgin's marble statues for Britain."

Evangeline had heard of it. The Earl of Elgin, a diplomat, had removed a large number of statues and carvings from Athens and shipped them back to England, where he had tried, with increasing desperation, to sell them to the government. Unsurprisingly he wanted a great deal of money, which was eliciting noisy protest from various people who didn't like the expense, the action, or Elgin himself. "Ah."

"It is," pronounced Mr. Wayles-Faire, "an atrocity."

Lord Edward's brows went up. Fanny looked delighted, Francesca ruefully amused.

Mrs. Murray leapt into the breach. "Surely that's a bit harsh," she said in gentle reproach. "What will become of the carvings if the government does not buy them?"

The artist turned toward her. "They should be sent back to Athens, where they belong."

"Elgin has spent a fortune bringing them here," put in Mr. Rieger mildly. "An Englishman always wants his money."

"Elgin is a Scot," said Lord Edward.

"Which means he *definitely* wants his money," murmured Fanny.

Wayles-Faire, also a Scot, scoffed. "Aye, and 'tis no excuse. He ought to have known better. He spent a fortune at his own choice! No one demanded he do it. In fact, I hear he has refused to pay several of the artists and workmen who assisted him—which is no more than they deserve," he added darkly. "They ought to have known better than to throw in with the likes of Elgin."

"What do you mean?" asked Mrs. Murray. "Surely it's an artist's dream to be invited to accompany a diplomatic mission, with permission to see all the treasures of antiquity."

"Aye," he replied, "but Elgin's intentions were well-known. They willingly joined a thief's raid."

Lord Edward sat forward. "Elgin had legal permission to take the carvings. As little as you may like it, he sought permission in the proper way."

Wayles-Faire's mouth twisted. "He wheedled permission from the Turks, who hadna any care for those pieces. They aren't so free and easy handing out their own treasures, but the ancient Greeks—!" He gave a wave of one hand. "They never cared for that bit, so o' course they told Elgin he could have it—especially once he offered a hefty bribe."

"But then it's still a legal transfer, no matter how little you may approve," said Lord Edward, frowning.

The artist gave him a look. "If I were to break into your house, fight you and beat you and lock you in your wine cellar, then throw wide the doors and sell your family trea-sures to anyone I pleased because I had claimed your property by force, would you call it legal? Or would you call me a thief and an invader, and consider yourself still the rightful owner of the pictures?"

"All right," agreed Lord Edward. "I concede that point."

"A great many things like that happen in war, though," said Fanny. "Bonaparte carted away all the art he could get his encroaching little hands on. Had Elgin left them in Athens, they would merely have ended up in Paris."

"That only proves my point," declared Wayles-Faire, his voice rising in pitch. "What did the treaty in Vienna say? That the French must return the art and antiquities stolen—*stolen!*—by Napoleon. The British government was implacable upon that point—except for the items the English army had subsequently captured! Why should the English be permitted to keep their stolen treasures, while the French may not?"

"Because they are French," said Mrs. Murray with a little laugh. "Bonaparte was awful, sir, simply awful."

"I submit that Elgin was nearly as awful," he replied. "It is British arrogance to force France to return what they stole, while keeping the antiquities and treasures taken by Englishmen."

"You will start a new war, Mr. Wayles-Faire," said Lord Edward in amusement.

The artist shook his head. "If you had seen the carvings as they were meant to be seen, on the Parthenon in the brilliance of the Mediterranean sun, you would agree with me. There, they are the history of an ancient and brilliant people. Here, they are singular novelties, gaped at by silly, idle people who have no idea of the history they represent."

"As one of those silly, idle people," Fanny replied with a smile, "I confess I was rather dazzled by them."

He ducked his head in apology. "I meant no offense. Of course many people see them and recognize their beauty. But I assure you, they were far more beautiful in their natural setting, before Elgin hacked them down with all the finesse of a butcher and absconded with them." He turned to Richard in appeal. "You ken what I speak of, aye? *You* did not bring home entire ships' worth of stolen artifacts from your travels."

Richard hesitated. "I never felt moved to bring artifacts home with me, no. Certainly not ones that required chisels to extract from their native setting."

"And why not?" prodded the artist, who clearly knew the answer.

Richard glanced at Evangeline. "Because they were not mine to take. They belonged to the people I encountered, and I wished to know the people far more than I wished to have their treasures."

"None at all?" asked Fanny, surprised.

He shook his head. "I never traveled in search of *things*. My desire was always first to see the beauties and wonders of the world, and second to meet the people who dwelt in those places. I certainly have seen wondrous and awe-inspiring things," he said as she drew breath to ask the question. "And some of my sponsors and benefactors would have been delighted, had I brought them back with me. But that, to me, is a false reason for traveling. I craved adventures one could not have in Europe. My pleasure came from the people I met and the experiences I shared with them." He made a face. "Anything else is more like . . . a shopping expedition at best, looting and pillaging at worst."

"Exactly!" Wayles-Faire nodded so hard his hair fell into his face. "Looting! 'Tis exactly what it was! Those pieces never should have left Athens."

"You brought nothing home, Sir Richard?" asked Francesca with interest.

"No, no." He smiled. "Naturally I purchased items—clothing, blankets, supplies. Some items I admired and they were given to me as gifts. In a few instances, I fashioned my own copies of their weapons or tools, often with guidance from friendly natives. But I had no interest in acquiring much that wasn't immediately needed. The thought of shipping it anywhere . . ." He held up one hand and shook his head, as if to hide from the very thought. "Also, I did not always know where home was, which certainly complicates ownership."

"You have always had a home here," cried his sister.

"Due to your generosity," he said. "Only now do I feel the pull of England." His gaze stayed on his sister, at the other end of the table from him, but Evangeline knew, with a prickle of warmth, that he also meant her. *Goodness.*

"But now that the Parthenon carvings *are* here," asked Francesca tactfully, "what can be done? I very much doubt they could simply be put back where they came from."

"Not without considerable effort and expense," murmured her husband.

"Even more than that," she replied, turning to the artist. "I understand they were chiseled from the plinths, in many cases. Would it even be possible to restore them to their original situation?"

"It would be difficult," Wayles-Faire admitted, mouth twisted. "Though not impossible! Elgin hardly cared for the difficulty of prising them from their native berth, why should we care for the difficulty of restoring them?"

"At the very least, they could be returned to the land they came from," said Evangeline. "Here, they will be set up as a museum, and all of us charged two shillings to parade past to view them. Surely the same could be done in Athens?"

"That would not be the same, but better than this display of spoils," grumbled the artist.

"But who would pay for it?" asked Fanny. "It *is* a crass question, I know," she said as Wayles-Faire turned to her, flushed and frowning. "Elgin could tell you how frightfully expensive it was to ship them to England. I daresay sending them back would cost no less."

"And then there is the matter of housing them, repairing them, safeguarding them . . . To whom would you even entrust them?" asked Evangeline. "The Turks who allowed Elgin to take them?"

"Sound arguments, Lady Courtenay," said Lord Edward. "The Greeks are agitating against the Ottomans. I wouldn't be surprised if they have a revolution of their own, now the French appear spent."

"If one always waits for peace, naught will ever be done," growled the artist.

"True." Richard raised his glass. "Having seen a few revolutions at close distance, though, I would not knowingly send anything so valuable into the teeth of one."

"Well." Evangeline gave the visibly frustrated artist a sympathetic look. "Perhaps we shall keep them safe in England for a few years, and return them at a more propitious time."

He sighed. "I canna argue with that, except to say that the longer they bide here, the harder it will be for the government to let them go. Now they've voted funds to pay Elgin, there's many who will come to think of the Parthenon sculptures as British property, bought and paid for."

"Goodness, is there anything in this world Britain doesn't allege some claim over? Surely this time it's remarkable only in that the government has actually paid," said Fanny lightly, and a ripple of laughter went round the room.

"You must console yourself that Elgin did not sell them to the Prince Regent," said Lord Edward to Wayles-Faire. "Then they would be not state property but the monarch's private possessions."

Wayles-Faire shuddered. "You'll put me off my dinner with that talk, sir. I beg you, say no more of the Regent taking possession."

Everyone laughed again, and the conversation moved on. Evangeline stole a glance at Richard as the plates were removed. Could he really mean her? That she was what drew him to England? That spoke of a deep, enduring attraction. How could he even know that, so soon?

The fact that she apparently felt something equally strong for him had not escaped her. She, who had engaged in flirts and affairs for years, had taken Richard to bed within hours of meeting him, then fallen right back into bed with him practically the moment they met again years later. Who was she to look askance at him?

When the evening ended and the guests were making their farewells, she lingered, contriving to be the last to leave. Richard seemed bent on aiding this, and Fanny eventually picked up on it and occupied herself with complimenting Mrs. Murray on the excellence of the dinner. Mr. Rieger seemed to know he wasn't wanted, and Evangeline was finally rewarded with a quiet moment in the drawing room with Richard.

"What a remarkable evening," she said lightly. "I cannot thank you enough for inviting me."

His blue eyes sparkled. "I believe you could."

She imagined it, and blushed. "Perhaps I might try . . . Would you care for tea, the day after next?"

"For the chance to drink it with you," he replied, "I would drink tea every day."

Her heart gave an unsteady, unexpected lurch. Was this really happening to her? It was too good to be true, too sudden to last. *Enjoy it while you can,* she reminded herself, letting him kiss her hand and escort her and Fanny to their waiting carriage.

"My dear," said Fanny when they were on the road rumbling back to Wyndham House, "has he improved upon you?"

That was hardly possible, Evangeline thought. "It was a very pleasant evening," she said primly.

"Pleasant!" Fanny laughed. "He was charm itself. His sister is delightful. His friends were entertaining. He keeps a very good table and did not stint on excellent wine. He even declined the chance to pilfer valuable antiquities on his travels. And never once did his attention and interest waver from you. I shall begin to doubt your sanity if you deny any of this."

She sighed, although it was warm and happy. "I can't deny a word. I couldn't imagine a better evening."

"On the marriage mart, he would be the catch of the season. Perhaps of the decade. I hope this evening has eased your conscience about seeing him, because I would consider it unconscionable if you reject such a fellow."

No, she wasn't about to reject him. She told herself he would tire of her sooner or later, and she was prepared for that. But in the meantime . . .

"Yes, Fanny," she said with a small smile, hoping her friend couldn't see it in the dark carriage. "I am finally prepared to take your advice and carry on an absolutely torrid affair with him."

CHAPTER 15

Richard hewed as carefully as possible to the agreement they had made, determined not to press his luck too far.

"Are you not to visit your lady?" asked Gerhard at breakfast, a fortnight after the dinner party.

Richard turned a page of the newspaper he was browsing. "It is barely eight in the morning, Gerhard. Many people are still abed at this hour."

His friend grumbled. "That has not stopped you from walking to her at dawn, other days."

He turned another page and reached for his coffee cup. He had indeed gone walking soon after dawn the other morning and found himself eventually at Evangeline's. He would have been content to gaze at her windows from afar, but she was out riding, as it happened, and crossed his path. They'd ended up back at her house for breakfast in the garden, and conversation, and then a walk, and then . . . He'd gone home in time for dinner, to Gerhard's immense amusement. "Ring for more coffee, since you are unoccupied at the moment."

Gerhard rang and asked for more coffee. "So," he went on, folding his arms. "What does she see in you?"

"You must ask her," said Richard from behind his newspaper.

"Is she to dine with us again?"

"Eventually, I hope. Or rather, I hope she shall dine with me. You, I have little use for at dinner."

Gerhard laughed. "But we are old friends! Who else would put up with your moods and ill humors? If not for me, you would be sitting here alone, since you do not intend to go to her."

"I have no objection to solitude. You are free to leave at any moment."

"No objection to solitude," said Gerhard thoughtfully, "yet you set out to make her acquaintance almost as soon as you took residence here. I suspect you took this house because she lived nearby. You held a dinner party—one of the events you claim to despise with a potent passion— merely for an excuse to invite her and gaze happily in her direction all evening. I sense a plot."

Richard put down the newspaper and looked at his friend. "Would you be dismayed if I were to agree to all that? Would it alarm you if I fell for a woman?"

"Alarm! No," retorted Gerhard. "Is this love?"

Instantly Richard remembered the bathhouse, the conservatory, the first night they had met. No, none of those times had been love, because he did not know her. It had definitely been something else: namely intense, all-encompassing lust.

He had experienced lust before; he had never been a monk. But something about Evangeline was different. He couldn't say exactly what, but there was a deeper attraction that pulled at him when he heard her voice, her laugh, her soft sigh of contentment. And even though he had used the word "love" rather rashly, it kept leaping to his lips, like the confession of a sin he couldn't keep himself from committing over and over again.

"Are you questioning my intentions?" he asked mildly.

Gerhard raised his brows with interest. "Should I?"

"I did not know you cared so deeply about my romantic adventures."

Still smiling, Gerhard looked at him for a long moment. "I am correct, I think."

"I suppose it might happen, now and then," replied Richard. "Regarding what?"

"You did take this house because of her. Mrs. Murray says you met her years ago, but you never said a word to me."

Richard lifted one shoulder. "I never knew it would fascinate you so."

"So you have known this woman, somehow, and now you are in love with her." Gerhard tilted his head. "How do you know?"

"I was not the one to use the word love," Richard pointed out. "That was you."

"And you did not scoff and push it away, as you normally do when I suggest something ridiculous," Gerhard observed.

"That hints to me that, even if you do not believe it is love now, it soon will be."

"And you do not wish me ever to fall in love?" Richard asked, smiling.

His friend shook his head. "I wonder at your haste, so unusual for you. What have you done to win this woman? How deeply do you know her heart? I only ask in concern."

Richard sighed. "Clemency has put you to this, hasn't she?"

The other man leveled a finger at him. "No. She has not. She is as puzzled as I am by the speed of this attachment, but she worships you. She wants you to be happy. She, perhaps, thinks that if you marry an Englishwoman, you will stay. No. I ask because I do not want you to make a grave mistake."

He grinned. Of course Clemency was behind it. Gerhard, ever protective of *her*, was worried Richard's affair would end badly and send him haring off to China or Brazil for several years, which would upset his sister dreadfully. "So speaks the man who followed me into the desert of Egypt and stood by my side in a monsoon. We have both risked many grave mistakes, in the most literal sense, and yet here we both are today."

But Gerhard didn't smile. Uncharacteristically somber, he wagged one finger. "You are treating her, this woman, as an adventure, a challenge to conquer, a trial to be won. Women are not like that. You do yourself, and her, an injustice to think so. And when you risk love as well, you could cause both of you great suffering."

It was uncomfortably close to what Evangeline had said: *This is too pleasurable to sully with talk of love.* Richard frowned. He had never been in love himself, but Gerhard had been dying of it for years, Clemency had loved and lost, and Evangeline thought it a fool's game. Perhaps they knew better than he did.

"I am not a fool," he said abruptly. "She is not a mysterious foreign land, tempting me to explore simply because she is unknown. There is something more, Gerhard, something I cannot even put into words, that pulls me toward her. No, I dare not call it love—that would be folly, on such slim acquaintance. But . . . I believe it is very possible that I will love her in the future."

Gerhard sat back in his chair, still looking unpersuaded but no longer frowning. "Then you intend to pursue her."

"I intend to become acquainted," he corrected, "as closely as she wishes to be."

"And you will work tirelessly to do that."

"I hardly view courting a beautiful woman as work," he said testily, and shoved back his chair.

"But it will be," called his friend after him as he stalked from the room. "It must be, or it will not last. You cannot expect to keep anything you do not earn."

Nonsense, thought Richard in ire. Earning and working did not come into matters of the heart. Gerhard didn't understand, and that was no doubt why he still had never bared his heart to Clemency—or to any other lady, though Richard knew that he also had not been a saint when it came to women.

All he meant to do was spend time with Evangeline, and not only in bed. He *wanted* to spend time with her. He did feel a strange certainty he would enjoy it, and he did sense that she was also drawn to him. Surely if both their wishes converged, falling in love would happen as easily as plunging over a waterfall.

And if it did not . . .

In the hall, he hesitated. He'd meant to proceed moderately, keeping his word to call upon her and talk to her until he knew her. He'd done so twice, but both times they ended up making love, despite his protestations that he wanted more.

But he didn't want it to fizzle out once they had sated their obvious desire for each other. He did not want to stand here in several months and realize he knew little of Evangeline except what pleased her in bed. Even if theirs was not to be a love affair for the ages, he still wanted it to be full and rewarding, an affair between equals, as she had said.

He went into his study and found another of his travel notebooks. She listened to his stories with the most bewitching attention and interest. Then he put on his hat and coat and headed out to call on her. To earn her trust and affection.

To *know* her.

Chapter 16

Evangeline found herself looking forward to Richard's visits with great anticipation, but he surprised her.

He did not come every day. When he did, he usually came on foot, a satchel slung over one shoulder and a walking stick in hand. He often brought flowers, cheerful bunches of whatever bloomed in the local lanes. And he insisted they would have tea and talk, opening his satchel to bring out a notebook or two which he'd kept on his travels. His handwriting was impossible to decipher, and many passages were in German, but he read them aloud to her, stopping for additional anecdotes and amusing stories—often involving his friend Mr. Rieger.

And the sketches. Evangeline stared, rapt, at the pencil sketches of towering waterfalls, wide plains under starry skies, lions lying in the shade of strange umbrella-like trees. There were spiral-horned creatures called kudus, and enormous hippopotamuses, and an entire herd of elephants.

"We only saw them from a distance," Richard told her.

"They are magnificent creatures, intelligent and feeling. When one of their own is in distress or dying, they all gather to help or to mourn. When a calf is born, the herd welcomes the young with almost congratulatory flapping of ears."

"How fascinating," said Evangeline, studying his drawing. There were several sketches of the large animals beneath a tree, with a river in the background, on the vast open land Richard called a savannah. Some of the elephants were obviously young, even babies. "I saw an elephant years ago, at Mr. Pidcock's menagerie. It struck me as magnificent, but . . . lonely. I wonder if an animal can miss his fellows, the way a man or woman would if confined alone in a small room. It is hard to lose one's society . . ."

Richard made a quiet sound, and she looked up at him. "What?"

He was watching her, thoughtful and quiet. "I think a single elephant must be very lonely. They are herd animals. And they are not meant to be caged. Perhaps no one is."

"But we cannot all journey to Africa or India to see them, as you did. And if we were to attempt it, surely that would frighten the poor beasts into hiding." She gave a short laugh. "I can only imagine it—carriages full of London ladies trundling across a savannah demanding to see the lions! The lions would flee in terror."

Richard did not laugh. "No, that would be unwise." He took the book back from her.

"People adore seeing the unusual," she said, draping her arms over the side of the chaise she reclined on, so she could better see him in the chair beside her. "And you must admit, the tales you and Mr. Rieger tell only incite the desire to see those foreign things and places. Yet most of us have neither the skill nor desire—nor the bravery, it must be frankly admitted—to go to Africa or to Athens ourselves, so we must content ourselves with menageries and museums."

"As Mr. Wayles-Faire scorned?" He closed the notebook. "I agree with him about the Parthenon sculptures. They would be better off where they were originally created, where they were designed to be. But I credit less cruelty to removing a statue than to capturing a living creature and bringing it far from its home to be an object of curiosity. Simply because it is a beast, without speech or human thought, does not mean it doesn't suffer when taken from its fellows and its land."

"Such as a dog bred for herding cattle in the mountains?" she teased.

Richard's head came up, and then he smiled ruefully. "Yes. Something like that, I suppose." He gave a theatrical sigh and looked at Hercule, who lay in a patch of sunlight on the conservatory floor, with Louis curled up next to him. Evangeline had invited him to bring the dog whenever he came to visit, since Louis loved the big beast. "She has hoist me with my own petard, Hercule."

The big dog raised his head and thumped his tail, but then lay back down when no bacon was forthcoming.

Richard turned to Evangeline. "He was the runt of his litter. The farmer said he would have no use for such a small dog. I saved him from being unwanted."

She glanced at the huge dog in surprise. "The runt!"

"Yes. I could hold him in one hand when I took him."

Richard looked toward the dogs. "Now he is ruled by the bacon you feed him, and look how he has grown."

She laughed. "He was quite that large before I ever saw him! You shan't blame his size on me, sir."

"Of course not," he said with a smile. "But I do think he has never been happier than with his new companion, Prince Louis."

"And is that why you come to see me?" she asked, still smiling. "So that your dog can be with my dog?"

"That is a very convenient benefit, but no." He put aside his notebook and leaned toward her. "It is much more selfish than that."

"Is it? How so?" She stretched her neck, turning her face up to his, almost begging him to kiss her. So far her plans to have a torrid affair were going splendidly; Richard had proven as generous and charming as she'd thought, and she certainly felt in command of the relationship. Both times he'd come before, she'd had to tempt him into lovemaking.

He smiled. "You know what. I want to be with you."

"You are," she whispered. "Right now."

"Hmm." He leaned forward and gave her the kiss she wanted, but then pulled back. "But so far you have listened to me talk about myself, when I wish to hear about you."

"A pox on that," she said lightly. "I'm not half so interesting as you are."

His faint smile had come back. "To me, you are fascinating." He kissed her again, deeper this time, and she melted. However, to her disappointment, he raised his head and glanced at the sky. "Alas, my darling. I must go. Perhaps you will join me for a visit to town tomorrow?"

Evangeline's smile stiffened. She had expected this affair to be conducted in discreet privacy, out in Chelsea. "I really have nothing to do in town, Richard."

"No?" He was smiling again. At some point he'd taken hold of her hand, idly stroking her fingers and wrist. Now he brought it to his lips. "My sister tells me there is a vast deal of entertainment to be found there. Won't you come with me? I must visit some shops, but I have heard tales of the ices at Gunter's . . . They are a great favorite of my nephews. And I must confess, Lord Edward has offered me his box at the Theatre Royale tomorrow evening, which I have accepted but I have no companion."

She hesitated. It would be one thing to join him for the theater, which she adored and made no secret of. She had been to the theater often, with many different people. But to stroll through London and do something so public as eat ices at Gunter's with him, and then attend the theater with him, would be highly suggestive to the gossips of society.

Did she dare announce it so clearly? It had only been a few weeks. She was still in the flush of infatuation, still enthralled by his company and humor and the stories he told her. And, obviously, by the multitude of pleasures he gave her physically.

Unaware of her inner turmoil, he rose to his feet, still holding her hand. "Will you? I could call for you at ten." At her continued silence, he leaned down, his lips curving in the coaxing smile that never failed to persuade her. "Come with me, Evie," he whispered, brushing a kiss over her mouth.

And despite her misgivings, she heard herself say, "Yes."

CHAPTER 17

As promised, he called at ten exactly.

"A very handsome carriage," she said as he helped her into the glossy curricle. "Is it new?"

He jumped into the seat beside her. "How did you know?" He clicked his tongue, and the horses moved forward without the slightest hesitation.

"It looks it." She ran one hand over the polished wood beside her. To her surprise a panel popped open under her touch, and when she edged it open and peeked inside, she caught the gleam of polished steel. "Richard, have you got a pistol in there?" she asked in amazement.

He looked mildly surprised. "Of course. I always have a pair." He glanced at her expression and asked, "Why? Does that alarm you?"

She didn't know. With one more lingering glance at the weapons, she closed the panel. "It's unusual."

"Ah." He grinned. "I'm afraid it is a habit with me. To be

without something to defend yourself is very foolish, in many parts of the world. So, I keep them close at hand."

Remembering some of the tales he had told her, she shook her head. "You are very unlikely to be threatened by Cossacks in Bond Street, or fall prey to an attack with spears in Piccadilly."

"No doubt," he said in good humor. "As I said, it is merely a habit. Think nothing of it."

It was a beautiful day, and he drove briskly but confidently. When she complimented him, he laughed and said it was far easier to drive trained horses than yaks, as he'd had to learn from the Mongols. But as they drew nearer to London proper, Evangeline felt a tension creep into her shoulders, and she had to consciously relax when he helped her down at the White Horse Cellar stable, where he was leaving the equipage.

"I thought we might walk," he said with a charming smile, offering his arm. "It is a fine day, and the traffic can be troublesome."

Green Park stretched to their left, verdant and quiet. Ahead and to the right lay the finest shopping London had to offer. It had been years since Evangeline had walked here regularly—not since Court had still been alive, and she'd lived in the Courtenay house in Portman Square. In her mind these streets were still tinged with the virulent unhappiness of those years, but she had enjoyed the shops, the tea rooms, the museums and theaters. Spirits rising, telling herself not to be a goose, she tucked her arm around Richard's, and they set off into Piccadilly.

She expected Richard to turn into Dover Street, where

Mr. Manton's shooting gallery was, but he didn't even glance that way. Court had spent hours there, exhibiting his skill at shooting the wafers. She'd heard he was quite good. Perhaps if he'd kept a pistol on him at all times, as Richard did, he wouldn't have been caught so unprepared by Lord Ambrose.

Then again, given what he'd been doing with Lady Ambrose when her husband had walked in, perhaps not.

"What would you like to see, my dear?" asked Richard. "I only know a few places still."

She summoned a smile. "I can never refuse a visit to Wedgwood's, nor the booksellers. If I were alone, I would spend hours buying everything in sight at Harding and Howell's and send myself right up the River Tick!" He nodded, listening closely. She pressed his arm. "But what do *you* wish to do? This outing was your suggestion."

He looked at her, his hair glinting fair in the sunlight, his skin still tanned from the Indian sun. His blue eyes twinkled at her, and that elusive dimple flashed for a second as he smiled at her. He was so handsome, so fit and virile, it made her stomach leap with excitement that he, this marvelous man, wanted to be with her. "My primary errand is to stop in at my tailor's, to order new waistcoats." He glanced down at himself with a comically dismayed expression. "My sister tells me I am hopelessly out of fashion, but my tailor is a genius and will soon put me to rights."

"I daresay it's not so hopeless then, but let us do that first," she said with a laugh.

"Very good," he said with a grateful glance. "And then, ices and sweets."

They strolled along, studying the wares in windows they

passed until they reached a shop in St James's Street. Richard swept open the door, and they went into the shop, where Evangeline looked around with interest. She'd never been in a gentlemen's tailoring shop. It was less formal than a modiste's shop, but still similar. Bolts of fabric lined one cabinet, and cutting patterns hung at the rear. Two tailor's apprentices were hard at work at a table near the window.

A man with long, wavy dark hair and olive skin came forward, arms open in welcome. "Signor Campion! Buongiorno." He clasped his hands and gave a little bow.

"Good day to you, sir." He turned toward Evangeline. "Lady Courtenay, may I present Mr. Federico Salvatore."

Evangeline dipped her head with a smile. "A pleasure to make your acquaintance, Mr. Salvatore."

"An unspeakable delight, madam," he returned, beaming. He turned back to Richard. "How may I help you today, sir?"

"Some new waistcoats . . ." The men moved toward the long table at the back, where Mr. Salvatore began taking down bolts of cloth and laying them out for Richard's inspection.

A plump woman about Evangeline's own age bustled through the drapes shielding the back room. "Won't you sit down, m'lady?" she asked in a broad Essex accent. She indicated a pair of armchairs tucked away in the window beside the door. "Would you care for a cup of tea?"

"Thank you, that would be lovely."

The woman nodded. "Shall I take your pelisse? A bit warm in here, with all these windows and the sun today."

Evangeline unbuttoned her pelisse and the woman hung

it up, then disappeared into the back again, emerging several minutes later with a small tray holding a cup of steaming tea. She set it down in front of Evangeline.

"Thank you, Mrs . . . ?"

"Oh! Mrs. Hutchins, madam, Henrietta Hutchins. I run the shop for Mr. Salvatore." Evangeline's surprise must have shown on her face, for the woman pulled a good-natured grimace. "Right brilliant he is, with cloth and scissors, not so much with the bookkeeping. I help him."

"Very good of you," said Evangeline in surprise.

The woman waved a hand. "Me husband were a tailor himself, and I learned how a shop ought to run. When Sal— Mr. Salvatore took this place, he had a spot of difficulty, what with being a foreigner, you know. He didn't know how London folk do things, and there I was, a new widow in search of something to occupy myself. So, I stepped in, and I've been here ever since." She nodded over her shoulder toward one of the young apprentices cutting pattern pieces. "My son Joseph," she said with pride.

"It appears he shall be learning from the best," said Evangeline warmly. "Sir Richard waxes almost rhapsodic about Mr. Salvatore's work."

Mrs. Hutchins beamed. "Right you are, madam!"

She excused herself and went to Mr. Salvatore. It appeared Richard had chosen his fabrics and Mrs. Hutchins made notes while Mr. Salvatore spoke at some length, his hands moving as if he were sculpting the garments in the air before him. Evangeline drank her tea and watched, entertained by this domestic view of Richard.

After nearly half an hour, the three nodded and came to

her. "Thank you for waiting, my dear," said Richard ruefully. "I have delayed this visit, but I should not have kept you so long."

Mr. Salvatore waved his hands again. "Apologies, signora!"

Evangeline got to her feet. "I expect to be dazzled, sir," she said with a smile.

"Of course, of course, I—" The man stopped short, his gaze sliding down Evangeline's dress, growing more horrified the lower it went.

"Sal," said Mrs. Hutchins in warning.

"What is it?" asked Evangeline, knowing the answer but feeling reckless nonetheless. She had seen that expression on Fanny's face, more than once. It merely irked her when Fanny criticized her gowns, but here was a professional—and one who appeared ready to give a blunt assessment. "Is there a fault with my dress?"

"*Sal*," said Mrs. Hutchins more stridently.

The man pressed his lips together as if to hold back a flood of words. "The work is fine," he said after a moment.

Richard's brows went up. Mrs. Hutchins closed her eyes, looking pained. Evangeline burst out laughing, that all he could compliment was the stitching.

"Yes," she finally allowed, "that is the best I can say for it as well. Alas!" She smoothed one gloved hand down the Devonshire brown carriage dress with knotted gold floss fringe. It was eminently respectable and appropriate for a woman of her age and rank, and Fanny would shake her head in pity over it. "It's from a very fashionable shop."

"Bah." Mr. Salvatore threw up one hand as if to shove the dress away. "Any one of my boys could do better!"

"But it's not your place to say so, Sal," put in Mrs. Hutchins firmly. "You don't make lady's garments."

"I could do better than this," he said to her. "You know it!"

"Of course," she agreed, to Evangeline's further amusement. "But the lady didn't ask you to make a dress for her, did she?"

He turned to Evangeline. "I could do it," he insisted. "I will show you." Without another word, he turned on one heel and strode into the back, flinging aside the curtain with a certain drama.

Mrs. Hutchins lowered her voice. "Never mind him, my lady. A bit hot-tempered, he can be."

"Is this dress so dreadful?" Evangeline asked.

The woman pressed her lips together, just as Mr. Salvatore had done. "It could be more flattering to your coloring and figure, is all. It's very staid for a woman of your looks—don't you think, Sir Richard?"

Richard, who had been watching with interest, started. "To my eyes, Lady Courtenay is a vision of beauty in anything she wears."

She gave him an appraising look. "Then you've never seen her in something better, have you?"

Richard blinked and said nothing.

Mrs. Hutchins waved her hands. "Never mind! None of my business, is it? Here's your pelisse, madam. Good day to you!"

When they reached the pavement, Richard paused. "Have I committed a grievous sin?"

Evangeline looked at him in surprise. "Such a guilty question!"

He glanced over his shoulder as they strolled away from the shop. "When I answered her question." He looked at her. "You are beautiful to me no matter what you wear—or do not wear."

She blushed in spite of herself. They were walking down a public street, for heaven's sake. He shouldn't say things like that, things that made her want to throw her arms around him and kiss him. She pressed his arm in both warning and gratitude. "Oh, no. Not in my opinion." She heaved a sigh. "I have accepted that I am not favored by fashions of the moment." She tipped her head to one side. "Would that I had been born in a Tudor century! I believe I would have looked quite splendid in a farthingale."

Richard laughed. "And a ruff? Is that the correct era?"

"With high-heeled shoes and codpieces." She put up one hand artfully beside her head. "And the false hair. Especially the false hair!"

"In that case, I am vastly relieved that we were both born in this era, for all its fashion shortcomings. I am very fond of your hair." They paused to wait for a sweep to guide them across Piccadilly.

"What kind of gown could he make, do you think?" she asked suddenly, unable to stop thinking about it.

"I haven't the slightest idea," said Richard warily. "I only buy coats and waistcoats from him."

"Hmm." She gave a quick laugh and waved one hand.

"What a lark! I suppose he's never made a woman's garment in his life."

She was still thinking about it several days later when Solly brought a letter out to her in the garden. She opened it to see a sketch of a dress. For several minutes she stared at it. It was not fashionable. There were no ruffles, fringe, or rosettes. The woman in the sketch was lushly curved, like her, and the gown emphasized every curve, clinging boldly where fashion expected a discreet drape of fabric. The colors were bold and surprising.

"Solly," she said, holding it out. "What do you think?"

Solly inspected the sketched gown, tinted green, with a skirt that cut away in front at a rakish angle to reveal a yellow underskirt. The bodice was formed of elaborate folds turned back, almost like a man's jacket, edged with silk ribbons to frame the neck and bosom.

"Blue would be a better color for it," was all she said.

Evangeline took the sketch back. "Do you think so? This shade of green is very bold, so bright—"

"Blue," said Solly firmly.

Evangeline gave it up. She liked blue. And before she could stop herself, she wrote a reply to the brief note from Mrs. Hutchins, enclosed with the sketch, expressing her approval. She gave it to Solly and asked her to include measurements, knowing her companion would also mention the color.

And her eagerness certainly wasn't due at all to the thought of what Richard might think of her in a truly flattering gown.

CHAPTER 18

Now that he had taken residence near London, Clemency began suggesting he join a club.

Richard had little interest in this. He'd seen how Englishmen carried on, away from ladies, and he found it ridiculous and frankly disappointing. They wagered immense sums of money on trivial things, when he and Gerhard had staked their very lives. They argued politics past the point of all reason, even when they agreed. They drank constantly, which mainly led them to behave like fools and idiots. And they gossiped worse than any women Richard had ever known.

"But it's the thing to do!" Clemency protested.

"You must know by now that I am not good at doing what is expected."

"You don't even know what you are refusing," she said crossly. "Have you ever been to a club?"

"Yes, I have been. I have dined at one and played cards at another."

Her mouth opened in a round O. "When?"

He turned and raised his voice. "Gerhard! To which club did Sir Harold Stephenson belong?"

"Watier's," said his friend from the desk by the window, where he was writing a letter.

"And Captain Bucking?"

Gerhard paused, thinking. "Brooks's, I believe. Far worse dinner fare."

Richard turned back to his sister. "And I did not care for either of them."

"There are others! Daniel was a member at White's, and I suppose Rafael will put his name down there as well."

He raised his brows. "Have you ever been to one of these clubs?"

She flushed. "Of course not. They are for gentlemen, not for ladies."

"You have missed nothing," he told her, "and I am content to miss them as well."

"What else will you do with your time?" she pestered. "Since you have taken a house, I presume you mean to stay."

He did. But he did not want to tell his sister so, partly because she was trying to manage him and he didn't want to reward that, and partly because he didn't want to tell her it was only somewhat due to her and her sons. And perhaps she had a point. He had already vowed not to make a nuisance of himself to Evangeline, for fear of giving her a disgust of him. Perhaps he ought to find something else to occupy his time. He had no need to work; he had an inheritance from his family that kept a single gentleman—who had no estate, wife, or children to support—in good comfort. But neither was he interested in another adventure now.

"I will find something," he told her vaguely. "Perhaps I will take up watercolors."

She sat with the frustrated look on her face that told him the battle had been paused, not ended, and certainly not decided. He returned to his book, but with only half attention.

Sure enough, she couldn't hold herself back for very long. "I took tea with Lady Allen at Mrs. Fitzwilliam's the other day," she burst out, "and she told me Lord Allen would give his team of grays if you would attend his club with him!"

Richard paused. Allen . . . "Henry Allen? We attended a ball at his home once."

His sister brightened. "We did! Years and years ago, but both Lord and Lady Allen remember it well. You left a lasting impression upon them."

As had Allen, on Richard. He'd wanted Evangeline's name and direction from Allen, and the man had refused to give it.

Gerhard's chair creaked as he rose from his chair and came to sit on the sofa across from Richard. His eyes gleamed with mischief though his expression was calm. "Surely you remember, Richard. I certainly do. It was only a few nights before we left for Copenhagen, in the year Twelve. It was a benefit ball. I remember it because—"

"Very well," interrupted Richard, sensing Gerhard was about to remark that Richard had left that ball early and not come home until late the next morning, looking rumpled and dissolute. "If Lord Allen wishes to have me to dine with him at his club, I suppose I shall say yes, since we are prior acquaintances." He didn't have fond memories of the man, but he also didn't want his sister to know he'd left her at a ball so he could make love to a woman he'd just met.

Clemency gave a happy chirp and clapped her hands. "I will mention it to Lady Allen! Oh, she will be so pleased."

"Why will it matter to her?"

She blinked at him. "Why—well, Richard, you're a bit . . . famous."

He rolled his eyes and Gerhard gave a snort of laughter.

"You are," insisted his sister, blushing pink. "Not everyone has raced ahead of Napoleon's troops through Russia and then had to skirt a war in India on the way home! Not everyone has been to Mongolia or Africa!"

"They are imagining you astride a yak, or milking one of those Kashmir goats," said Gerhard, and Richard finally laughed.

"Gerhard has done all those things as well," he told his sister. "Let him be famous. He was nearly as brave and daring as I was."

"In truth, I saved him from many a disaster," countered Gerhard to Clemency. "But only for your sake. I knew you would miss him too deeply if I allowed a Gurkhali to cut him down, or a crocodile to eat him."

She beamed at him. "Oh, Gerhard. *You* ought to be famous, too."

The big man turned pink and lowered his eyes. "Ach, no. I would not be good at it."

"Of course you would!" She leaned toward him and put

her hand on his. "You are every bit as daring as Richard, and so much more sensible besides. You deserve more credit." She turned to shoot an indignant glare at Richard, and so missed the searing glance of helpless adoration Gerhard gave her before averting his eyes again. "You should credit him more, Richard."

She was still holding Gerhard's hand and he seemed perfectly willing to sit there, in that chair, until he turned to stone, as long as her hand was on his. Richard, seeing it, only smiled. "I believe I have done Gerhard some favors in my time." And his friend sent him a look that agreed.

EVANGELINE WAS VERY glad she had told Richard not to fall in love with her, because she was in grave danger of doing just that with him.

He came to see her every few days—not often enough for her to feel he was always about, but not infrequently enough that she got used to his absence. He brought flowers, and poetry, and once a basket of freshly picked strawberries, asking if she had any cream. Then he fed them to her, one by one, and licked the cream from her skin when it dripped.

He was, as Fanny kept hinting, practically perfect.

"Dine with me tonight," she said one afternoon. The words left her lips before she even knew she was thinking them.

He put down the book he'd been reading aloud, a new Waverley novel called *Guy Mannering*. It was outrageous and full of adventures and schemes and twists of fate, and they were both enjoying it tremendously. They were, as usual, in the conservatory, with the dogs dozing by the door that stood open into the garden, now filled with the buzz of insects in the late afternoon sun. Earlier they had taken a walk, arguing good-naturedly over some point of political drama she didn't even recall, then enjoyed a sumptuous tea before settling down for a quiet read, lying relaxed and lazy beside each other on the chaise. A practically perfect day, in other words.

"Do you mean it?" he asked, his lips brushing the hair at her temple.

She nodded. It was the first time she had asked him to dine with her. She had resisted that so far on the theory that, if he came to dinner, it would be just the two of them at the table, late into the night, and it was very likely she would invite him to stay even longer, and then he would spend the night in her bed, and she would have crossed a line she'd drawn for herself.

But still she'd asked him, and even though her heart seemed to patter a little more frantically than before, she didn't withdraw the invitation.

"I would be delighted," he murmured, nuzzling her ear. The book fell to the floor with a soft thud as he rolled toward her. Then he went still. "Alas." He sighed. "I cannot. A prior engagement."

"Oh." Flustered, Evangeline sat up. "Of course."

He also sat up. "I could cancel."

"Goodness, don't do so on my account!" She put up her hands to fix her hair, which had begun to slip from the pins.

"I would rather dine with you."

She flapped one hand at him, forcing a laugh. "Nonsense. I wouldn't wish to steal you from your friends and companions." She wondered whom he was dining with; a party of ladies and gentlemen? Only other gentlemen? Or perhaps a ball or soirée, the likes of which she was rarely invited to attend?

She got to her feet, wincing as her back complained. Lounging on the chaise with a man's arm around her was extremely pleasurable, but she was getting too old for it. Refusing to show any discomfort by stretching or rubbing her back, especially when he rolled lithely to his feet in one swift motion, she summoned a smile. "Forget I asked. An impulse of the moment, I'm afraid. You lulled me into such a state with your dramatic reading, I forgot myself."

"No, no, it was a marvelous impulse!" He ran one hand over his head, looking torn. "You should always give in to such impulses, regarding me." He looked up, more determined. "Ask me again. I will make a better answer."

"Don't be silly, darling. I couldn't possibly tear you away from the company of your fellow men. Or the ladies," she added hastily, reminding herself that she had nothing to be jealous or envious of, by her own decree.

"No ladies," he said at once. "Only gentlemen. I don't even like them much. I shall send my regrets. I only accepted because my sister persuaded me—" He stopped, and something about his expression told Evangeline he hadn't meant to tell her about the dinner, or the companions, or why he was going.

Which was his right. And it was not her right to know.

"Then I completely withdraw my invitation," she said lightly. "I wouldn't dream of disrupting Mrs. Murray's plans for you. Of course your companions would miss you." She made a little face of amused resignation. "And I should hate to be blamed for taking you from them!" She went to the open door and peered up at the sky. "It begins to look like rain again," she said, wishing she'd never asked him to stay.

Richard followed her, touching her arm. "Clemency wants me to join a gentleman's club," he began.

She turned and tapped one finger on his lips. "You don't owe me an explanation, or any information at all about your activities. I am not your keeper, darling."

He caught her wrist. "No, I—I will tell you. Not because I must, but because I don't wish to keep anything from you." He paused, searching her face. "I am to dine with Lord Allen and some of his friends this evening, at White's."

Allen. Her stomach dropped. She suspected Allen knew about her first tryst with Richard, four years ago; it had been his benefit ball, for goodness' sake. She didn't know *how* he could know, as she and Richard had slipped out separately and Fanny, the one person who did know, wouldn't have told a soul, especially not Henry Allen.

But somehow, immediately after that ball, there had been a renewed burst of gossip that Lady Courtenay was up to her old tricks, seducing decent men at fashionable parties and tempting them toward ruin. Her own sister-in-law had written to her about it, half indignant that it might be false, half worried it might be true. Evangeline had tried to reassure her, but she knew Marion—who was respectable, social, and very fashionable—would have listened to every whispered word.

And Richard was dining with that treacherous, beastly

man. She forced a pleasant look to her face. "I hear the new chef at White's is an improvement on the previous. I shall be very surprised if he is better than your cook, though."

He was still looking at her with an odd expression. "My sister believes it is a very English thing to do, dining at a club. I agreed to it, to please her, but I have grave doubts I will enjoy it."

"Well, you cannot know until you try it, can you?" Her smile felt more confident now, and she gave his chest a little pat. "Allen has a reputation for knowing his wine, so in that respect at least it should be an enjoyable evening."

A thin line formed between his brows. "You don't object to my going?"

Of course she wished he wasn't going to dine with Allen —*Allen*, of all people, Court's dear friend who had blamed her for Court's miserable demise, whose wife would happily spread vitriol about her around all of London. If Evangeline had her way, her world would never again intersect with that of the Allens.

She raised her brows. "Why should I? He's obviously an admirer of yours, and your sister approves. If you wish to dine with him, you should. My opinion hardly matters."

"It does," he said in a low voice. "To me."

She hesitated. The temptation to say *don't go* was powerful—but she had removed those words from her vocabulary, with him. He was not hers; she was not his. She was not in love with him, and didn't want him to fall in love with her. She didn't.

With a poise she didn't feel inside, she looked him right in the eye and said, "Go, by all means."

CHAPTER 19

Richard regretted it the moment he walked into White's.

Instinct had told him not to go, this afternoon. He'd noticed Evangeline's mood dim the moment he said Allen's name; too late he remembered what Allen had said about her, four years ago. It was idiotic to think she didn't know how the man felt about her.

But she'd told him to go, and he, riven with indecision, had gone, because not going would have meant telling Clemency and having to endure her pestering about why. She knew about his infatuation with Evangeline, obviously, but he hadn't gone out of his way to tell her how much time he spent with his lover. His love.

The line between lover and love was becoming thinner and fainter with every hour he spent with her. She'd told him not to fall in love with her; how could he help it? She was beautiful. She was clever, and funny. She would argue with him about topics both trivial and weighty, and then burst out laughing at the end. She was kind, especially to animals —Richard lived in daily expectation that he would wake to find Hercule had slipped out of his house and gone to live with her and Louis—and warm and so sensual in bed that he would swear his skin grew electrified when she touched him.

And here he was, dining with a man who didn't like or respect her.

"Is it too late to reconsider?" he muttered to Gerhard, whom he had pressured into coming with him.

"He has seen us," reported Gerhard, peering over Richard's shoulder as they relinquished their coats to the footman. "It is too late."

"Damn," he said under his breath, straightening his shoulders and striding grimly into the club. It was old-fashioned and stuffy, to his eyes, the sort of place where men whose families had been indolently wealthy for generations would feel at home.

"Campion!" cried Allen, beckoning with his free hand. His other hand already held a glass of wine. "Marvelous to have you join us, what? And Rieger! Welcome, welcome! Come, I've taken a private dining room this evening."

Allen introduced them to his friends. Sir Paul Brentwood. Lord Arthur Dunstan. Mr. Edward Parker-Philips, and Viscount Halesworth. They all seemed particularly English to Richard, with their schoolboy nicknames and casual arrogance. Brentwood was called Woody, Parker-Philips went by Stumps, and Halesworth was Swole. Dunstan apparently had the ridiculous title of Nimblesticks. Allen alone seemed to have escaped. Richard didn't look at Gerhard, who would find it all as ridiculous as he did.

But they had done this before. Granted, he had been more enthusiastic several years ago, talking about his travels and where they hoped to go next, mindful of the fact that sponsorship would be immensely useful, but he had not forgotten how this game was played. He summoned a cordial smile and greeted each of them as if they were destined to be real friends.

Sir Paul was keen to hear about their journey into Mongolia, while Parker-Philips kept asking about their improvised flight through Russia, when Napoleon had invaded virtually on their heels. He was very disappointed when Richard told him they had been able to move much faster than the French army, and had only seen Moscow burn from a safe distance.

"A bit less dramatic than I expected," he complained. "Not having to exchange fire with the damned French."

"But far more beneficial to our health, not to be shot on the Russian steppe," replied Gerhard.

"A principal goal of every expedition is to return home whole and well," added Richard with a smile. "Gunshot wounds are a great hindrance, even if not fatal."

"Have you ever been shot?" asked Halesworth. He'd been quiet so far, listening and watching with a faintly patronizing expression.

Richard didn't like him, and it was a stupid question. Still, he looked evenly at the man. "Twice with a bow, once with a pistol. Those did not unnerve me so much as the time a Gurkha nearly cut off my head, though."

Halesworth's amusement faded. He looked back stony-faced.

"Decapitation!" Parker-Philips was delighted. "*That's* adventure, right there! Don't you say so, Woody?"

Brentwood nodded. He'd listened, rapt, to Richard's story.

"India, was it?" Parker-Philips pressed. "Quite a lot of brutal savages running around there."

Richard inhaled deeply. "Yes. You can know them by the red coats they wear."

There was a moment of stunned silence, then Allen broke out in guffaws. "Well, we did send a load of rabble to India, Stumps," he said jovially. "Campion must have run into them. If Wellington's men were the scum of the earth, I daresay the Company's men were virtually savage."

"How did you escape decapitation?" Dunstan wanted to know. "The Gurkhas are reputed to be beastly in battle."

"We had engaged a young man from Kathmandu to guide us through the valley, and he cried out before the man reached me." Richard shook his head ruefully. "They believed we were English, but once he assured them we were Swiss . . . They were happy to let us pass."

Allen gave another bark of laughter, and even Halesworth smiled.

Dinner was finished and Allen had sent for cigars and brandy before things took a bad turn.

"I hear you've been slaking your thirst for adventure in another way lately," remarked Halesworth.

Richard smiled. "That explains my presence here tonight: a desire to see the Englishman in his native surroundings."

Allen and Brentwood chuckled. Dunstan grinned.

Halesworth's eyes gleamed. "No, no. Or rather, not the Englishmen, but . . . a particular English *woman*."

Richard didn't move, but the smile froze on his face. Beside him, Gerhard shifted in his seat and made a soft *tsk*. "One thing you must know about the Swiss, sir . . . Women are at once more delicate, and yet also fiercer, than any man, and I have learned to treat them all with cautious respect, rather than scrutiny. We will not discuss a woman."

"Oh, but this one is exotic and fascinating to all of us," said Halesworth, now openly enjoying himself. "One can't help but indulge in some scrutiny, or even, perhaps a little more . . . *intimate* examination, if one dares." Parker-Philips choked on a snicker, and Allen smirked a little. "I merely wanted your opinion of the creature, since rumor holds you've been making a close study."

Richard imagined gutting him and leaving him staked on the ground for animals and insects to devour. He knew the man meant Evangeline, but he refused to engage. "I've no idea what you mean, Halesworth."

"Why, my Lady Courtesan, of course." Halesworth leaned forward, one elbow on the table, a malevolent twist to his lips. "The Countess of Cunny. Lady Lightskirt. You know the one."

Richard turned his head toward Allen. "Of whom is he speaking?"

The question, asked so calmly and plainly, flustered their host. He cleared his throat and muttered, "Why, Lady Courtenay. I warned you about her, you know, years ago."

Richard had an excellent memory. He remembered that.

"Ah, yes. The lady you said you would like to fuck, when she was married to your own friend?"

Allen flushed purple. Halesworth chuckled. "Of course he wanted to fuck her. All of us did."

"But only Swole here managed it," put in Parker-Philips, who looked more eager than ever.

Halesworth had the smug smile of a viper. "That's true." He raised his brandy glass in Richard's direction. "Man to man . . . It was worth it, wasn't it?"

Richard glanced to his left, where Gerhard sat in apparent stunned silence. Gerhard caught his eye and gave the slightest nod.

Richard rose, sliding one hand inside his jacket. "I thought you would all like to see a souvenir I brought with me from our most recent journey. You in particular may find it interesting, Swole. I shall call you that, since it is appropriate. Swelled and puffed up, I believe it means?" He unsheathed the knife with a faint, supple *zhing*.

Allen's brows shot upward. Parker-Philips's mouth hung open, as did Dunstan's. Brentwood seemed rather drunk, so he just nodded earnestly, staring at the knife in unblinking fascination. Halesworth didn't move.

"This is a khukuri," Richard went on, turning the knife so the light gleamed along the razor-sharp curving steel. "The weapon of the Gurkhali soldiers in the Kathmandu Valley, whom we discussed earlier. It likely began as the tool of a farmer, meant to clear brush and skin game, but it is also known as a fearsome weapon. There is an interesting legend that says it must draw blood before being sheathed." He looked up at Halesworth, the candlelight still burnishing the blade. "Perhaps you will oblige me, Swole?"

"Put it away, please," said Allen in discomfort. "For God's sake, Campion!"

"So, you *do* think it was worth it," said Halesworth softly. He didn't look alarmed, but almost triumphant. "We should form a club, of all the men who've had her. She is a remarkably enthusiastic whore, isn't she?"

Richard swept out his arm. The blade flashed and the candles wobbled, causing Dunstan to give a shout of alarm, but nothing happened. Allen put his fist to his mouth, eyes on the knife.

"Those words do not become a gentleman," Richard said calmly, holding up the blade to examine it closely. "I will overlook it, as you are clearly gone stupid with drink this evening. In the morning, surely, you will regret ever uttering them."

Halesworth climbed to his feet. "I don't regret it," he snarled. "I meant it as a favor to you. Know what you're getting! Forewarned, and all that."

Inhale, exhale. Richard felt his breath like the force of the wind against a mainsail, straining under the pressure, driving him toward the man across from him. "Perhaps I should persuade you to regret them," he said. "Tomorrow, at dawn."

Dunstan goggled at him, and Allen gave an awkward laugh. "Now, no reason for that!"

"I'd like to see you try," growled Halesworth.

With a loud sigh, Gerhard shoved back his chair and got to his feet. "Not again, Richard! Too many times have I done this. Duels are such an inconvenience, so early in the day. If you mean to kill him, do it now, please, and leave me to my sleep."

"What, what? *Again?*" asked Parker-Philips, startled.

Gerhard turned toward him as a tutor might turn to a student who had asked a question. "Three times . . . or is it four? I cannot recall them all now. I know he does not need my assistance with the actual shooting of someone, but I have found other seconds rarely manage well, with all the blood. One man wet himself and began weeping, he was no use at all. I could almost call myself a surgeon, after all the wounds I have tended." He turned to Halesworth. "Can you not apologize? Are you a complete idiot?"

Halesworth was furious. "I apologize for nothing!"

Gerhard threw up his hands. "Another idiot! Who is your solicitor? He will have a copy of your will, correct?"

Halesworth flushed, but his eyes flickered toward the knife in Richard's hand. "You'll see, Campion, you'll see—"

Richard reached out and poked the top of the candles in the candelabra in front of him, one by one, with the tip of the khukuri. The top two inches of candle, wick still burning, toppled to the table. The second candle top rolled toward Dunstan, who instinctively seized it in his napkin to extinguish it. The third candle top fell into the tray of cigars, causing Allen to yelp. The fourth candle top landed upright and continued burning, a trickle of wax running down the side.

"Beeswax will do, for tonight," said Richard quietly. He slid the long blade back into its sheath. "Shall we try again tomorrow, Halesworth?"

The viscount's furious gaze jumped from the blade, to

Gerhard, to the candle fragment still burning on the table. In the reduced light, the whites of his eyes stood out. "No."

Richard kept a steady gaze on him, like a hawk watching prey. Gerhard cleared his throat. "A retraction, if you please."

Halesworth clamped his lips together and looked mutinous.

"My pistols are in my carriage," said Richard in an even softer tone. "We could settle it tonight. This very hour."

Halesworth, with several glasses of wine and brandy inside him, hesitated. He glanced at Allen in appeal, but that man only shook his head emphatically. Halesworth inhaled, then closed his eyes. "I regret my earlier implication of any impropriety committed by Lady Courtenay," he muttered.

Richard bowed his head. "Of course. Drink makes one rash and foolish, prone to misstatements. I accept your apology." He turned toward Allen, who sat rigidly upright, his back pressed hard into his chair. "Good evening, Lord Allen. Thank you for dinner."

He turned on his heel and walked out, Gerhard behind him, and just caught Brentwood's gust of drunken laughter as a servant closed the door of the private room behind them. "Good Lord, Halesworth! I say, *four* duels! And not even a limp to be seen!"

Gerhard did not speak until their carriage had been summoned and they were safely alone in it. Then he asked, in his deceptively mild tone, "That may prove unwise."

Richard glared out the window at the gaslit streets around them. "And yet I feel no regret."

His friend heaved a sigh. "The man did deserve it. He is a

cretin. But I suspect none of them are as discreet as they should be. What will you do if the lady hears of it?"

He closed his eyes. She would be mortified. If she heard of it, of him threatening Halesworth with a dagger—in White's, of all places—then other people would hear of it. Clemency would hear about it. He didn't care what people thought of him for doing it, but he quailed at the thought of his sister being scorned for it. But he positively dreaded what Evangeline might do, now that he had exposed her to gossip and scorn yet again.

"I don't know," he told his friend, and didn't speak again, his mind in torment.

Chapter 20

Mrs. Hutchins brought the dress herself.

"Sal's not got a place for a lady to try on a dress," she said. "And I know how to fit a dress better than he would!" She winked at Evangeline as Solly opened the dressmaker's box and folded back the paper.

"Oh, my." The words evaporated in her throat as Evangeline stared at the dress. It was brilliant, literally. The bodice and overskirt glowed like a garnet in the sunlight, deep and luscious. The blue underskirt was brighter, the brilliant blue of a late summer twilight. She'd never had such a colorful dress.

"Sal wanted to do it in parrot green and some shade of yellow." Mrs. Hutchins made a face. "I told him, you'll never! What that lady needs is blue, to make the most of her complexion. See!" She held up a scrap of the blue silk next to Evangeline's face. "Don't you think?" she appealed to Solly.

The other woman tilted her head and nodded. "Yes. I told her blue is a good color for her."

Mrs. Hutchins nodded decisively. "So it is, and the red will give her a nice pink in the cheeks. And they go so well together, although I did have to make Sal order it. He had the blue already, on account of gentlemen wanting it for waistcoats and such, but they're not so much for this mulberry color, the gents. Sal's got quite the eye for cut and silhouette, I'll give him that, but his color sense . . ." She rolled her eyes.

Solly helped Evangeline out of her day dress and into the dazzling new creation. Evangeline hesitated to look at herself in the mirror, realizing it had been a long time since she'd done so with a real hope of being impressed. She was accustomed to straining seams, extra fabric in the skirt, and muted colors that somehow never looked as good on her as they did in the dressmaker's sketchbook.

"Look, madam," urged Solly, tugging the overskirt into place.

Slowly she turned and almost gasped aloud. The dress didn't attempt to minimize her bosom or hips. If anything, it emphasized her curves. The intricate folds of the bodice settled low across her breasts without appearing strained, and the skirt skimmed closer to her waist and hips than more fashionable dresses did, making her appear . . . not slender, but more trim than before.

"You might have a petticoat made to fit it better," noted Mrs. Hutchins, fussing over the bodice seams with a chalk. "Long and light until the height of a garter. Then add some fullness, to carry the hem."

"Yes," agreed Solly, inspecting the dress from the front. "And the stays as well."

Mrs. Hutchins joined her and they studied Evangeline's figure as if she were a mannequin of wood. "You're right. Who made this corset?" she said, before checking herself and looking abashed. "None of my business."

"Mrs. Tipton in St James's Street," murmured Evangeline, still staring at herself in the mirror. Her mother had always scolded her about her posture, so she did not slump, but this dress made her want to stand taller. Her neck looked elegant, rising from the jewel-bright fabric. Even the sleeves were flattering, not the popular puffed sleeves but a closer fitting cap topped with delicately rippled silk, to give the same look without the volume.

Mrs. Hutchins scoffed. "Mrs. Tipton! She does fine work, if a body is a willowy reed. Well, you can't stuff a stocking with apples and call it a sausage." She nodded once. "Go to Louisa Turnbull, in Leicester Square. Not so fashionable as Mary Tipton, but she knows how to make a proper corset."

"Very well," said Evangeline, beginning to feel something like giddiness. "I will. And I'll take another gown from Mr. Salvatore, along with four day dresses."

"Four—? Truly, m'lady?" gasped Mrs. Hutchins, taken aback.

She nodded. "Send the sketches as soon as Mr. Salvatore can make them."

As she went about her day, she thought about those dresses. Of course they were just clothes, and she already had plenty of clothes, most of the highest quality. But that gown had felt different. It looked nothing like the restrained, respectable garments filling her wardrobe, and she'd loved it.

She'd felt at ease in it, not constricted or awkward. Even more, she'd felt beautiful.

She returned from her visit to Fanny to find a note from Richard. "He delivered it himself," Solly told her. "And the picture of anxiety he was. He waited nearly an hour before saying he had to go, and begged me to give this to you at once when you returned."

Evangeline paused before opening it. He'd dined with Allen and his friends the night before; who knew what those men might have told him? Then she shook herself for attributing her own fears to Richard, and broke the seal.

My dearest Evangeline-

My nephew has fallen ill while visiting his friend in Lyme Regis, and my sister is pleading with me to take her to him. I shall return as soon as she is delivered, and I must speak to you when I do. In the meantime, I beg you not to credit too fully any story you may hear about me or my actions at Lord Allen's dinner. Please allow me to explain before you render judgment.

I remain, as ever, your servant—

RC

She read it again, eyebrows raised. What had he done? And why was he worried what she would think of it?

Because it's about you, whispered a nagging voice in her head. *Somehow.*

Oh Lord. She folded the letter and shoved it into her desk, out of sight. She didn't want drama from Richard; he seemed so sensible, so even-tempered. She'd had more than her fair share of volatile men, including one man who pursued her with excessive zeal even after she refused his advances. That one had been rather terrifying. Her brother George had had to speak to the man before he turned his attentions elsewhere.

She sighed. It was her own fault, she supposed, for carrying on with men like that. Leaving aside the husbands, she'd only had two lovers. Other widows, she knew, had had more, and many were far more public in their relationships.

But for all that she'd tried to be discreet, both affairs had gone spectacularly wrong. One man had been charming until he lost a considerable sum at a gaming hell. Then he began hinting, before suggesting, and finally demanding she pay his debts. She had refused, and he had grown threatening and angry, calling her ugly names and snarling that she deserved to be lonely.

The other man . . . Well, things had begun well, but Evangeline had broken it off when she discovered he'd got his parlormaid with child and turned the poor girl out. They'd had a blazing argument; he'd been annoyed that she cared, and she'd been incensed that he didn't.

After that, she had told herself she was done with all men . . . until Richard. There had been no one else since he walked out of Lord Allen's ball with her, not even in the four years he'd been away and she'd had no thought at all of there being any future contact.

Well. There was nothing she could do about it, so she resolved to do nothing, and to forget about it until he returned to explain.

• • •

Richard's intention to tell Evangeline was thwarted almost from the start.

A frantic message from Clemency had arrived before breakfast the day after his disastrous dinner with Lord Allen. Gabriel, who had gone with a school friend to Lyme Regis, had come down with a fever after swimming in the ocean. The friend's mother, Mrs. Putney, had written to her that he was asking for her, and Clemency had flown into a state of pure terror. *It's just how Daniel died,* she'd written in her tear-stained letter. *I must go to my precious boy. Oh, Richard, you must take me to him!*

Of course he would. Of course he must.

He'd planned to call on Evangeline and disclose all his sins of the night before; now he had only a few hours. He went to Wyndham House as soon as he'd made the directions for his hasty departure, but she was out. He waited as long as he dared, then was forced to leave a letter begging her to give him a chance to explain.

There hadn't even been a chance to explain to Clemency on the drive to Lyme Regis. Her fears for Gabriel had driven everything else from her mind, and he wasn't about to upset her further by telling her he'd likely offended not only Allen, but several other gentlemen as well. That knowledge had lodged like a stone in his heart as his sister worried and wept over something far more important: her son's life.

After driving his horses harder than he should have, and changing teams at every available posting inn, they reached Lyme Regis at twilight the next day. The Putneys received them with relief. Gabriel had been ill for three days now, and the doctor was worried. Clemency ran into the sickroom, where Gabriel opened his eyes and smiled weakly at her, and didn't even protest when she gathered him into her arms as if he were still an infant and stroked his hair and called him her little lamb.

Mr. Putney ushered Richard into his study. "The lad didn't seem that poorly for the first day," he explained. "The two of them were at the shore with my son's tutor, young Gabe and my William. They came home pink from the sun but nothing worse, both of them tired unto exhaustion. But Gabriel woke early in the morning complaining of a headache, and stayed in bed. When my wife looked in on him, she discovered he was hot with fever. We summoned the doctor, of course, but he said it looked mild and not to be alarmed unless it persisted more than a day. Well, the moment it did, my wife wrote to Mrs. Murray. We've been worried fair out of our minds."

Richard nodded. The man did look anxious and worried. "It sounds as though you did everything correctly. Boys get fevers. I am sure my sister would have done precisely the same, with the same effect." He paused. "Do not tell her I said that. All the way here she wept of him needing his mother's care."

Putney smiled in relief. "And so he does! I would never suggest otherwise. If there is anything she requires or wants for his care, you have but to ask."

"Thank you."

He went to the sickroom. Gabriel looked small and pale in the white bedlinen, with Clemency almost lying next to him. At the sound of the door, Gabe opened his eyes. "Ahoy, Uncle," he said in a whispery-soft voice.

"Shoals spotted," returned Richard. "Steer carefully, Captain."

The boy grinned. "Hard to port, mate."

Richard laughed quietly. He came to sit beside the bed. Clemency looked at him with anguished eyes, and he tried to exude calm in reply. "It seems you've run aground, Captain Gabriel."

"I have, sir." The boy looked at his mother. "But I'll come about, Mama. I promise."

"Oh, Gabriel." She petted his hair and he closed his eyes. "Of course you will, my darling."

Richard picked up a cup sitting on a nearby table and sniffed it. Weak tea. "Have you been eating and drinking?"

Gabriel made a face without opening his eyes. "Some. I'm tired of tea. And my stomach hurts."

"Perhaps you would like some switchel," Richard said.

The boy forced his eyes open. "What's that? Is it from a foreign land?"

"Naturally," said Richard, knowing this would make it appealing. "A ship captain taught me the receipt, and said it was the best thing to drink in hot climates. But I also found it excellent for settling an unruly stomach. Would you like some?"

Gabriel nodded. Clemency stroked his hair a moment more, then rose and took herself into the hall, motioning for Richard to follow. "Will it help him?" she asked anxiously.

"It can't hurt him, and the more he eats and drinks, the stronger he should be. He is awake and lucid, Clemency. Those are very promising signs."

She seemed to wilt with relief. "They are, aren't they? But he's still so pale and weak—"

"So let us get some food into him. The switchel should calm his stomach and allow him to eat more."

She nodded. "Thank you, Richard. I know you think I am worried excessively—"

"Nonsense," he soothed. "He is your child."

"But after Daniel . . ." She bit her lip, tears welling in her eyes. "I know you have no wife or child, so perhaps there is no way to explain it to you . . . It's as if a piece of my own heart lies in that bed, and I feel his suffering like a physical pain here." She laid one hand on her bosom. "It's not like when Father died, or Mama, or anyone else. I think it was only because of Rafael and Gabriel that I survived it when Daniel . . . But it would be so much worse if *Gabriel*—" She choked back a little sob, and Richard put his hand on her shoulder in comfort. "Thank you," she whispered, and ducked back into the room where her son lay.

Richard stood there for a long moment. Of course he didn't know a parent's anguish, with no children of his own. And he had no wife, but he'd seen enough marriages to know that didn't always indicate strong attachment.

But he was beginning to know the feeling that a piece of his heart had cleaved to someone else. That his happiness would be permanently reduced without that person in his life. And unlike Clemency, he also knew the dread of knowing that he might be the reason she left him.

Time would tell; it always did. If Evangeline flew into a rage over his actions at White's . . . she wasn't the woman he thought her, and it was best to know now. If it mortified her and she could never speak to him again . . . perhaps it had always been doomed, eventually. But if she waited and gave him a chance to explain . . .

Finally he turned and went down the stairs to ask Putney where he could find ginger root and cider vinegar for the switchel. Tomorrow he would promise to send Gerhard, because he was going home to see Evangeline.

CHAPTER 21

For the next several days, Evangeline did her best to do as Richard asked, and wait for his explanation of whatever he'd done. She finished embroidering the handkerchiefs she was making for her niece. She read a whole novel and enjoyed it very much. She discovered a nest of baby rabbits in her garden, and enjoyed watching the tiny bunnies hopping around, even though she had to shut up Louis in the house to keep him from chasing them, and her gardener muttered that they'd be eating her favorite flowers. And she visited Mrs. Trumbull in Leicester Square and ordered a new corset, with a pair of new petticoats for good measure.

And after four whole days, she was about to lose her mind, wondering what on earth he'd done and when he would be home to tell her about it.

In the end, she learned that answer not from Richard, but from her sister-in-law.

"Marion," she said warmly as Solly showed her in. "What a lovely surprise."

Marion came to embrace her. She was petite and slim, with chestnut brown hair just beginning to show threads of gray. Evangeline hadn't known her well before Marion married George, because Cunningham had kept them at his Scottish estate all winter, and they'd only come to London that spring. Then Cunningham had died and Evangeline had gone into mourning.

"How are you?" she asked as they settled on the sofa. "I was just working on some handkerchiefs for Joan." She reached for the embroidery basket nearby.

"How lovely," said Marion with a smile, inspecting the stitching. "She does so like lilies."

Evangeline laughed. "Just like her aunt! One of my favorites."

"She will be delighted." Marion accepted a cup of tea. Solly had brought the tray just before Marion's arrival, and had rushed to bring a second cup. "Evangeline . . . I hope this isn't an intrusion . . . But I've come to ask you about Sir Richard Campion."

Evangeline paused in the act of serving her guest a piece of cake. "Oh, my," she said with a light laugh. "Whatever can you want to know about him?"

Marion took the cake but set it down, while Evangeline took a bite of hers. She had a feeling she was going to want it. "I understand you are acquainted with him."

Evangeline took her time eating her cake, and then a long sip of tea. "I am."

Marion stirred her tea, looking awkward, which was unlike her. "I—I don't mean to pry," she began haltingly. "I did not come to berate you. I only . . . I only wondered if you knew what is being said about you? And . . . about him?"

She took another bite of cake—her cook's caraway seed cake, one of her favorites—even though it tasted like nothing in her mouth. "I'm afraid I have no idea."

Marion flushed a becoming pink. She was a very attractive woman, and had been considered a minor beauty of the ton when George married her. "I don't know a gentle way to tell you, so I'll just say it. George reports to me that, several nights ago at White's, Sir Richard threatened a man with a sword and challenged him to a duel over you."

Oh Lord. She had to sip more tea to wash down the dust-dry cake. "What on earth would cause him to do that?" she finally croaked. A *sword*, in White's?

Marion fiddled with her cup. "Hasn't he spoken to you about it?"

For the first time in four days, she was intensely glad he was gone, that she could disavow all knowledge of this. "Not a word. I've not seen him in several days." She paused, then decided to spike at least one gun. "He has taken the house beyond my garden and woods. We are neighbors, and as such I have seen him several times. But I believe he has gone away recently."

Marion's eyes widened. "He—He lives next door?"

"Some two miles away," said Evangeline with a careless wave of her hand. "I understand his sister, Mrs. Murray, entreated him to take the house. He invited some of the neighbors to a dinner party, where Mrs. Murray was hostess."

"Oh, my," murmured Marion, her brow furrowed.

Evangeline longed to ask what was wrong with that, but had a feeling she wouldn't like the answer.

"Then perhaps it was more in chivalry than . . . something else," murmured Marion. She looked up. "You say you are barely acquainted with him?"

Evangeline willed herself not to blush. "I did not say that, but may I ask what happened? If it is about me, I deserve to know what is being said, and by whom."

Marion's eyes darted sideways. "I'm not entirely certain. George wouldn't tell me, and my friends haven't heard every detail."

But they had heard about the sword, and a near duel. Evangeline felt a surge of dislike for Marion's friends. Whatever had been said, she was certain they would hear it eventually—or more likely, some exaggerated, corrupted version of the truth—and then they would pour bile into Marion's ear.

"Sir Richard mentioned that he was to dine with Lord Allen," she remarked, giving her sister-in-law a contemplative look. "*He's* certainly no friend of mine."

"No," said Marion, cheeks pink. She did share Evangeline's dislike of the Allens. "But a duel—! Especially after—"

She stopped, but Evangeline could fill it in. "After Ramsdale? Or Court? Perhaps Sir Elias—or do you mean Halesworth?"

Marion looked annoyed. "Any of them, Evangeline. It's rather difficult to keep up with your scandals!" Her face blanked in horror, and she flushed a deeper red. "Forgive me," she said swiftly. "I never should have said that!"

Evangeline waved one hand, though her other hand,

hidden in her skirt, was balled into a fist. "But you were thinking it, so might as well have it out."

"I know they were not entirely your fault," said Marion, who appeared to be fighting both embarrassment and distress. "But you do seem to have a way of attracting the worst men."

She reached for the teapot and refilled her cup, each action measured and deliberate. "And why is that my fault, rather than the fault of the men for being scoundrels and worse?"

"It's not your fault," said Marion at once. "But once you know, it's best to discourage such men immediately!"

"I never gave Ramsdale the least encouragement," she said evenly. "Court, who was a very eligible man until his ignominious death, was forced upon me by my father. Sir Elias is still widely received, even though you know how abominably he behaved. Halesworth . . . was a mistake, but no greater a mistake than many a lady makes. I was taken completely by surprise, and broke with him the instant I discovered his true nature. You yourself told me you had no idea he was such a gambler."

"That's true, but . . ." Marion bit her lip. "It is a distressing pattern, don't you think?"

"Yes, Marion, I do," snapped Evangeline, her temper slipping a bit. "It is humiliating to be made a fool of, or worse, by men I believed to be gentlemen. I certainly don't set out on a mission to find the worst men in London!"

Marion bowed her head. "I know," she said stiffly. "And if you say there is nothing between you and Sir Richard, I will respect that. I could not blame you for a man's actions."

Evangeline sat back on the sofa, wishing she had Louis with her. Marion wasn't fond of dogs, though, and Solly had taken him out into the garden when Marion arrived. She wished *she* could go into the garden and avoid this. She took another bite of cake instead.

She was fond of her sister-in-law, who was a loving wife and devoted mother. Marion had a good heart—but she was also prone to being influenced by gossip, and her very fashionable friends were some of the worst gossips in London.

"I never said that." She knew it was her temper speaking, but she didn't care. Richard wasn't like the others, her mistakes, and she didn't want to be accused of lying. If only she knew what exactly had been said at White's, and by whom, and what exactly Richard had done and why.

Marion's brows snapped together. "Then—then you *are* having an affair with him?"

Evangeline fought off the temptation to roll her eyes. "As if there is no space between acquaintance and lover! But since you ask so plainly . . . yes. I am."

She hadn't meant to do this. She'd meant to keep it to herself, her own lovely private affair of the heart. Or body. She hadn't quite decided which it was, but something inside her rose up instinctively to Richard's defense. Whomever he'd waved a sword at had probably deserved it.

The other woman grew agitated. "What? Oh, why?"

"Have you met him?" Evangeline returned. "He's utterly charming, and quite popular in fashionable circles as well— among ladies *and* gentlemen."

Marion flushed. Evangeline would have wagered good

money that even ladies in Marion's circles felt a flutter whenever Richard walked by. "But is he good for you?"

So far, she thought. So far he had been wonderful for her. But as she had no idea what he'd done in this matter, perhaps she was fooling herself. As Marion had pointed out, she'd been wrong before about a man. "I expect he'll explain himself when he returns," she said. "And if his explanation is not satisfactory, be assured I will turn him out at once."

"May I suggest," began Marion, with the air of someone choosing every word with care, "that you do so anyway? Not only is there bound to be talk, over this . . . whatever it is, but . . . My dear. You are *neighbors.* It's unseemly."

"That we can walk back and forth to visit each other without anyone spotting us? How is that worse than Lord Everton leaving his carriage outside Mrs. Armstrong's house, in the heart of Berkeley Square, for hours every night?"

Marion flushed again, looking a trifle annoyed. Mrs. Armstrong was a member of her circle. "That's also not well done, but—"

"It is far more brazen, and right in front of the ton, too."

"Be that as it may." Marion's face was still pink but her expression was serious once more. "Campion's a bit *young* for you, isn't he?"

"Cunningham was far too old for me, and that didn't stop anyone," she said before she could stop herself. "Perhaps Fate is attempting to make amends for it."

Marion blinked, then gave a shocked gasp of laughter. Evangeline grinned, but the moment didn't last.

"You would certainly deserve it, but my dear . . . at our age . . ." Marion paused delicately. "What I mean is, a man of his age will, sooner or later, want to marry . . . and . . . have children . . ."

Evangeline rose, tired of the visit. She did not want to argue with her sister-in-law. She did not want to think of Richard with another, younger, woman. She did not want to be left amid the wreckage of another scandal while the man who caused it walked away untouched.

She burned to storm over to Richard's house and see if he had returned, or perhaps to see Mr. Rieger if he were about and shake some answers out of him. Surely he would know. "Thank you so much for calling, Marion. Do give my best to George, and remember me fondly to Joan and Douglas."

Marion stood, clutching her reticule. "I am worried for you. But also . . . for Joan's and Douglas's sake. I know you haven't a mother's sensibility on these things, but children are so impressionable . . . I would hate for them to draw the wrong conclusion."

Evangeline raised her brows. Joan was about to turn eighteen, and Douglas was twenty-two or twenty-three. Hardly impressionable children. "I wouldn't dream of speaking to either of them about my love affairs."

She looked away, her chin working back and forth. "But they will hear, and when everyone learns he's bought the house next to yours . . ." She bit her lip and fell silent.

"Yes, how devastating it will be if they learn Sir Richard has taken a house in the country." Evangeline had no idea how Marion planned to protect her children from rumors and gossip, particularly since she herself enjoyed them immensely. And really, there was nothing Evangeline could do to prevent people talking about her; she'd learned that well enough over the years. If she'd ever had children, she liked to think she would have erred on the side of telling them everything, in her own way and time, rather than trying to shelter them from anything she disapproved of.

But again, perhaps she was wrong. She'd never had to test it.

"Come, let me walk you out." Evangeline rang for Solly, who appeared at once, as if she'd been lurking nearby and heard the raised voices. "Bring Lady Bennet's things, please, Solly."

Marion gripped her arm when she would have led her out. "Break it off with him," she said with sudden passion. "Please. At least until next year. Joan's just made her debut. Please don't let there be any unkind gossip to distract from that."

Evangeline all but gaped at her. Next year? "Why would anyone hold *Joan* responsible for my actions?"

Marion set her chin. Evangeline knew the answer was that the gossips—even Marion's own friends among them—included some vicious harpies who spared no one. "Not responsible, but associated. You know how these things spread."

"They would say such things about your own daughter?"

Now Marion flushed. She knew they would. "Please, Evangeline. She is my only daughter. Perhaps I am being over cautious, but I—I could not bear it, if I were too lax and my daughter suffered the consequences."

Would she feel this way, if Joan were her daughter?

Perhaps. She sighed, trying to be sympathetic to a mother's anxiety. "I understand. Really, I do. But surely that is extremely unlikely—"

"Break it off," repeated her sister-in-law, her voice tight with anxiety. "Or I shall have to break with you."

She blinked in alarm. "But why? I'm not in London, flaunting anything! And he's a very respectable man, lauded in society! How can we possibly bring disrepute on Joan?"

Marion's fingers dug into her arm. *"Please,* Evangeline."

She stared at the other woman. They were about the same age, and though they hadn't been friends as girls, Evangeline had always hoped for a sisterly relationship. Her disastrous marriage to Court had derailed that—Court's affairs being both widely known and thoroughly scandalous, and thus a horror to Marion—but this . . .

"I'm sorry, Marion," she said quietly. "I can't. I—I find Richard excellent company, and I care for him a great deal. We shall always be discreet—"

Her sister-in-law released her as if scalded. "Very well," she said. "I understand. You do as you wish." And she turned and walked out, leaving Evangeline staring after her, speechless.

Chapter 22

Richard strode up the drive to Wyndham House, heart thudding.

Lately he'd begun walking through the woods, arriving to her garden with Hercule at his heels. Not today. Hercule was at home, and Richard walked up to the front door and rang the bell, like any visitor uncertain of his reception.

When Solly opened it, she gave him an appraising look. "Welcome back, Sir Richard."

I hope I am welcome, he thought as he came in and removed his hat. "Thank you, Solly. Is she in?"

"I think she will be, to you," replied the woman, gesturing for him to go into the front drawing room. "Wait here. There is brandy in the cabinet, if you feel in want of any."

He did, but he smiled and shook his head. She closed the door behind him, and he let out his breath.

He liked this room. It was the most formal in Evangeline's house, but even here it was relaxed and comfortable. By now he had seen enough drawing rooms in London to know that hers was different. It was the room, he realized, of a woman who had decided to live life on her own terms, regardless of what fashion and style dictated. Who didn't mind leaving out her embroidery spilling across the table, or a little basket of toys for her dog, or hanging a watercolor of haphazard skill on the wall.

He knew the last had been done by her niece as a girl and given as a gift, and Evangeline had hung it in the most public room of her home, opposite a large painting he suspected was by Canaletto. On the mantel beneath it was a roughly carved wooden ship. She had told him that her nephew had made it with the penknife she'd given him for his twelfth birthday, all the while beaming proudly at the carving as if it were a priceless sculpture.

She cared for those children as he did for his nephews. Surely she would understand why he'd been away so long. His actions at White's . . .

Perhaps she would not understand those.

Behind him, the door opened with a bang. "What did you do?" she demanded without greeting.

Richard turned, and his heart soared at the sight of her. She wore a new dress of soft peach, with her hair tied up loosely, and he'd never seen a more beautiful sight in his life. But her expression was severe, and he knew without asking that she'd heard about the disastrous dinner at White's.

"You mean at Lord Allen's dinner," he said. "I lost my temper. I was rude to Allen's guests, and I can only humbly apologize."

Evangeline shook her head. "Not that. I don't care a fig for Allen's guests. What did you *do*?"

For answer he took the khukuri from his jacket and held it out. "I showed them my souvenir of Nepal."

Eyes wide, she closed the door and came into the room and touched the sheath gingerly. "I heard it was a sword."

"No." Holding it well clear of her, he drew the knife. "It is a soldier's knife. They wanted to hear of my adventures, so I took it to show them the weapon of a Gurkhali soldier. That is all."

She gave him a suspicious look. "Then why did you leave a note begging me to reserve judgment until you returned?" Then her face changed and she quickly said, "Oh no—how is the boy? I quite forgot . . ."

"He is recovering and will soon be well again," he told her. "My sister was frantic with worry, but with her care, he has come through it. When I departed, Gabriel was playing cards with his mother and asking for pudding again. Gerhard will bring them home from Lyme Regis in a few days." He hesitated. "I came back as soon as I could, after assuring myself he would recover."

Evangeline closed her eyes for a moment. "Thank heavens. I am so glad to hear it." Then her face fell, and she looked tired for a moment. "What happened at White's, Richard? I've heard . . . stories."

He had rehearsed how he would explain, for four straight days. Now that the moment had arrived, his mind was a blank. "It is no excuse for my behavior," he said at last, "but I was provoked. I was wrong to allow my anger to get the better of me," he added quickly. "I am deeply sorry."

She just looked at him, brows arched. He slid the knife back into the sheath and laid it on the table behind him. She waved one hand, and he sank into his usual chair while she seated herself on the sofa.

"Allen invited several of his friends," he said. "Sir Paul Brentwood, Lord Arthur Dunstan, Mr. Edward Parker-Philips, and Lord Halesworth." He saw her color fade at the last name. "Gerhard accompanied me. As I anticipated, they wished to hear tales of our journeys, the more daring and dangerous the better. Many Englishmen do. I brought the knife, thinking it would impress them.

"But one among them began . . ." Again he paused. "He began talking of other matters, and making crude and indecent insinuations."

"About me," she whispered.

He bowed his head. "I attempted to deflect him by pretending ignorance. When he refused to cease, I took out the knife, thinking it would distract him, or perhaps intimidate him into silence. Still he persisted. Gerhard even attempted to reason with him, but he only grew more offensive. That was when I . . ."

"What?" she asked warily as he paused again. "Please just tell me, Richard. I have heard so many dreadful things."

"I slashed the candles with it," he muttered. "Four candles were decapitated, very neatly. That is all the harm that was done." She looked at him with wide eyes. "And I assured him I would be pleased to meet him at dawn," he added with some reluctance.

Evangeline gasped and clapped one hand to her breast. "You challenged him to a duel? Over *me?*"

"No!" He lurched to the edge of the chair. "He apologized. Gerhard is a very diplomatic fellow when he chooses to be, and he persuaded the man it was all very foolish. Halesworth apologized, and we left."

She stared at him a moment longer, then shot to her feet and paced away in a swirl of peach skirts. He sat tense and unmoving, not sure if he had been dismissed or was still being weighed in the balance.

"What did he say?" she asked, a slight tremor in her voice.

He shifted uneasily, not wanting to say it, and she repeated her question in a sharper tone. "What did he *say?* It was about me, I know it was, and I expect it's being whispered in every drawing room in London by now. I deserve to know!"

"I won't say those things aloud," he growled. "Not to you, of all people!"

"Why not?"

"Because they were vile and disgusting, and I would have called out any man who used those terms for a woman—you, my sister, or your friend Lady Woodville!" he snapped, finally losing his temper. "You don't want to hear them. He's filth of the lowest order and I would have gladly shot him, then and there. For you, I refrained." He closed his mouth, breathing hard.

She stared at him, open-mouthed.

Richard sighed and flexed his hands, which had curled into fists. "It was not my intent to expose you to scurrilous gossip," he said tightly. "Very much the opposite. But that— that *Drecksau* persisted, and yes, I threatened him to make him stop." He took a deep breath. "I suppose you heard of all manner of dreadfulness on my part."

Evangeline was pale. "I was told you drew a sword on Allen's party over some slight to me. They said you threatened several members and were thrown out of the club. Rumor says you threatened to challenge any man who approached me, but for a price you might grant them my favors, like a—"

"No," he exclaimed in shock. "God above, no! Never! Not a word of that is true!"

For a long moment they looked at each other, he in dismay, she in shock. Then she gave a gasp of laughter, then another. "I know," she gasped, holding her side. "I knew you couldn't have done that!"

Impetuously he charged across the room to her and seized her hand. "Who said I did? Tell me, and I will—"

She laid her other hand across his mouth. "Never mind them," she whispered, still smiling. "They don't matter."

"You believe me?" he asked cautiously.

She nodded. "I told myself to be on guard, because men have lied to me and I believed them, to my detriment. But I *do* believe you. I can see all of it happening just as you said, and I couldn't say that for the rumors." She put her hands on his cheeks and leaned in to kiss him lightly. "Forgive me for doubting you."

"Forgive me for giving you cause," he said, kissing her again, feverishly. "Forgive me for being so stupid—"

She laughed. "You haven't been any more foolish than I have been. Oh, Richard." She let him pull her into his arms, and as she rested her cheek on his shoulder, the tension seemed to drain out of him. He held her close, gently, breathing deeply of her soft perfume.

After a moment she raised her head to look at him. "Tell me, please. Fanny and my sister-in-law told me what some of the gossip is. I would like to know the truth."

"I will tell you only because I keep no secrets from you." He drew a breath. "Halesworth called you names: Lady Lightskirt. The Countess Courtesan. He said you were an enthusiastic . . . whore, and he suggested forming a club of men who had—who had—"

"Been my lovers?" Evangeline's mouth twisted. She sighed. "What a mistake I made with Halesworth. I wonder if he ever managed to pay his debts, after I refused." Richard glanced at her in astonishment, and she nodded, two spots of color in her cheeks. "It was a long time ago," she said quietly. "Not long after Court . . . Well, I was widowed, and somehow a rumor got around that Court had left me an enormous fortune. It wasn't true, of course—he left my widow's portion and no more. I suspect his heir started the story because Court had drained his own fortune pursuing various pleasures, and the heir preferred to think I'd made off with his money rather than that it was gone on drink and cards.

"But obviously Halesworth put enough credence in that rumor to have a go." For a moment she was quiet, her face shadowed with hurt. "He was so engaging and solicitous, in the beginning," she said with some bitterness. "I thought, perhaps he would be different . . . But he wasn't. He expected me to pay nearly twenty thousand pounds in gaming debts. He was . . . He didn't take it well when I refused."

Richard had to will his breathing to stay regular. He wished he *had* shot Halesworth, or at least cut him. Evangeline stepped back and he let her go. Belatedly he realized there was a desperate scratching at the door, which Evangeline opened. Louis burst into the room, leaping and barking frantically. She scooped up the dog and sat on the sofa, hugging him to her bosom while the Pomeranian licked her hand.

"I suppose I should tell you the rest," Evangeline said, sounding self-conscious and resigned. "Perhaps it will give you a disgust of me, but you might as well hear it now."

He sat beside her and gripped her free hand. "Never," he vowed in a low voice.

"Well." Flustered, she stroked Louis's head until his eyes closed in satisfaction. "I had a flirtation with Sir Elias Burton, but he turned out to be a man after Court's heart, not mine. Fortunately I discovered it before things had progressed too far. He got his parlor maid with child and sacked the young woman when she began to increase. I called him a lecherous goat and refused to see him ever again." She took a deep breath. "The poor girl. He'd turned her out without a reference, and I still suspect he coerced her. He was very handsome and couldn't believe any woman wouldn't yield to him."

She sighed again. "And then there was Ramsdale, who decided he was in love with me and refused to take no for an answer. He persisted until he frightened me. I tried to persuade him kindly, and then firmly, but in the end my brother had to speak to him. I don't know what George told him, but he finally went away." She looked at him. "And that's all, the complete, wretched history of my unlucky love life."

"Until me." He brought their clasped hands to his lips and kissed her knuckles. "I will never betray you like they did."

Her fingers tightened in his. "No?"

He shook his head. "I swear it."

She bit her lip and leaned against him. It felt so good, so right; his eyes burned, and he kissed the top of her head before he could stop himself.

"I admire this dress," he said. "It suits you."

Her expression grew a shade brighter. "Do you? Your Mr. Salvatore made it, with Mrs. Hutchins's oversight."

"The man is a genius," he declared. "First waistcoats, and now gowns worthy of the most beautiful woman in London."

She smiled a little. "Would you really have faced Halesworth over pistols?"

"I would. Gerhard stepped in. As he keeps telling you, he has saved me many times."

She gripped his hand tighter. "You think Halesworth might have prevailed?"

"No. I would have shot him in the heart and been obliged to go abroad again. That is what Gerhard saved me from, not death." He kissed her soft hair again. "I have no desire to go abroad. Not while you are here."

She looked up at him, misty-eyed, and he kissed her mouth. It was all that needed to be said.

That night he stayed to dinner. He didn't go home until after breakfast, and within days that became their pattern. He walked to her house through the woods, and she beamed with joy when he arrived. Sometimes she would walk over to Humberton Hall for tea, or they would share a picnic by the pond while the dogs splashed in the water. Hercule loved the water, while Louis danced along the edge, barking in excitement and making them both laugh until their sides hurt. It was more than enough for him, even if all of London called him a savage and a maniac.

Gerhard eventually took lodgings in London, explaining that he might as well be in town where there was more chance of finding company, and Richard hardly noticed his absence.

Don't fall in love with me, whispered Evangeline's voice in his memory.

Too late, my darling, was his silent reply.

Evangeline never told Richard about Marion's visit. She never told him what Fanny related in the days after, that wagers had been placed on their relationship, and that they were now fixtures in the gossip rags, with all manner of wickedness and indecency ascribed to both. She never told him that she had chosen him over her family and society.

He had stood up for her. Not with a stern word in private, as George had done with Ramsdale, and not by countering ugly gossip, as Fanny tried to do. Richard had pulled a foot-long knife on Stephen Halesworth, in a dining room at White's, of all places, and told him—in front of

Lord Allen and other men of consequence—to close his mouth about her, or Richard would make him. And his friend had not talked him out of it, but had backed him up.

No one else had ever done that for her. Marion recoiled from anything scandalous, and pressed George to do the same. Her own father had sold her into marriage to an old man and a rakehell, on the grounds of preventing scandal. Her mother had offered nothing but empty expressions of the gratification she should find in doing her respectable duty, which had been the biggest load of tripe Evangeline had ever heard.

Richard chose her, publicly and unreservedly. He was wrong to act as he had, of course—he'd all but told White's entire membership, and by extension the entire ton, that they were lovers, and implicitly threatened anyone who spoke ill of her. Sooner or later the proximity of their respective homes would become public knowledge, and the gossips would feast on it.

But she . . . did not care. She didn't care if every living soul in London believed him to be her lover; he *was* her lover, and she had never felt a moment of anything other than satisfaction or delight at that fact.

She stopped going to London. Instead, they rode together and took long, rambling walks. They took holidays to Cornwall instead of Brighton or Bath. Solly, with some encouragement, created a theatrical group with the servants of both households. Sometimes Richard's nephews, on holiday from school, would participate, too, and send them all into gales of laughter. They attended private parties and dinners hosted by friends, and occasionally an opera.

Neither ever mentioned it, but both knew and understood that theirs was an attachment that excluded all others. Evangeline had never been so happy in all her life.

She didn't spend time pining over what could never be. It hurt that Marion was willing to cut her off over something as unreliable and cruel as gossip. She supposed she ought to be angry at George for allowing it, but she expected he had done like she had, and chosen his wife over all others. She did miss seeing Joan, but every time she thought of her brother or her niece, the entertainments in London she had exiled herself from, she would catch sight of Richard and remember that she had made the right choice.

Until six years later, when a letter arrived in the hand of a Bennet footman. She tore it open to see a plea from her brother. Marion was ill—dangerously so. George was taking her to the seacoast immediately. He needed someone to chaperone Joan in their absence.

There is no one else I can trust so well as you to see that she is not sunk into melancholy or grief about her mother, he wrote. *Please help me.*

Included was a brief note from Marion herself: *I would be forever in your debt, Evangeline.*

It was forgiveness, acceptance, a chance to return to the embrace of her family—everything she had told herself she did not regret losing, but somehow still yearned for, deep in her heart. Evangeline clutched the letter to her breast for a moment, before calling for Solly to pack her trunks as she wrote her reply: *Of course I will come.*

Then she went to tell Richard.

CHAPTER 23

1822

"Solly! Goodness, where did my straw bonnet with the blue ribbons go? Do you think I shall want it, if we drive in the park?"

"I'm sure I don't know," returned her companion, who was folding stockings. "But it will be possible to send for it, if you want it later."

"What? Oh, yes," said Evangeline in distraction. She went into her bedroom, then turned around and came back out. "And my satin slippers. I suppose it's very likely I shall have to attend a ball—"

"They are already packed," Solly assured her.

Evangeline pressed one hand to her temple. Good Lord. One would think she was moving her entire household permanently to London, instead of just herself for a few weeks. "Do you think—?" she began at the same time Solly held out her bonnet and gloves.

"Perhaps," said Solly gently, "you should go on, and I will follow with the baggage."

Evangeline looked at her and grimaced. "I'm interfering terribly with the packing." Solly agreed with a wry smile. "Then I shall go. Oh! I must deal with Louis . . . Louis! Where is he?"

"He must be here. Perhaps he has tucked himself into a trunk and hopes to be spirited along."

Evangeline laughed, but it was bittersweet. She couldn't take the dog with her. Marion would never want a dog in her house. But Louis was a perceptive little creature. He was almost surely hiding from the tumult in the house, afraid of what it presaged.

She told her coachman she wanted to go to Humberton Hall before departing for London, then went in search of Louis. She found him in the conservatory, under the chaise. "There you are," she said, getting down onto her knees and leaning down to look at him. "Come out, sweet pup."

He just looked at her.

"Come here, my Louis," she crooned, extending her arm under the chair to stroke his fur. "Come to your mama."

He gave a little whimper and refused to move.

"Oh, darling." She sighed, resting on her elbows. "You cannot come with me. You've realized that, haven't you? But you're going somewhere even better, I promise."

Richard had agreed to keep the dog. He was being very good about the whole thing, not making any protest when Evangeline said she must cancel plans to attend dinner at his sister's, and that she would not be going to the opera with him next week, as they'd planned. Opera was the one public entertainment they still attended together, where they could sit together in the privacy of a dark box.

"Come with me to Richard's," she said to her dog. Louis looked at her, then put his head down on his front paws. "And Hercule," she coaxed. "Wouldn't you like to stay with Hercule?"

His tail gave a twitch.

"I'm sure Richard will have bacon for you," she went on in the same warm, confident tone. "He always does. He scolds me for spoiling the pair of you, when he is far more generous with the bacon. And the cheese, now I think of it."

Louis's head came up. He knew the names of all his favorite treats.

"Come," she said eagerly. "Let's go to him now."

Louis stood and gave himself a full-body shake. Slowly he came out from under the chaise, sniffing at her hand and giving it a lick before letting her scoop him up. She kissed his furry little head and cuddled him close. She would miss him.

She went into the hall, and saw with relief that the carriage was waiting. She had already packed Louis's things— his sleeping basket, his cushion, the old bit of wool blanket he liked to chew on and the rope toys she had knotted for him. She had also made a list of his favorite things and his habits, as if Richard didn't already know these things perfectly well.

On the drive over, Louis stood in her lap and put his paws on the window, peering out and panting with excitement. He did like carriage rides, even more than he liked walks in the woods. She made the most of petting him and telling him how much she would miss him, and she resolutely blinked away the tear that formed in her eye.

"Ah, our guest has arrived," said Richard when she reached Humberton Hall. "Come in, Prince Louis, come in." Hercule trotted forward, tail wagging, and the two dogs sniffed each other complacently. "You are leaving," Richard said to her.

She nodded. "Solly has cast me out. I am too much in her way, fretting over what to take. She pointed out that I am only going four miles into town, and anything I want later can easily be fetched, and so I should stop pestering her to death and simply *go*." She smiled as she imitated her companion's stern tone.

"As usual, she is correct in every detail. And the same applies to me: if ever you want me, simply send word and I shall come at once." He raised her hand to his lips.

She sighed, but happily. "You are too good to me. I'll write to you as soon as I arrive and acquaint you with the lay of the land."

"To let me know when it is safe for me to show my face about town," he teased.

Evangeline laughed. "That's too harsh!" He cocked a brow, and she laughed again, a little more ruefully. "She's very ill," she said in apology for Marion. "I don't wish to upset her even by asking—"

"I know. I admire your generosity." He squeezed her hand and released her. "Now, how shall I occupy this fellow in your absence?"

Louis was standing watching them, and at Richard's regard, he gave a little yip.

"Long walks, every morning," said Evangeline firmly. "No bacon. And he must be combed from head to tail every other night."

Louis barked in disagreement, and both laughed.

"Thank you," she said.

"I know how important this is to you." He drew her into his arms. "I hope Lady Bennet recovers swiftly and is home soon, although my reasons are partly for her family, and partly for my own selfish gratification."

She leaned against him, sliding her arms around his waist. She would miss this—him. They had been separated before, naturally. He had delivered his nephews to their various schools. She had gone for a fortnight's holiday at a spa with Fanny. They would be only four miles apart, a distance easily covered in a day. But still it felt different. Perhaps because she was facing a nebulous but daunting task, chaperoning a young lady on the ton with no warning or chance to prepare, for who only knew how long. It would all seem so much easier if Richard would be with her, laughing with her over her inevitable mistakes, comforting her if she and Joan didn't get on as well as she hoped.

But he would not be there, because that was a favor too much. Marion was trusting her, and Evangeline didn't dare push her luck.

"I will miss you," she whispered, to keep her voice from breaking.

"And I you." He tipped up her chin. "But I have faith you will be a marvelous chaperone and an excellent companion to the young lady. I hope you enjoy it immensely.”

“I hope so!” She kissed him quickly, beginning to smile. “I am sure you can come visit at least once. I’ll write and tell you when.”

“Rest assured, I will come.”

She stepped away, blinking hard, and scooped up her dog. “Be a good dog,” she told Louis, who wriggled wildly. She handed him to Richard. “I fear he will run after me.”

Richard took the protesting Pomeranian to the morning room, deposited him inside, and closed the door. Louis began barking, and Evangeline blinked again as she turned to the door. “Good-bye.”

“One more thing,” he said, and caught her in his arms and kissed her, deeply, passionately, and when he finally released her, Evangeline could barely hear Louis’s barking.

“You do know how to make a woman miss you,” she said unsteadily.

“It would be only fair,” he replied. “I will be desolate without you.”

It was almost noon by the time the carriage turned into South Audley Street, where the Bennet house stood. Evangeline found herself peering out the window, curious to see it again. It had been several years since she’d last been there.

She’d grown up in that house, with the curving staircase she and her brother had rolled balls down and pretended to be pirates climbing aboard a ship and once slid down atop a large atlas. Her nephew Douglas must have heard the story, for he’d done the same as a boy. Unfortunately, he’d done it when George and Marion had guests for dinner, and Evangeline would never forget the expressions on their faces when he crashed into the entry hall with a mighty shout of triumph. Marion had been shocked, her face white with embarrassment. But George . . . Evangeline had seen him smile for a moment before agreeing with his wife that it was of course very naughty behavior.

She sighed. It was wrong to think of the times Marion had been too strict, when the woman was so ill now. Even though she had stopped inviting Evangeline to dinners or parties, she still wrote to let her know how Joan and Douglas were getting on. George still came to see her now and then, so the breach had never been complete. And now, finally, was a chance to put it behind her.

She straightened her shoulders, summoned a smile, and climbed down from the carriage. She was here for Joan, to comfort her and guide her and offer an understanding ear for any of Joan's worries. She was not here on her own agenda. She was going to keep Marion's feelings and strictures in mind at all times, and not do anything that would upset her.

IT TOOK her only twenty-four hours to smash that resolution to bits.

When the butler came to take her pelisse, she recognized him as the young footman she had schemed with in her youth. "Smythe," she'd cried in delight, and then told Joan how Smythe had helped her sneak around her parents, years ago.

When Joan cast a covetous eye on her dress—a new one of saffron cotton, with some charms Mrs. Hutchins had found in a warehouse on the India docks—Evangeline had heard herself saying "You mustn't tell your mother . . ." before telling Joan all about Mr. Salvatore, who made all her gowns with the same disregard for conventional fashion, and then offered to take Joan to see him about a dress of her own.

And when a handsome young man came to call the next morning, she took one look at him and lost her mind, along with all her vows not to interfere.

"I hope I've not ruined things already," she fretted to Solly, who had arrived with her trunks and hatboxes.

"What did you say to him?"

She sighed. "I told him to come to tea."

"Why?" Solly would have made an excellent attorney, with her patient tone and open questions.

Evangeline checked that Joan wasn't nearby before answering. "What else should I say? A handsome, well-dressed man calls on my niece—and she never sent for me to join her, by the by—and departs looking enormously pleased about something."

Solly raised her brows. "Isn't that what every young lady, and her mama, wants? A handsome, eligible gentleman coming to call?"

"Yes, but I don't know that she would approve of this gentleman." Evangeline sighed. "He said my nephew asked him to call on Joan and see to her contentment. Was I supposed to call him a liar and throw him out?"

Solly raised a brow. "If your actions were purely logical, why are you alarmed?"

She bit her lip. Viscount Burke had been the young man's name. She remembered his father, who had been one of the most dashing—and outrageous—gentlemen in London when she was a girl. Despite not being in London anymore, Evangeline still heard some of the gossip; Fanny brought it with her on her weekly visits for tea. She'd heard Burke's name, which meant he'd done something scandalous, though she couldn't remember what. "He might be a rake."

Solly just looked at her. She knew very well that Evangeline knew plenty of rakes and enjoyed their company at times.

Evangeline threw up her hands. "How do I know? I don't. If he is, I shall have to throw him out." She paused. "If he is not . . ."

"If only you had some way to learn more," said Solly somberly. "If only you had someone you trust, who would tell you anything and everything you want to know about a man. That would certainly be very useful, at times like these." The woman was definitely laughing at her.

"You're right." She sat down at the desk and took out paper, aware that she was about to break another of her own guidelines for this stay in London. "I must ask Richard."

Chapter 24

The sky was barely light when Richard set out with the dogs for Mayfair. It was only four miles to the Bennet house, but he had been told to arrive as early as he could, and he had had difficulty restraining himself this long.

He was impatient to see her again.

When she had come to him, saying her brother had asked her to return to London to chaperone her niece, he had understood. He didn't have the highest respect for Sir George Bennet and his wife, but he knew Evangeline loved her niece and held her blameless for the rupture in their family. Richard had smiled and said of course she must go, and had sent his best wishes for Lady Bennet's health. He had even agreed to keep Louis, as Evangeline didn't think her sister-in-law would like the dog in her house.

The Pomeranian had not been pleased to be left in Chelsea. Richard had had to shut him up, barking hysterically, in the morning room when Evangeline left, dabbing at her eyes with a handkerchief. It had made him smile wryly, how devoted she and her spoiled little pup were. "I feel the same way," he'd told the dog, once she was gone and Louis had exhausted himself.

And now she had been away for a week. Humberton Hall had never felt so dull and dreary. Richard was mildly unsettled by that. It wasn't as if they had never spent time apart. There had been illnesses, guests, visits with Clemency to see the boys at school . . . Still, knowing that he *couldn't* walk through the woods past the pond and see her, just for a few minutes, cast a pall over his days that he hadn't expected.

Louis trotted eagerly at his side. The dog had been reluctant to get up from his cushion by the hearth until Richard said Evangeline's name, at which point Louis leapt up and ran to the door, barking excitedly and raring to go. Again, he found himself in complete agreement with Louis.

They reached South Audley Street in good time, though Louis began to flag after the third mile. Richard slowed his pace and was beginning to think he would have to carry the little beast when they encountered a pack of geese, being driven to market. The Pomeranian exploded in a flurry of barking that sparked an uproar among the geese, a flurry of shouting from the boy shepherding them, and Richard scooped up the incensed Louis with a hasty apology.

"Stop that," he scolded the dog, thankful for Hercule walking placidly alongside him.

Louis gave one last bark, his short tail wagging fiercely, then licked Richard's hand.

"That will not work on me," he said sternly. "You must behave."

Another lick, then Louis rested his head on Richard's arm with a gusty sigh.

"We are almost there," he said in amusement. "I suspect she will have bacon waiting for you." Louis perked up and barked happily, and Hercule danced a few steps, having also recognized the word.

South Audley Street was quiet at this hour, with the rising sun just peeping over the neighboring rooftops. He knocked instead of pulling the bell, as instructed, and it was swept open at once. "Good morning, sir," said the butler. He didn't blink an eye at the orange dog in Richard's arm, now wriggling fiercely because Evangeline had come into the hall.

For a moment Richard felt stunned immobile. God, she was beautiful, her dark hair pinned up loosely in the soft way he liked so much, wearing a rose dress that flattered her curves. He'd missed her *so* much.

"Good morning," she said, coming forward, her dark eyes glowing with welcome.

Somehow he managed to bow, and then he set Louis on the floor. The Pomeranian was too excited to bark, and was making desperate whining noises. His claws scrabbled on the marble floor as he ran to his mistress and jumped at her skirts until she scooped him up in her arms and got her hands licked thoroughly.

"And good morning to you, my sweet boy," she said, laughing, as she tried to fend off the licking. She put down the dog as Richard handed off his coat and hat to the servant, then beckoned him into a small but bright breakfast room, where the table already held several steaming dishes. Hercule trotted in after Louis, and got his head and ears thoroughly scratched, too. Evangeline closed the door behind them and turned into his open arms.

"Mein Gott," he breathed, pressing his face to her hair and inhaling deeply of her perfume. "I've missed you."

She tugged at his jacket, tipping her smiling lips toward his. "Show me."

He smiled and kissed her. He intended it to be brief, because they were standing in someone else's house and who knew when servants might walk in, and he knew very well that he'd been invited to breakfast at dawn because Evangeline was nervous about her niece meeting him. He suspected he wasn't supposed to be here at all, given the stray remarks she'd made over the years about her sister-in-law.

And yet, when she caught his face in both hands and kissed him, all that faded away. He pulled her close and bore her back against the door. She made that sound in her throat, the one that conveyed surprise, delight, and desire all at once, and he felt as flushed and reckless as a boy.

Louis gave a sharp bark. Evangeline started, and Richard raised his head.

"Goodness," she whispered, her mouth still red from his kiss. "What a bad influence you are, Sir Richard."

He laughed and loosened his grip on her, raising her hand to his lips. "Have pity on a man who has been starved for affection and companionship."

She blushed, but her dark eyes danced with laughter. "Starved! It has been six days."

"It has felt like six years."

"Pooh!" She shook her head, but she was still smiling

intimately at him, and she let him lead her by the hand to the table. "I would swear it felt like no more than *four* years."

He pulled out her chair. "Ah, but you have had much to distract you, while I was abandoned, with only poor Louis to remind me of you."

Evangeline wrinkled her nose at him as she sat. Louis, hearing his name, emerged from beneath the table where he'd been hunting for crumbs, and put his paws on her skirt.

"See," said Richard, taking his own seat. "He and I have been two sad and lonely wretches, doing our best to console each other."

The dog was already on her lap, his little eyes scanning the table and his tongue hanging out as he panted in excitement. Evangeline stroked his head. "But now here you both are, much to my delight." She paused and glanced at him. "Thank you, Richard, for being so understanding."

He waved it aside. Now that he was here with her again, the inconvenience faded from his mind. "I do understand. How have you enjoyed your time here?"

She fed Louis a bit of bacon from the platter, and a larger piece to Hercule. "Very well. Better than I expected, to be truthful. George and Marion had already left by the time I arrived, and poor Joan looked quite dazed and unsettled by the entire affair. But she and I are getting on very well, much to my relief."

He smiled. "Were you truly worried?"

"I didn't know," she said. "It's been so long since I saw her, and her mother . . ." Her smile faltered, then returned more determined. "But she's a darling girl and I'm so delighted I can do this for her."

"Was the information I sent helpful?"

She nodded. He had been serving them from the dishes on the table as they talked, and now she took a bite of berry compote. "Oh, yes. I didn't want to trust my memory. It put my mind greatly at ease to learn I was not wrong."

She had written to him the day after she arrived here, asking what he could discover about Viscount Burke. Burke, a friend of the Bennets' rather rakish son Douglas, appeared to have taken an interest in her niece, and she wished to know more about the young man before deciding how she should proceed. Clemency had been all too willing to share a veritable flood of gossip and innuendo, and Richard had had to ask at his club for the truth. He'd sent a long letter two days ago.

"Very good." He poured his coffee, then hesitated. "Perhaps that is all you should do, on that count."

Evangeline blinked at him in surprise. "All? What do you mean?"

He held up one hand in surrender. "You have satisfied yourself that he is not a rogue or a fortune hunter. Is that not enough?"

She gave him a narrow-eyed look. "I'm sure I don't know what you are suggesting."

He grinned. "You know very well. You believe Miss Bennet fancies the fellow, and you are tempted to a little matchmaking."

"Oh, Richard," she said, then spoiled her stern tone by laughing. "And what if I *do* think she fancies him? It's as plain as day that he fancies her."

"Then he will not need your help," he replied. Everything he'd heard of Burke indicated the man was not shy about pursuing what he wanted. Richard hadn't passed on the most salacious bits of information, but if anything, he suspected Evangeline might have to protect her niece from the brash young viscount, rather than encourage her to accept any advances Burke might make.

She made a face. "Perhaps not. But I like to know what I'm dealing with."

"Then he has approached her?"

From the way she busied herself with buttering a piece of toast, Richard knew. "He called upon us," she finally said. "Douglas, the scamp, urged him to do it, before he also left the city. That must count for something, don't you think? Douglas is a bit of a rogue, but he would certainly know if anyone of his acquaintance was unacceptable to his mother, and I notice he hasn't sent any other of his friends to call." She looked at him in appeal, and he gave her a wry look. Her lips quirked and she waved one hand. "Anyway, I met Lord Burke as he was leaving, after he had spoken to Joan, and I must say, he looked very pleased by the encounter. I invited him to tea—"

"Evie," he said with a soft sigh.

She gave him an unrepentant look. "Why shouldn't I? I had only just arrived, and here was a handsome young man on the stairs, saying he'd been bidden to look after Joan! I needed to size him up. What else ought I to have done?"

"Nothing," he replied. "Allow him to leave, then speak to the young lady. Perhaps she did not wish to see him."

"Richard," she said in reproach. He met her gaze with a raised brow. With a guilty look over her shoulder at the door, she lowered her voice. "How could I? Joan is four-and-twenty, and no other suitors have been to call. I don't know much about him, but I know who he *is*, and I felt it would be wrong to turn away a potential, very eligible, suitor." She sat back with a tiny shrug. "If Joan takes a disgust to him, of course I would put a swift end to things."

He shook his head, but with a rueful smile. Even after her own disastrous experience of marriage, Evangeline was still a romantic at heart. Somehow that pleased him, even if he thought she ought to stay out of any courtship involving her niece. "But I presume she has *not* taken him in dislike."

Her eyes brightened and she leaned forward. "No! Quite the opposite. And having seen them together, I believe the fascination is mutual."

"'Let me not to the marriage of true minds admit impediment,'" he said in amusement. "Of course I would not wish to spoil a young lady's happiness." He put his hand on hers. "I merely hope you will make very certain that the interest is mutual, and not likely to upset or alarm Lady Bennet. She has always been a woman of firm ideas." More like rigid and inflexible, to his thinking, but he didn't say that. "Miss Bennet is not your daughter, after all, and the decision is not yours."

Evangeline sobered. "True. I have no wish to anger Marion. And I swear upon my life, the moment Burke puts a toe out of line, I will whip him from this house and never allow him back in."

"I shall send a warning around to the man, that he will have you to face if he trifles with the young lady," said Richard with a grin.

She slapped his hand lightly. "If he needs a warning like that, he's not the man for Joan. You know I would never allow her to be hurt."

"Of course not," he said, putting aside his reservations. Everyone said Burke was no idiot; he would know the rules of society. He was also a friend of Miss Bennet's brother, which ought to temper his actions further. Richard guessed Burke was like a great many other single young gentlemen— willing to be wild and carouse for a time, but with some measure of honor to keep him from crossing the line, and a nebulous plan to settle down into respectable marriage eventually.

"Clemency is attempting to persuade me to give speeches again," he said, not wanting to argue over Lord Burke any longer.

"Oh? Do you intend to?"

He lifted one shoulder. "I don't know." He glanced at her. "Would you also attend, if I were to give a speech?"

"Perhaps," she said with a coy look. "If the evening promised to be entertaining."

He leaned toward her. "What if I assure you . . . that it would end in your complete satisfaction?"

She tilted toward him, too, one hand still stroking Louis's fur. "You would personally guarantee it?"

"I would see to it myself," he replied.

She smiled, one brow arched. "How could I refuse? One is so rarely guaranteed *complete* satisfaction."

He ran his fingertip over her wrist. "I hope you wouldn't refuse. Your presence would assure *my* satisfaction."

She smiled, the same dreamy smile that had captivated

him from across Lord Allen's drawing room years ago. "I don't wish to deny you any such pleasure."

"I hope not," he returned, "since my pleasure is vested in bringing *you* pleasure."

Her eyes grew soft. "Silly man! You must know you bring me more pleasure than anything else in this world."

His heart gave a solid thump. His exact feeling about her. The last several days away from her had driven home to him how much so.

He had agreed to a discreet, almost clandestine, relationship because she'd wanted it, and he'd wanted her badly enough to agree to virtually anything she asked of him. He'd had no way of knowing where things would lead, though. Instead of his attraction burning itself out eventually, like a flame consuming oil-soaked rags, it had become something integral to his very being. He couldn't imagine being without her, and more and more it chafed that they must keep a discreet distance.

Clemency had told him once that everyone whispered that they were living together in sin, which had given Richard a stab of unease. He'd listened and watched closely, but had seen no sign that it afflicted Evangeline. He himself suffered no ill effects, though they would have had to be crippling to deter him. Perhaps the gossips had finally had enough of them.

He wanted more. More of her, more of *them*.

If she were willing to go to a salon with him, on his arm, it would be a tentative first step toward a public declaration. He loved this woman. His heart and mind had been pledged to her for some time, but only in private. He wanted to say it aloud; he wanted everyone to know. He wanted her hand on his arm when he attended some pompous aristocrat's salon, he wanted her as his dinner partner at every ball, he wanted to help her into his carriage at the end of the evening and take her back to their home, where he wouldn't need to slip away in the first blush of dawn through the garden.

Behind them, the door opened. A tall young lady with dark hair stood there, fairly gaping at them—at *him*. Richard hid his grimace of dismay behind a polite smile. This must be Joan, whose mother thought him scandalous and dangerous.

He did not wait, but took his leave after a few pleasantries. He'd had his moment with Evangeline, and it would carry him through a few more days without her. He walked home with the dogs, Louis protesting all the way, and considered his next act.

CHAPTER 25

Despite Richard's words of caution, Evangeline felt a wholly unexpected excitement over her new role as chaperone.

Lord Burke had called twice, sent flowers—to Joan *and* to Evangeline—and asked to take her niece driving. He also looked at Joan with the sort of veiled fascination Evangeline recognized. He might not think himself the marrying kind, but he likely soon would.

Of course she'd written to Richard for intelligence of the viscount. He'd reported back favorably, as far as these things went. And Evangeline, not unaware of the delight Joan was trying desperately to hide at being noticed by one of the handsomest, most eligible single peers in London, made her first grievous error.

When Lord Burke had written to her, very properly, asking permission to take Joan driving, Evangeline had seen the smile that lit Joan's face when she read it. She'd given her permission. And Joan, despite blushing furiously and muttering about Lord Burke's general unreliability, had accepted the invitation.

As a result, two days later, Evangeline was pacing the drawing room, with no idea where her niece was or when she would be back. Smythe, the Bennet butler, could only tell her that Lord Burke had called very early that morning, that Joan had been inexplicably up and dressed to go out, and they had driven off together.

That was not what Evangeline had envisioned. She had pictured Burke calling at a decent hour, coming inside like a proper gentleman, and answering her questions about where they intended to drive and when to expect them back. She had been prepared for that, even though it had given her a spark of incredulous amusement that she, of all people, was such a starchy chaperone. Still, she told herself not to worry; a turn or two around the park was as respectable as Marion could wish, and would only take an hour.

An hour had gone by. Then another. And another.

Joan and Lord Burke did not reappear.

Even as she told herself not to panic, that rushing to the park in her own carriage in search of them would be a mistake, Evangeline couldn't stop agonizing over where they might be. And what she would tell George. Where had Burke taken Joan? What could they be doing? She wore a path in the carpet, pacing from door to window.

Smythe silently brought tea, with the brandy decanter alongside the pot.

Evangeline laughed bitterly when she saw it. "You've read my mind, Smythe."

"Don't fret, my lady," replied the butler gently. "Miss Bennet is a sensible young lady."

She glanced sideways at him. "And Lord Burke?"

He conceded that hit with a dip of his head. No one knew, for certain, about Lord Burke.

She picked up the decanter and poured a healthy splash into her cup of tea. "What do you think Sir George would do to me, if there were a scandal? Drawing and quartering, or pistols at dawn?"

He smiled, just a little, at that. "He's not at home, madam. Who's to say he'll know anything about this?"

She smiled reluctantly. Smythe had said much the same thing to her decades ago, opening a scullery window to let her climb back into the house after a night out as her father furiously searched the attics. Smythe had become the second footman when Evangeline, only a year younger at thirteen, was just embarking on her wild phase. In Sir Robert's strict household, they'd been complementary spirits. He'd helped her avoid several punishments, usually when she'd slipped out of the house for one madcap adventure or another, and she'd helped him along in his post, letting him know her parents' preferences and even slipping him her pin money when once he'd accidentally spoiled some table linen and needed to replace it before it was discovered.

She waved at a chair. "Will you sit with me?"

He hesitated.

She got up and strode to the drawing room door and closed it firmly. She didn't need to compound her mistakes by compromising his authority in the household. "*Please*, Denny," she said, massaging her temples with her fingertips.

"I need company . . . to stop me from doing something very reckless indeed . . ."

He perched on the edge of a chair. "If I may be so bold . . ."

"Please!"

"Miss Bennet does not receive many callers," he said. "Gentleman callers, I should say. I was struck by how pleased she was to see Lord Burke this morning. She must have expected him, to be awake and dressed so very early of a morning, but she also looked surprised to see him." He cleared his throat. "I've known the young lady since she was an infant. Her delight was obvious." He darted a quick glance at her. "She reminded me of you, Miss Evie, when something unexpectedly turned your way."

Evangeline scrunched up her face ruefully. "Never say so! She's much cleverer than I ever was."

"As I said," he replied with a straight face, "she's a very sensible young lady."

She laughed. "Not like me at all, then!" Then she threw herself into a chair. "And I can only pray my brother isn't much like my father, where his daughter is concerned."

"He's not."

She looked up in surprise. He seemed to realize how confident he'd sounded, and cast his gaze up to the ceiling, giving him a vaguely pious air. "What I meant to say is . . . Sir George is a thoughtful gentleman. His temper is . . . far milder than Sir Robert's."

"Thank heavens for that," she said with feeling.

Another small smile crossed his face. "And he's a devoted father. Beyond fond of Miss Bennet and her brother. Much more . . . tenderhearted than Sir Robert, if I may say so."

"You may," she told him warmly, "and I'm very glad to hear it."

Smythe rose to his feet. "Chin up, ma'am," he said bracingly. "I've been in this household for nearly forty years, and I've never yet told tales when I shouldn't." He pressed his lips together in exaggeration.

Evangeline smiled ruefully. "To my inestimable benefit! Thank you, Smythe. You're invaluable."

He bowed. "I do my best, ma'am. I daresay all this will work out well enough, with a little time, and no need for anyone to do anything reckless or inappropriate." He left her there, and finally Evangeline heard the rattle of carriage wheels outside the house, drawing to a stop. She flew to the window and spied Joan's bonnet as Lord Burke handed her down from the curricle. Both appeared unhurt and perfectly proper.

Thank God. Thank every saint in heaven. She pressed one hand to her breast and made a silent vow not to be so negligent again, when it came to Joan's safety. She must keep a closer eye on the girl, for Joan's own sake—and her own.

Then she took a deep breath before going into the hall to meet her niece.

CHAPTER 26

The next time Lord Burke came to call, Evangeline was ready and waiting for him.

It was plain to see that Joan was infatuated with the fellow. The viscount had taken her *ballooning*, of all things, which nearly gave Evangeline heart palpitations, but Joan . . . Joan had been enthralled by it. Her face had lit up as she described rising through the morning air and gazing over the whole city of London, from St. Paul's to Chelsea, and she'd called the viscount by his Christian name.

When Evangeline had raised a brow at that, Joan had blushed scarlet and mumbled something about knowing him since childhood, and then she'd gone silent when Evangeline prodded her about, perhaps, possibly being courted by the viscount.

It didn't bother Evangeline; quite the contrary. It gave her a small thrill of her own that her dear niece might have fallen in love—with a handsome, charming gentleman, no less, who was clearly just as caught by Joan—and she resolved to do everything in her power to oversee this potential courtship with the utmost propriety while also doing absolutely nothing to inhibit the progress of it.

Marion couldn't fault that, surely. Burke was a very eligible gentleman, and his hijinks weren't really any worse than what George had got up to—nor worse than what Douglas, Joan's brother, was still actively getting up to. Burke was in fact a close friend of Douglas's, as Joan had told her several times. But perhaps it was time to make certain Burke knew he was being evaluated as a suitor.

"How kind of you to call again," she said to Burke when Smythe had shown him into the drawing room.

Lord Burke's gaze, which had strayed to the door, jerked back to hers with some evidence of alarm.

Evangeline had purposely not sent Smythe to tell Joan about their caller until after he'd shown Burke into the drawing room. "I've wanted to have a chance to have a word with you, sir."

"Indeed, ma'am?" He was a big fellow, tall and broad-shouldered and exceedingly fit. But today he perched on the edge of the sofa, his hands between his knees like a boy who'd been caught doing wrong.

Which he had done. "Ballooning?" she asked dryly.

Incredibly, he perked up. "Did she tell you about it? I hope Miss Bennet enjoyed it as much as I did."

That was very interesting. He still looked like a boy, but now one who had a ripping good tale to tell. Much the same way Joan had looked, when relating the same tale. "How much did *you* enjoy it?" she asked curiously.

"Enormously," he said with relish, and then began

waxing enthusiastic about gas burners and balloon ropes. He also slipped and started to call Joan by her Christian name before catching himself with another covert glance at the door.

Joan had not yet appeared. Evangeline knew that some new dresses had been delivered that morning, and hopefully Joan was trying on one of them. The colors promised to go very well with her coloring, and the styles were elegant and only the slightest bit daring. One sight of her, dressed flatteringly, might clarify Lord Burke's mind.

"I never would have asked her to go up if I weren't completely satisfied it was safe," he ended.

"And you *are* persuaded it was safe?" It didn't really matter now that they were back on terra firma, but Evangeline wanted to know how considerate he was of Joan.

"Absolutely," he said without a flicker of hesitation.

She took a breath, and pressed a little. "In all ways?"

Richard had delivered the men's gossip about the viscount; Fanny had told her the ladies' view of him. He was indeed one of the most eligible men in London, but he was also one of the most elusive. He was never seen in the company of ladies, let alone unmarried ones; he was rarely seen at fashionable society events at all. Many a hostess had torn out her hair trying to lure the viscount to her party, where one of her single daughters or sisters might catch his eye. If there had been a ranked list of the biggest prizes on the marriage market, Burke would have been near the top. Handsome, titled, and rich—very, *very* rich.

His attentions to Joan had so far escaped anyone's notice, but taking her ballooning and continuing to call on her would change that. If, by some incredible chance, Burke hadn't thought of it, and had no intention of courting Joan, he ought to be warned off as soon as possible.

But if, on the other hand, he was considering just that . . .

"Take care not to create any expectation you don't plan to fulfill," she told him.

He bristled at this, taking her meaning. "Are you warning me off?"

Oh, very interesting. He wasn't taken aback, or revolted. He was affronted that she might be trying to deter him.

Evangeline smiled a little. "Rather the contrary! Merely letting you know the scope of the . . . challenge ahead of you." George. Marion. He would need to impress far more than Joan or even Evangeline.

"What challenge?" he demanded, looking both irked and determined, but then the door behind them opened, and Burke shot to his feet, a strange expression on his face.

Evangeline knew it would be Joan. She turned and saw her niece, wearing a turquoise dress they'd ordered a week ago. She was pleased to see that the color did flatter Joan's coloring, and the cut was infinitely better for her curvy figure than the beruffled and beribboned dresses Marion had dressed her in. Joan looked like a woman, not a little girl dressing up.

And Lord Burke looked like a man who'd just been struck by a thunderbolt to the forehead.

Well, well.

She sat quietly and watched them strike sparks off each other. Joan was teasing him—something about a wagered shilling—and Burke's eyes practically glowed with fascination. Evangeline had seen that look in a man's eyes before. In Richard's, when she'd stood up in the pond and opened her eyes to see him watching her, breathless and entranced.

Within days of that look, they'd been lovers.

"My niece tells me you are rebuilding your house," she blurted out, feeling suddenly as if she ought to redirect things. Mentally she sighed at herself; house building? But it was the only thing she could think of that might cool the sizzling air. She'd not heard Joan mention anything of his taste in music, books, theater, sport, even politics.

But it turned out that Lord Burke was as enthusiastic about his house improvements as he was about ballooning. Even more remarkable, Joan was as interested in the subject as she'd been at the modiste, asking questions and hanging on his answers about plasterwork and rooflines.

"Would you like to see it?" Burke asked of a sudden.

Evangeline seized the moment. "I should like it above all else," she said warmly. Joan gave her a startled look. "I've often contemplated improvements to my own house, but it's so difficult to picture them. Have you installed any water closets?" she asked Burke.

He cut a swift glance at Joan. "On every floor."

Her niece smiled, and soon they were on their way. Evangeline prattled on about the water closets—which she *was* interested in seeing, actually; such a convenience they would be—to cover her racing thoughts.

He owned a house in Hanover Square. A very good address, even if his house was currently not the most elegant on the square. Marion couldn't object to that in the slightest. Inside, the smells of plaster, paint, and sawdust hung thick in the air, but the rooms taking shape were very pleasing. Another point in his favor. Evangeline strolled through, listening with half an ear as Burke talked about his plans, and Joan responded with far more enthusiasm for new woodwork than one might expect from a London young lady.

She paused just inside the doorway of a parlor. She'd deliberately left them alone in the dining room. What were they saying?

"That was one of my favorite holidays from school," Burke was saying, almost wistfully.

"Why?" exclaimed Joan. "I meant to say . . . I'm glad you enjoyed your time there . . ."

Her lips parted as she realized they were talking about Helston Hall, the Bennet property in Cornwall. Evangeline had loved that house, and all of Cornwall, where she could run free and swim in the ocean and ride ponies on the dunes. But her mother had thought it too rustic and so they'd spent little time there.

Shamelessly she eavesdropped harder. Burke had been there as a lad, invited by Douglas—and it sounded as if they'd got into a great lot of trouble. Evangeline inhaled as something Joan had told her finally made sense.

After the ballooning trip, Evangeline had made a concerted effort to discover how deep and true Joan's attraction to Lord Burke ran. Joan had admitted that her mother disapproved of Burke, very strongly. Marion considered him wild and arrogant and—worst of all—indifferent to propriety. It all rang true to what Evangeline knew of Marion, but at the same time . . . Burke was young, handsome, eligible, and wealthy. Virtually every mother of the ton would be delighted if the viscount began paying attention to one of their daughters. The unkind thought that perhaps Marion didn't really want to see Joan wed had crossed her mind, for there were vanishingly few men in London who could possibly meet Marion's standards, yet still be acceptable to Joan.

But now, listening in on Burke's and Joan's conversation, Evangeline realized precisely why Marion didn't care for Burke. It wasn't anything to do with Joan, or his behavior now. He'd encouraged Douglas's wilder instincts when her son was still a boy and not yet a rakish rogue. How much easier it was to blame an outsider, a boy with no parents or protective family to defend him, for her son's wild behavior rather than admit that she had little sway over his actions.

Evangeline would have laughed, if it hadn't been such an important point. Perhaps back then, Marion hadn't fully realized that deviltry was bred deep in the Bennets.

She made herself move away. She *was* interested in the improvements to the house, and she'd heard enough. There was genuine trust and feeling between Joan and Burke. He showed Joan something that made her niece exclaim in delight, and Evangeline smiled ruefully when she realized it was a coal lift, to bring coal straight from the cellar to the parlor.

Decidedly not a rakish seduction in progress.

When they met her in the hall a few minutes later, she looked at Burke with fresh eyes. He was boyishly enthusiastic, pointing out the skylight above the stairs and the new banister, stealing glances at Joan every few minutes to judge her reaction. He seemed positively thrilled to show Joan water closets and pipes and new floors—and even more promising, Joan was thrilled to see them. Again Evangeline drifted away, this time to think.

Burke was *so* eligible. Roguish ways aside, that was undeniable. He had an old title and a healthy fortune, soon a very handsome house in a fashionable neighborhood, and he gave every sign of falling hard for Joan. George, she reflected, had been much the same, although he hadn't yet inherited when The Honorable Miss Marion Douglas caught his eye.

She blew out a breath. She had been caught up in her own troubles then, and hadn't paid much attention to how George went about his courting. But she knew he had reformed his behavior; he gave up some particularly dissolute friends, and curtailed his drinking and gaming. And he had settled right down after his wedding. Thirty years later he was still a devoted husband and attentive father. Surely Burke could be the same.

Her companions had gone into the main bedchamber, which smelled of wet plaster. Their voices were low, echoing indistinctly in the empty room. Evangeline wished she knew more about Burke, or London society. She felt the weight of ignorance pressing down on her. Should she encourage this suit, or dissuade the young man because of Marion's animosity? Perhaps he would be undaunted; perhaps he, like George, would change his life to win his love's favor.

Or . . . perhaps he would be offended, and turn his attentions elsewhere. Joan was twenty-four years old and had been out for six years. Fanny reported that she was generally liked, but also something of a wallflower. Joan's reactions alone were enough to tell Evangeline that suitors were unusual for her.

She stared out the window at Hanover Square for several minutes before realizing how quiet it had become. Joan and Lord Burke had not emerged from the bedchamber, but they were no longer speaking. Evangeline felt a start of alarm. She had suggested Joan let the viscount kiss her, but now she was doubting everything. She strode after them, determined to keep a close eye on her charge, but with no clear idea in her mind how to proceed.

Chapter 27

"It would really be the most thrilling thing in London this year," Clemency said earnestly. "Please say you'll consider it."

Richard made a face, accepting some biscuits from the plate his sister offered. "I have no objection to attending a ball. I have no desire to give a speech there."

"But your adventures are so interesting!" she protested. "They all told me so, when you spoke of them years ago."

"Yes, I already spoke of them. Today no one cares that I have climbed mountains," he told her. "It was years ago, and I am no longer interesting to society."

"You are," she protested. "You could be!"

Richard made a face.

"You know she may be correct," said Gerhard mildly. "The English are wild for travel again, and you have been places few of them have seen."

"That's true," chimed in Clemency at once. "And no one

remembers your speeches from years ago. Why won't you do just one, to see how it is received?"

Richard stirred his tea to avoid answering. They were in Clemency's drawing room, with a warm breeze drifting through the sunlit windows opposite him. It was a splendid day out today, and he wished his nephew would hurry home so he could be out in that sunlight.

He'd found himself at loose ends more than usual, in Evangeline's absence, and had ended up at his sister's more frequently. Her sons were home from school on holiday: Rafael from Cambridge and Gabriel from his last year at Harrow. Rafael had asked him for shooting lessons, and Clemency had finally agreed. But the boy was not home yet, and Richard had been lured into having tea.

"Lady Brentwood would be delighted if you agreed to speak at her upcoming ball," Clemency pressed on, more cautiously but also more hopefully. "Sir Paul was always a supporter of your travels. He would be well pleased to have you."

Richard raised his eyes to his sister's. Her face was flushed pink. "Clemency. You cannot invite me to someone else's ball." Her blush deepened, and she flicked a glance at Gerhard, who gave a tiny nod in encouragement. Richard sighed as understanding dawned. "Unless Sir Paul or Lady Brentwood has enlisted you to persuade me."

"Well, Lady Brentwood did mention that Sir Paul would like it very much," his sister defended herself. "And Gerhard thought you might agree, since it's been so long, and—and—"

"And?" he snapped.

"And because Lady Courtenay has also been invited, with Miss Bennet." Clemency's chin came up as she played her trump card.

Richard stared at her. He and Evangeline did not attend society events together. Mostly because Evangeline didn't attend many, and Richard didn't care for them anyway. They went to the opera and the museums together. They dined with friends and rode out and swam in the pond and took long, leisurely walks together.

But the balls and routs and soirées and breakfasts that made up social London . . . They never went to those. By unspoken agreement they were almost never in each other's company in public situations.

And as a result, he had only ever danced with Evangeline on the night they met.

She had not mentioned this ball to him. Of course he knew she was taking her niece out into society, as Miss Bennet was an unmarried young lady and was accustomed to parties and balls. It shouldn't surprise him that she would attend such an event, particularly if Viscount Burke continued to pay Miss Bennet attention.

He hadn't seen her in what felt like an eternity. They had exchanged letters, but paper and ink were a poor substitute for her warm laugh, her exasperated smiles, the arousing little gasp she made when she kissed him. When she'd told him that she meant to chaperone her niece for several weeks, he hadn't realized how hard her absence would hit him. It was now obvious that his entire life revolved around her.

"How do you know that?" he finally asked.

Clemency's expression lit with triumph. "Lady Brentwood mentioned it. She is dear friends with Lady Bennet and has every expectation they will accept."

Every expectation. Meaning Evangeline would be welcomed as she should be, not whispered about as she feared. This time Richard glanced at Gerhard. "Are you in favor of this public exhibition of our narrow escapes from death and dismemberment?"

Gerhard, who had been watching Clemency with a tinge of worship, glanced at him. "Why would I object?"

Richard ate a biscuit and thought. Clemency wanted him to go, therefore Gerhard wanted him to go. Saying a few words about their travels would be no hardship; he did it often enough at dinner parties when people asked him about traveling the Nile or the Ganges. And if he agreed to speak, he would be considered a guest of honor, which meant he would be expected to dance with ladies in attendance.

That, Richard knew, would be akin to a public announcement. But also, one that his hosts would have no choice but to approve, which meant other guests would also not disapprove.

"Very well," he said abruptly. "Yes, I will attend and give a speech, if it pleases you."

Clemency gave a little exclamation of joy and Gerhard gave him an approving nod. Outside in the hall, the front door opened, and Rafael charged in.

"Apologies, Mama, Uncle, Mr. Rieger," said the boy breathlessly. He gave a quick bow. "I didn't mean to be so late."

Richard, who thought Rafe's timing was excellent, was already on his feet. "We had better be off. Clemency." He nodded to his sister, ignored Gerhard, and waved Rafe out the door ahead of him.

"I really am dreadfully sorry." Rafael was flushed and a bit windblown, as if he'd run home from wherever. "I was with some fellows from university, and we quite forgot the time . . ."

"Apology accepted. Your mother had something to tell me, and the time was not wasted." They went out into the street, where the groom walking his team and curricle appeared in a few minutes.

"I want to thank you for taking me out," said Rafe almost shyly as Richard started the horses. In the last two years he'd shot up to Richard's own height, but was still slender and rangy, with Clemency's dark hair and eyes, his father's diplomatic sensibility, and a wit that was all his own. He had just finished his first year at Cambridge.

Richard smiled. "Of course. I was honored to be asked. It is not every day we old men are invited to spend time with young bucks like you."

Rafe laughed. "You've confused me with Gabe! Not that you're old, Uncle."

Richard glanced at him. "The fact that I can look you in the eye now, when you used to sit upon my shoulders and pull my ears, proves that I am indeed getting old."

His nephew grinned. "You don't seem it."

"Praise indeed," said Richard gravely.

"I mean, all the blokes at school have heard of you, and they're in awe," went on Rafael with enthusiasm. "They want to know if you're planning to take me and Gabe to China or Africa."

"Your mother would have me drawn and quartered. No —she would do it herself." Richard was sure of this. It had taken several days of careful argument on Rafael's part for Clemency to allow *this* outing.

His nephew fell quiet. Richard glanced at him, noting the young man's pensive expression, and they drove the rest of the way to Humberton Hall in silence.

They left the curricle at the stables and walked down the rolling lawn. It was away from the pond at the far edge of the property, the ground cleared ahead of where the trees grew thickest and the brambles wildest. For further protection, an earthen berm had been heaped behind the primary target area, and beyond it was more woodland. Over the years he had owned the property, he'd got it just the way he liked it, and this was where he took his nephew for his first shooting lesson.

One of the servants had set out a table with shot and powder. The sky was cloudy, but there was little wind and no threat of rain. Richard opened the polished wooden case set on the table, and removed one pistol from the felt-lined interior.

His pistols were magnificent pieces, ten inches of blued steel with rifled bores and walnut stocks, made by one of the finest gunsmiths in London, a Swiss fellow by the name of Durs Egg. Richard was inordinately fond of them. He handed one to Rafe, who nearly dropped it.

"It's heavy," he exclaimed.

"Yes. Weight dampens the recoil." He showed Rafe how to load the pistol, then had him load the second. The young man bent his head over the task, his face set in concentration.

Richard talked him through the steps, then directed him how to stand and hold his arm. A tree some ten or twelve yards distant had a large blue patch painted on its trunk, with a red circle in the center, right at the height of a man's chest. Rafael raised the pistol, squinted down the barrel, and pulled the trigger.

"A good first effort," said Richard.

"I missed it entirely," muttered his nephew.

"But your form was good for a first attempt." Richard handed him the powder. "Reload."

After half an hour, during which Rafe managed to hit some part of the tree once, Richard told him to put down the pistol. "Rest your arm," he said, taking up the powder and his own pistol.

"Do you get used to the weight?" Rafael flexed his hand after laying down his pistol.

Richard smiled. "Yes, although I would consider it a very bad sign were I ever required to take more than two shots in short order."

"In a duel, you only shoot once."

Richard gave him a sharp look. "In a duel, you only shoot at all if you are hot-tempered and impatient."

Rafe gave a huff of laughter. "You sound like Mama."

"Well," said Richard, tamping the ball into place, "unlike your mother, I have actually engaged in a duel."

"Three, wasn't it?" asked Rafe eagerly.

"Yes. Three times I have shot a man because he would not listen to reason." Richard raised his arm, still and steady, and pulled the trigger. Bark flew from the edge of the red circle. He turned to his nephew, whose admiration was mingled with shock.

"You shot . . .?" he faltered.

"Twice in the leg, once in the shoulder," replied Richard. "None of them died, though I believe two of them were left considerably injured. And all of it could have been avoided if they had mastered their tempers and behaved as sensible men."

"What do you mean?"

Richard laid down his pistol. "A duel results when one fellow feels his pride has been insulted beyond bearing, yet often the insult has been dealt only out of drunkenness, temper, or thoughtlessness, not out of real desire to wound. Sometimes the act is merely perceived as an insult because it strikes too near an unflattering truth. But whatever the incitement, a duel results because one, or perhaps both, parties would risk death or disability rather than humble themselves to make up the slight." He paused with a significant look at his nephew. "And do not listen to any nonsense about honor being outraged. The victim of the grievance is as likely to suffer as the perpetrator, and what honor is satisfied then?"

"Then why have you fought three of them?" asked Rafe.

"Once, because a captain of our ship thought we should continue on when a storm threatened. I refused. He feared to look a coward, so insisted and eventually challenged me. I accepted for the sake of the entire crew, who were cowed by him. His shot went wide, my shot pinked him in the flesh of his thigh, and a hurricane blew in the next day and did such damage, his officers came to me to apologize. We would likely all have been killed had we continued into that storm.

"Second, when I came upon a man beating a woman, his servant. I stopped him and he flew into a passion, insisting I meet him." Richard smiled slightly. "I did not try hard to avoid that one. Him, I shot in the shoulder, and he never could raise his arm again, to a woman or anyone else."

Rafe was listening, wide-eyed.

"And third, on one expedition, a chieftain offered to sell us some people he had captured as slaves. One fellow, a merchant who had joined our party, thought that a fine idea. Several of the captives were young, boys and girls about Gabriel's age. This man . . ." Richard stopped, remembering the frightened eyes of the children as well as the expression on the merchant's face as he eyed them. "I knew why he wanted to buy them. I declined the chieftain's offer, and this fellow protested. I said we would leave him behind if he attempted it, and he called me out. Gerhard tried to reason with him, but he held fast to his belief that I had not only impugned his honor, but that I had cost him valuable . . . servants." He glanced at his nephew. "I shot him in the leg, breaking it badly, and *then* we left him behind."

"Oh," said Rafe softly. "But . . . those *do* sound honorable, Uncle."

"Only because they were against men of no honor at all."

"How did none of them hit you?"

Richard snorted. "One did!" He drew his finger a few inches along the side of his abdomen. "Right here I have a scar. The ball did not penetrate, but it left a bloody gash that took weeks to heal."

"How were you able to hit all three of them?"

"I stood my ground and did not lose my head." Richard picked up one of his pistols. "Also, the barrel is rifled, which makes for a more reliable shot."

Rafe looked uncomfortable. "Oh, but . . . Aren't rifled barrels unsporting?"

"Cheating, you mean?" asked Richard in amusement. "Only the English think so, and none of the duels I described took place in England." He shook his head. "Only the English would prefer to be shot at by a pistol which might discharge the ball in any direction but the one where it was aimed."

Rafe grinned hesitantly.

"The important point to remember," Richard went on, "is that duels are not mere sporting events, but life and death contests where either man, no matter how grievously wronged or how innocently accused, might pay with his life. They are not to be entered into lightly. If you are ever challenged, you should do all in your power to reconcile the matter peacefully, and I hardly need say that making a challenge is rarely the wisest strategy."

"Has Mr. Rieger fought any duels?"

"No," said Richard. "When anyone has challenged Rieger, he has chosen a bare-knuckled brawl as his preferred contest, and the offended parties have always discovered that their honor was not aggrieved so seriously after all."

Rafe laughed. Richard grinned.

"Gabe wants to join the army," said Rafael abruptly.

Richard's brows went up. "Does he?"

His nephew nodded. "Instead of university."

"He's rather young for the king's shilling," said Richard wryly. Gabriel was only fourteen. "And I do not think your mother would be pleased."

Rafael huffed in reluctant laughter. "She is why he wants to go into the army. Or the navy. He says they take cabin boys younger than he is now. He . . . He wants adventure, and daring, and action. He wants to explore the world, as you did." He shot a nervous, sideways glance at Richard. "And he knows Mama would never approve."

"Until he is a grown man, he must consider what she says. Even I hesitate to argue with her judgment, and a boy of fourteen can have no justification at all." Richard took his own pistol, now loaded and primed, and turned his shoulders. "Stand straight and lean," he said. "Feet apart just so. If you are ever being shot at, present the slimmest possible target." He cocked his pistol and raised it. "If you ever must shoot at someone, aim carefully." He pulled the trigger, and again bark splintered away from the red circle. "And hit what you aim at."

Rafe stared at the tree. "It must take some nerve, to meet a man and know he's going to take a shot at you."

Richard smiled. "I have rarely been accused of lacking nerve."

His nephew laughed, the tension breaking. "By God! Not at all! The bravest fellow I know, Uncle."

Richard fell silent as the young man loaded his pistol, adjusted his stance, took aim, adjusted it, checked his stance, readjusted his aim yet again, and finally pulled the trigger. Rafe exclaimed as bark blew off the tree; he put down his pistol and charged across the grass to see for himself how close to the target he'd come.

Richard stayed where he was.

Rarely accused of lacking nerve. No, rather the opposite, his entire life, even when his life had been the thing at risk, on the ocean, exploring jungles and forests, climbing mountains. His mother had once scolded him that *some* fear was healthy in a man, and that he was sending her to an early grave with his utter lack of it. Richard had laughed and kissed her cheek, not even cowed by that. So why was he dithering over a London ball?

He took a deep breath and let it out. He wasn't—dithering, that is. He was going to that ball, and he would give as long a speech as Sir Paul wanted to hear, and then he was going to dance with Evangeline in front of all London.

Let everyone make of that what they would.

Chapter 28

When George had asked her to chaperone Joan, Evangeline had thought she was reasonably well prepared for it. After all, she'd once been a young lady of good family making her debut. Even if she hadn't cared to obey all the fussy rules, she knew what they were.

Too late she was realizing that adhering to those rules was rather like exercise; too many years without, and even the most seemingly trivial thing made her want to tear out her hair in frustration. An invitation to a ball had arrived from Lady Brentwood, most gratifyingly—but with a note that incensed Evangeline.

"I know Catherine Brentwood and I were never friendly," she raged to Fanny over tea. "But how dare she!"

Fanny raised one brow. "How? She thinks very highly of herself, that's how. She always has."

Evangeline made an exasperated noise and poured another cup of tea, adding a drop of brandy. "And with what reason? We were girls together—not close, but cordial. But more to the point, she would be insulted beyond belief if I said anything like that to her!"

Fanny took her time replying. "She is friends with your sister-in-law."

This time Evangeline made herself count to ten before speaking. "Of course. I would not have expected *any* invitation otherwise. And I am pleased she's invited Joan. I just . . ." She snapped her mouth closed and shook her head, wildly irked.

The note lay on the table between them. Evangeline planned to burn it, but she'd had to show Fanny, because she needed someone else to see for themselves. Lady Brentwood had written that she hoped they would attend, but that she trusted Evangeline not to cause a stir—"for Miss Bennet's sake, if not for mine or my guests'," as she put it.

A *stir*. What did that even mean? Did she think Evangeline meant to burst out singing bawdy tavern songs over supper? Seduce a married man during the quadrille? Arrive with a troupe of circus performers in tow and ruin the ball?

"I expect she felt she had to invite you," said Fanny, "as Sir Richard Campion is rumored to be one of the guests of honor."

She started. "What?"

Fanny regarded her calmly over the rim of her teacup. "Surely you knew."

Flustered, Evangeline drained her cup and set it down. "No. Why would I?"

Her friend rolled her eyes.

"I have kept a careful and deliberate distance from

Richard since I came back to London," Evangeline defended herself. "For Joan's sake."

"And you've had no contact of any kind with the man."

Evangeline flushed. "Only letters." Fanny waited. "He came to breakfast once, very early, bringing Louis for a visit. Over a fortnight ago! I've not seen him since then—not once, not even in passing."

"Ah," said Fanny dryly. "No wonder he's finally agreed to speak at one of Sir Paul's parties. The man must be desperate to see you."

"No, why—?" began Evangeline in puzzlement, before she stopped. Once, Richard had regularly attended those sorts of events and spoken of his travels. She'd met him at one, after all. But Fanny was correct: he hadn't done any of that in recent years. But surely it wasn't because of *her* . . .

Fanny smiled, a touch grimly. "While you have been fortunate enough to be spared Catherine Brentwood's society, I have not. She's been attempting to lure him, and other dashing gentlemen like him, to her soirées for years. Somehow she's got it in her head that it will elevate her parties to rarified glory, and as Campion refuses every invitation that doesn't include you, she's been wildly frustrated." Evangeline gaped at her, and Fanny nodded once. "Miss Bennet offers a convenient excuse, but *you* are the one she really wants to attend. If you are there, he is sure to follow."

"Don't be ridiculous." Her face burning, Evangeline reached for a tea cake to cover her confusion. "Why pen such an insulting note if she really wishes me to attend? Which I do not believe she does, by the by," she added quickly.

The countess sighed and put down her plate, now devoid

of petit fours. "My dear. Which part mystifies you? That it is galling for Catherine to admit she needs you, or that that man of yours is both devoted to and fiercely protective of you?"

"Oh, I believe in the gall," she said, and Fanny gave a snort of laughter. "But Richard isn't mine, and he can go where he pleases. I've never once suggested he not attend an event."

"He only pleases to go where you are."

"But I don't go to London society events!" She wasn't usually invited, but she'd thought that was partly due to her relationship with him.

"Nor does he." With an air of victory, Fanny chose another petit four, one with a sugared violet on top.

"Fanny." Evangeline sighed, rubbing her temples. "There is a reason we aren't in public together."

"Perhaps, just perhaps," said her friend gently, "the reason no longer exists. If it ever did."

"It most certainly did," said Evangeline under her breath. Her sister-in-law had explained it quite clearly, if delicately. The scandal over Court's death had died down, but mention of it flared up every time she went out, like the embers of a fire she could never entirely extinguish. She suspected Lady Ambrose of fanning the sparks, hoping to drive her away. Every mention of Evangeline, after all, resurrected the tale of Lady Ambrose being caught in bed with Court, and of her husband killing Court in their bedchamber. Marion had agreed that it wasn't fair, but it nonetheless *was*, and Marion was worried about any of the scandal clinging to her family.

So Evangeline had gracefully given in, kept her distance,

and held her tongue. Not because she agreed, but because she didn't want to do anything to hurt Joan. Then she'd found she preferred life without the stress of society and their criticisms, and it hadn't really mattered.

"Are you going to attend?" asked Fanny, rousing Evangeline from her thoughts.

She sighed. "Of course. For Joan's sake. I cannot imagine what Marion would say if I kept her away from Catherine Brentwood's ball over a trifling little note."

Fanny's eyes fell on the noxious paper. "It *is* offensive."

Evangeline took a deep breath. "It is. And I must rise above it, mustn't I?" Then she ruined it with an angry exclamation. "Though I'm very tempted to let slip how besotted Catherine was at age seventeen with her brother's tutor, and how very like him her oldest son looks!" Evangeline had no evidence the boy wasn't Sir Paul's child, but he did bear a passing resemblance to the tutor.

"Those who live on spiteful rumors are just as likely to be felled by them," observed Fanny. "On the bright side, you will have Sir Richard's company to console you."

"Speaking to him would likely be judged a *stir*," said Evangeline, still in a simmering fury.

"Nonsense," Fanny retorted. "Speak to one of the guests of honor? How impolite, should you *not*." She leaned forward in her chair. "Take your niece. Speak to Richard. Dance with the man! Do not act guilty of a sin you never committed. In a just world, you would be every bit as welcome at these parties as Cynthia Ambrose is."

She thought about that. She did have to attend the ball; if she did not, Catherine would likely write to Marion, who would be upset. And really, no one could possibly blame her if Catherine also invited Richard, and as Fanny said, it would be only polite to speak to him—to dance with him.

He'd been such a wonderful dancer. So wonderful, she'd ended up in bed with him less than two hours later.

"Yes, all right," she said at last. "Of course I shall go. I've already accepted. I told you I would at the beginning, didn't I?"

"Good." Fanny rose. "I will see you there."

After her friend left, Evangeline picked up the note and the invitation and studied both. *Don't cause a stir.* She tapped it against her palm. Nonsense. The only stir she meant to cause was with her lovely niece, now dressed in flattering garments and beginning to find her confidence as a woman. She would wager good money there would indeed be a stir when Lord Burke fell over himself to ask Joan to dance. Evangeline had made sure to tell the viscount they would attend.

Her spirits rising, she went to tell Joan—and to be certain her niece had an absolutely stunning gown to wear.

CHAPTER 29

Richard walked through the Brentwoods' door with a fully formed plan.

He'd enlisted Gerhard's and Clemency's help. There was no man he trusted more than Gerhard, and now, on this matter of such importance to him, he'd confided all in his friend, whom he knew he could count on.

"You are in love with this woman," was Gerhard's only comment. "Of course you must try to win her."

Clemency, of course, had been delighted. "Oh, Richard, how wonderful! We shall do all in our power to help."

Gerhard had agreed that he would divert Sir Paul Brentwood and anyone else who appeared to interfere with Richard's plan. It was a simple one, after all: charm everyone in sight and then approach Evangeline, once he had cut the legs from under any potential gossip. All he wanted was to dance with her, preferably the supper dance, when he would then be able to escort her in to dine. He would have her on his arm and at his side, in full view of London society.

Since the day their affair began, he had accepted and understood the need for discretion. Lolling in her steaming bathhouse years ago, he had heard everything she said, and surmised a few things she hadn't said. Her marriages had been awful, and both times she had been blamed for it. She had no faith that society wouldn't paint her the most scandalous of wicked widows for associating with him. He had no reason to doubt her fear; he remembered his own sister's initial reaction to her name.

And for six years, it hadn't mattered. She rarely went to society events, so he rarely went, either. His friends quickly learned to invite her to any dinner or private soirée, if they wanted him to come. With their properties bordering each other, he saw her almost every day—or night. The path from Humberton Hall to Wyndham House was an easy one to travel even in the dark of night, now that he had his gardener maintain it.

But then she'd gone away to London, to her brother's house in South Audley Street, where he could not come and go discreetly, or at all. "I wish it were different, but my sister-in-law is so mindful of propriety," she'd told him, biting her lip with regret. "I don't wish to cause her any unease, especially when she is ill."

"Of course," he'd told her. "I understand completely."

Her face had shone with relief and gratitude. "Oh, Richard, thank you," she'd said, squeezing his hand. "I do so want to do this, for Joan's sake."

And for her own, he thought. It had meant so much to her, and he wanted her to have the family connection she'd missed and craved for years, but the truth was, he had missed her even more than he'd expected to. Being deprived of her company for a mere month had driven home to him how deeply he cared for her, and how galling it was that the upturned noses of some matrons could cause such trouble in his life.

And in Evangeline's. She might not crave their good opinion, but it had still cost her dearly. He'd had enough of that.

He headed right for his hostess, one of those matrons of upturned nose, and took her hand in his. She was a slender woman with pale eyes and a pointed chin. "My dear Lady Brentwood, how very kind of you to invite me to your gathering." He kissed her knuckles, letting his lips actually brush her glove.

"Oh, my!" She blushed scarlet. "Why, Sir Richard, we are *most* delighted to have you! I know you do not often attend society events . . ."

He gazed into her pale blue eyes and gave her an intimate smile. "Ah, but this one is not the usual society party, is it?"

Her mouth sagged open for a second before she recovered. "Why, how good of you to notice! My husband and I do so enjoy these honorarium balls. Don't we, Sir Paul?" she asked as her husband stepped up beside her.

"What? Yes, yes. Campion, capital to see you tonight." He bowed, looking quite pleased with himself, and Richard returned the greeting. While most of Lord Allen's friends had kept a distance from him since the night he'd dined with them at White's, Brentwood had seemed to be even more impressed with his daring and nerve.

"My dear, I was just telling Sir Richard how much we

treasure our honorarium balls," said his wife, waving her closed fan about as she spoke, giving her the air of a conductor. "How very beneficial it is to our spirits to host a selection of guests who might broaden all our horizons, by sharing their knowledge and fascinating experiences."

"Quite right, Lady Brentwood," said Sir Paul with a benevolent smile. "Why simply dance and drink with our everyday society? No, I say, bring in the adventurers, the artists, the geniuses who will show us the future!"

Richard laid one hand on his heart and bowed his head. "You honor me."

"Oh, sir, *you* do honor us, with your company," she trilled back.

"Perhaps you will grant me a dance, madam?"

Lady Brentwood turned pink again. "It would be my pleasure, sir."

"And mine," he said with a smile.

Sir Paul laughed. "And it would be *my* pleasure to introduce you to some people, Campion. Shall we?"

"Of course." To Lady Brentwood, he bowed. "Until later, madam."

They left her preening behind her fan. Richard did his duty, greeting everyone Sir Paul introduced him to, but always with one eye on the door. He had deliberately come early, but expected Evangeline and her charge to arrive at a more fashionable hour.

Clemency arrived, Gerhard in tow, and exclaimed in delight when she saw him.

"Oh, you *did* come," she cried, giving him her hand.

"I told you I would." He raised a brow. "What made you think I would not?"

She blushed. "You so often don't! I'm just delighted to see you."

Richard looked at Gerhard, who gave a tiny shrug. "Would you like some champagne?" he asked his sister.

"Oh, yes," she said, with an artless glance at Gerhard. The man turned on his heel at once and plowed through the throng toward a footman with a tray of flutes.

"Neatly done," he said in amusement. "I hope he brings some for me as well."

She swatted his arm. "Don't tease me, Richard. Have you seen Lady Courtenay?"

His gaze skimmed once more over the crowd. "Not yet."

"I believe she and her niece were arriving as we were climbing the steps."

He barely heard her, scanning the guests more closely. She was here, somewhere, or would be at any moment. He felt as eager as a child on Christmas Eve. "Excellent," he murmured.

"Richard." Startled by her tone, he looked at her. She pursed her lips and straightened his cravat. "If I may give you a word of advice . . . Ask Miss Bennet to dance first. I understand she is not one of the popular young ladies, and it will seem quite heroic in her eyes, and likely in her aunt's."

Richard looked at her in surprise. That was an excellent suggestion. "Brilliant thought, Clem. Thank you."

She flicked something from his sleeve, fussing over him as if he were one of her sons. "And be very gallant when you ask her. Lady Brentwood will have no choice but to approve, but the more regard you show for the proprieties . . . Well, it may sway the other dragons watching." She smoothed his lapel and gave it a pat. "Good luck."

He covered her hand and pressed it. "Thank you."

Over her shoulder he caught sight of Miss Bennet, who looked decidedly more elegant than usual. Richard had only met her once, but tonight she wore a gleaming gown of gold that gave her a new sophistication. Her face was bright with excitement as she came into the room, and there, a step behind her, was Evangeline.

God above. He stopped breathing for a moment at how beautiful she was. Her gown was deep blue, as if she had planned it as a foil to her niece's shine. Around her neck and at her ears, he recognized the sapphires he had given her a year ago.

And it hit him that he loved her—he would always love her, only her, and he would never feel complete without her. No other woman had ever moved him, amused him, intrigued him, comforted him, warmed him to the very bottom of his soul the way she did.

Sir Paul interrupted his realization with an inane question, and then Lady Brentwood came over to lead the opening set with him. He smiled and flattered and danced, and finally made his way toward her.

Miss Bennet had been talking with a pair of young ladies, but they left as Richard approached, to his relief. His sister's suggestion was a good one, even if he could see that Miss Bennet was covertly searching the room—for Burke, no doubt. Richard had spotted the viscount lurking behind a pillar earlier.

He bowed in front of the ladies. "Good evening, Lady Courtenay. Miss Bennet."

The young lady beamed as she curtsied and returned the greeting. Evangeline gave him a simmering look as she dipped her head.

"You look exceptionally lovely tonight," he said.

"Did you come over here just to express the obvious?" she said with a smile. "My niece looks magnificent, and I warrant everyone recognizes it."

He smiled back. From the corner of his eye he saw Miss Bennet blush, but he couldn't take his eyes off Evangeline. He felt starved for any sight of her. "I recognized it from the most distant corner of the room." With effort, he turned to her niece. "I wonder if Miss Bennet would do me the compliment of partnering me in the next dance?"

The girl's eyes went wide. "I would be delighted. Thank you, sir."

Evangeline sent him a look of adoration that made his heart leap. Richard said another silent thanks to his sister. He led out her niece, and reminded himself to make polite conversation. "Are you enjoying the ball?"

"Yes," she said, "but I wish my aunt would enjoy it more."

He froze. She stared back at him expectantly, almost hopefully, and a strange buzzing sensation filled his head. This girl knew what he was doing, and what he wanted, and she was trying to help him. "How so?" he asked cautiously.

She glanced at Evangeline, who was watching them. "I think she gave up much she holds dear to play at chaperone."

She'd said her niece was clever, and took after her. He

ought to have remembered that. But he couldn't forget that the young lady's mother had reproved Evangeline for her behavior, and virtually cast her out of their family. "Has she expressed any discontent?" he asked cautiously.

She bit her lip. "Not a word."

He wondered at that, and turned the conversation toward her. Evangeline had told him about Miss Bennet's unexpected ballooning trip with Viscount Burke, which had caused her great anxiety. But the young lady surprised him again. "Would you do me a great favor, sir?"

"Of course," he said politely.

"Would you ask her to dance?"

He looked at her sharply, but her expression was open and guileless. And it aligned too well with what he'd planned, so in the end he decided to risk it. "I would ask her for every dance, if she would consent to just one. I am not the party you need to encourage," he murmured as he led her off the floor at the end of the quadrille.

Her face lit up and she gave him a small, happy nod as he bowed and excused himself. He went back to Clemency, who was fending off polite conversation from Sir Paul Brentwood.

"How did it go?" she whispered.

"Perfectly." He paused. "She told me to ask her aunt to dance."

His sister clutched his arm in excitement. Richard could see Miss Bennet, holding her aunt's hand and speaking to her very earnestly. And there was Burke, at last, carving his way through the crowd toward them without subtlety. He had a waiter with champagne at his heels, and for several minutes the three chatted, appearing in very good charity with each other.

Richard knew Evangeline wanted to bring off this match, if there was a match to be made, and so he stayed where he was. Clemency whispered in his ear about something or other; he didn't listen.

And then Miss Bennet looked directly at him, and when their eyes met, she gave him a confident nod. *Do it,* he could almost hear her say. *She'll say yes.*

When Sir Paul spoke to him, it was all Richard could do to understand the words. Gerhard came back, wine in hand, and Richard let him step into the conversation and carry on with their host. Clemency obligingly piped up and chattered about something.

Suddenly, his sister jabbed him in the ribs. "It's almost the supper dance," she hissed. "If you are going to ask her, do it now!"

Without hesitation he turned on his heel and went.

They were drinking champagne and laughing as he approached. Burke wore a look of focused fascination as he spoke to Miss Bennet. Richard wondered briefly if there would be a proposal this very evening. Miss Bennet glowed with happiness.

"Your pardon, Lady Courtenay," he said. "I beg you to honor me with the supper dance."

She turned, her face soft with surprise.

"Oh, do!" burst out Miss Bennet. Her color was high, and she swung the champagne flute loosely in her hand. "As you know, I am already engaged, so you are quite free to dance yourself."

Richard silently thanked her, even though she was likely tipsy and high-spirited because of Burke's attention.

Evangeline gave her niece a look, then slowly put her hand in Richard's. "I would be delighted, sir. I will see you in the supper room, Joan."

He shot a look of rapturous gratitude at Miss Bennet, who beamed back, and led Evangeline to the edge of the dance floor.

"Everyone will be watching us," she breathed as she went into his arms. It was to be a waltz.

"Because they, like I, are transfixed by how beautiful you are tonight."

She smiled wryly, looking more like herself. "Flattery!"

"Well, it is certainly the truth in my case, and who is to know what all these strangers are thinking? I rate it even odds that I am correct."

"Even odds! Then you are just as likely wrong."

He smiled, darting a glance at Miss Bennet, who was safely in Viscount Burke's arms. "Perhaps some are distracted by the very great coup de grâce you are about to execute, snaring the most elusive bachelor lord in London for your niece."

She turned her head to look at the couple. "Yes," she said softly, "I do believe he's snared."

"Burke has been watching for her, and then watching *her*, all evening."

She looked at him in surprise. "How do you know?"

"It was difficult not to notice. He's a large fellow and cannot hide behind the pillars no matter how hard he tries. I gather he doesn't usually attend affairs like this." Burke might not have even been invited; Lady Brentwood had gasped aloud at the sight of him when he arrived. Sir Paul had chuckled awkwardly and made a comment about Burke being a friend of his son's. As if he needed to explain the viscount's presence.

She laughed. "No, I gathered he is not much for society balls."

"Yet here he is, enraptured by your niece." Richard glanced at the girl in question. "And she looks very striking this evening. You've done wonders with her."

"Nonsense," she said, her cheeks pink. "She was lovely all along."

He smiled. "Can I not pay you any compliment at all?"

She looked at him, her lips quirked. "Of course you can."

"Good. Evie . . ." He had been angling them toward the doorway, away from most of the dancers. "I have something to speak to you about."

Her brows went up. "What is it? Something serious?"

"Only in that I am serious about it," he said lightly.

"Then I shall take it seriously," she replied in the same vein. "Now I am terribly eager to hear it."

He grinned. "Then let us speak at once." The orchestra was still playing, but he spun her off the dance floor and stood still.

She glanced over his shoulder at the couples still dancing. "Joan . . ."

He looked over the crowd, picking out Burke's dark head about the rest. "They are near the musicians, still dancing. Come with me. Only for a moment," he said as she hesitated.

The waltz was winding down. In a few minutes the

crowd, including Miss Bennet and her partner, would turn toward them and head for the supper room. A few people had already trickled that way, as footmen had just swept open the double doors to the room.

"Just a moment," she agreed, her cheeks pink. "I mustn't be away long."

"Of course not." He took her by the hand and led the way around the corner away from the supper room, to the small chamber where he'd been received by Lady Brentwood when he'd called the other day to accept Sir Paul's invitation to speak tonight. As expected, it was dim and silent, and he closed the door gently behind them.

"What mystery! You do intrigue me, sir," she said, smiling.

He crossed the room to her and took her face in both hands. "You do enchant me, madam," he breathed, and then he kissed her, deeply, passionately, as he'd been longing to do for weeks now. And she clung to him with as much enthusiasm as he had, wrapping her arms around his neck and kissing him back so hungrily, he almost forgot why he'd brought her here.

"I've missed you so," he breathed against her lips.

"And I you." She kissed him again. "I am very glad to be able to do this for Joan, and I've adored the time spent with her, but . . ." She ran her finger over his lips. "It has not been the easiest month of my life. In fact, it's been rather wretched to be away from you."

He smiled, his heart skipping a beat. "I am delighted you came tonight."

He felt her flinch, but then she relaxed against him. "So

am I. Of course it's for Joan's benefit, and I do believe young Burke may screw his courage to the sticking point soon, if not this very evening." She rested her temple against his jaw for a moment. "But until tonight I didn't even realize how *desperately* I missed you, my darling."

He caught her hand and brought it to his lips. "I have wanted this forever," he said in a low voice. "To spend an evening with you. To dance with you. To be by your side in front of everyone in London, and to revel in it. I love you, Evangeline. I can't bear to be without you, even for a few weeks."

She raised her head. In the dim light he could see her wide eyes, and he tightened his grip on her hand, holding it against his heart.

"I remember what you said when we began. I have done my best to follow your lead, and respect your wishes," he went on. "All I am asking is that you might . . . consider it."

"Consider . . . what?" she inquired carefully.

He swallowed, suddenly nervous. "Evie, I want to marry you."

Her indrawn breath was loud in the still room.

"I am not asking now," he said swiftly. "I know your reasons against marriage, and I would never try to pressure you into answering immediately. I can only swear on my life that it would be nothing like before."

She was quiet for a long minute, then asked, softly, "Why?"

"Because I cannot stand to be apart from you. Because I want everyone to know, not that you are mine, but that *I* am *yours*. I have been for years now. How dare these London matrons, most of whom are no paragons of virtue themselves, cow us into hiding, when any one of them would give her right arm to be as adored as you are?" He felt her gather breath to speak, and he squeezed her hand again. "I came tonight to see you, but also to prove to each of them that I am not ashamed of our relationship. I would shout my devotion from the rooftops or print it in the *Times* for all the world to read."

She stepped back and he let her go at once. She clasped her hands together and paced a short path away, then back. "Are you not happy with how things are?"

"I *am* happy," he said. Sweat beaded on the back of his neck; his palms felt damp inside his gloves. "I only want more. I want to share a home with you. I want to breakfast with you without needing to arrive at dawn. I want to walk into every ball or soirée or theater box with you on my arm, and I want to take you home with me at the end of every evening, without secrecy or sneaking."

"Has it been so terrible?" she asked hesitantly.

He couldn't help a rueful smile. "No. Nothing with you could be terrible, to me."

Slowly she came back up to him, and laid her hand on his chest. "You want to marry me," she said, as if she weren't sure that's what he had said. "You."

"I do."

Her fingers stroked small circles. "I never thought to marry again . . ."

"All I am asking tonight," he said quietly, "is that you consider it. Marrying *me*, not anyone else—who would most certainly not deserve you."

She smiled at that, and his heart took a leap. "Very well," she said after a taut moment. "I will . . . consider it."

He inhaled and warmth flushed through him. "Thank you, my love." He bent to touch his forehead to hers, and for a moment they simply stood, breathing in each other, a small cocoon of happiness.

"How long do you think is a good length of time to consider?" she whispered.

His pulse leapt. "A fortnight? Or perhaps a month or two," he added quickly, not wanting to seem hasty. He had waited years to ask her this; he could wait another year to hear her answer.

She took her time replying. "Yes, I think a fortnight sounds a reasonable time for considering," she said at last. "Should I expect to receive any . . . persuasion in that time?"

"Only," he replied, "the sort of persuasion I would exert on any ordinary Wednesday."

She laughed. Richard smiled, as he always did when she laughed. "I remember one Wednesday when we only left the bed to eat and soak in the bathhouse."

"As I said," he agreed.

She laughed again, then went up on her toes to kiss him once more, tenderly this time. "Why now?"

"What do you mean?"

"You said you had wanted this forever." She waved one hand. "Why ask now?"

Richard let out his breath slowly. "For the first time I have been deprived of your company—not by ill health, or by travel, or even by your desire or my own, but by the narrow minds of people I do not care about. You did nothing to earn their scorn. My love for you is not a sordid secret."

She rolled her lip between her teeth at that. "No, it is not sordid . . . or secret."

Something in her voice made him frown. "What is it?"

She sighed. "Lady Brentwood . . . Never mind. It doesn't matter."

"Evie."

She gave him a look of reproach. "Never *mind*, Richard."

He held up his hands in surrender. "As you wish."

She took a deep breath. "We'd better return. Joan will wonder where I've gone."

He nodded, a little let down. What had Lady Brentwood done to discompose her? "The young lady looked very pleased with her situation, when we left."

The shadows in her eyes lightened. "She did, didn't she? I do think Burke is in earnest."

"If he is not," Richard replied lightly, "I will be happy to show him the error of his ways."

She laughed. "Oh no! I believe my niece would be capable of putting him in his place, if he needed it."

He grinned. "Let us go see. I wager you a farthing she'll not have noticed your absence."

Evangeline grinned back at him. "I hope so, darling."

Her hand around his arm, they left the quiet parlor and returned to the supper room. It was full now, crowded with guests at long tables. Footmen were bustling about with plates of food and trays of drinks, gentlemen were fetching wine and punch for ladies, and the chatter filled the room.

They did not spy Miss Bennet or Lord Burke at once. The supper was being served across three rooms, with doors wide open between them. Richard and Evangeline strolled through the first room, stopping more than once after being hailed by someone or other. Sir Paul Brentwood appeared out of nowhere and tried to divert them to his table, but Richard put him off.

This was what he longed for. She walked close beside him, where he could smell her perfume and feel the warmth of her touch on his arm. To his silent satisfaction, not one person blinked at the sight of them. Everyone greeted them equally, and warmly. He hoped Evangeline had also taken note. No vicious rumormongers would spoil this evening. This could be their life.

In the second room, Evangeline pointed out some of her niece's friends, the Misses Weston. "Oh my," she said in surprise. "I thought Joan would certainly be near them . . ."

The two young ladies, one dark and one fair, sat at a table with two gentlemen and a pair of other ladies. The blonde girl looked openly bored, and the dark-haired girl more politely bored, nodding slightly as one of the gentlemen spoke to her. At a nearby table sat an older couple; their parents, from the looks of things. The father kept shooting glances over his shoulder at the girls, only to be tapped on the knuckles by his wife.

"Perhaps Burke wished more privacy to declare himself," Richard said, having to lean close to speak to her. The conversational roar around them had grown louder in this room.

Evangeline brightened. "Yes, very likely. But let's look in the next room just to be certain."

They went into the third room, where the rogues and scoundrels had made themselves at home. A pair of dandies in tight coats were balancing champagne glasses on each other's heads, and at least one seduction was being waged in the corner, where a rake was whispering into a young widow's ear as she smiled coyly.

"I don't see her," said Evangeline slowly.

"We must have overlooked them. Let us go back."

But they didn't see Miss Bennet or the viscount on their second trip through the rooms. Even more people tried to stop them, asking Richard if he meant to speak about Egypt or Delhi after supper, and Richard had to put them off as Evangeline grew increasingly tense. In the first room once more, he spotted Gerhard, and made for the man in relief. "Perhaps my sister or Rieger has seen them," he told Evangeline.

Gerhard greeted Evangeline warmly, as did Clemency. Richard leaned close to his friend. "Have you seen Burke recently?"

"Ja, he was dancing with her young lady." Gerhard nodded toward Evangeline, meaning her niece.

"Since the dancing ended," Richard clarified.

Gerhard's eyes slid toward Clemency, who was speaking to Evangeline. "We came in here as soon as the music stopped, to secure seats. I lost sight of them."

Richard nodded.

"Mrs. Murray hasn't seen them," Evangeline whispered, plucking at his arm.

He led her out of the room, back into the blissful quiet of the ballroom. Servants were scurrying around, tidying the room, and the musicians had laid down their instruments and gone to have a bite in the kitchens. "Perhaps they stepped outside for a breath of air." Tall French windows led onto a narrow terrace outside.

Her face softened with relief. "They must have."

But when Richard opened the door and stepped out, the terrace was deserted. There was no garden, merely a stand of trees to screen the view of the outbuildings. He went to the railing and looked down, but saw no one. Miss Bennet's shimmering golden gown would be visible in the moonlight. He turned back to Evangeline, but saw from her face she knew.

There was no sign of Miss Bennet or Viscount Burke.

Chapter 30

Evangeline wasn't initially worried when they couldn't find Joan.

Her niece had proven herself trustworthy and well-behaved, after the ballooning incident. Evangeline thought she'd put Burke on clear notice that he was being weighed in the balance, and that he did not want to be found lacking. But any suitor would crave a private moment to express his feelings, and she was inclined to grant Burke that much, for Joan's sake.

If she could help Joan find as much happiness as she felt herself right now, Evangeline would happily face down George and Marion.

Evie, I want to marry you. She had never thought to hear those words and feel anything other than panic and alarm. But when Richard said them . . . her heart had leapt. *I want everyone to know that I am yours.* She had seen the glances their way, as she walked with him and danced with him. Some were surprised, but most were merely curious; fire and brimstone had not rained down upon her head, as she'd somehow feared.

This could be my life, she thought, stealing a glance at him beside her. No more fixing her gaze straight ahead and pretending she didn't see the wide eyes or hear the flurry of whispers. No more pretense of leaving separately, even when he intended to walk through the woods from his house to hers for the night. No more pretense at all, because marriage would make them uninteresting . . . and respectable. It was an unfamiliar concept, but one she found surprisingly appealing.

However, as they searched all three supper rooms and did not spy either Joan or Lord Burke, thoughts of Richard faded under the wave of concern rising inside her. A private moment was forgivable, if not fully permissible, but now it had been almost half an hour since she'd seen her niece.

When Richard opened the terrace doors and turned back to her, his face grave, a flare of panic shot through her. Where could Joan be?

"I'll ask her friends," she said as Richard came back into the house. "We saw them eating."

"Of course."

They went back through the supper rooms. She made her way toward the Misses Weston, and tried to catch the elder girl's eye. Abigail Weston jumped up and hurried over, leaving her sister to entertain the two young men at their table.

"I do apologize for interrupting," Evangeline told her with a smile, "but have you seen Joan?"

Miss Weston blinked. "No, Lady Courtenay. Not since before the waltz."

"Ah." Evangeline kept her smile firmly in place even though her stomach lurched at this news. "She must have gone to the retiring room. She tried a new hairstyle this evening and was worried it would need repair." The hairstyle was new, but it was simpler than the usual curls and braids; it should have been fine all evening.

Miss Weston looked skeptical but didn't argue. Evangeline bade her farewell and returned to Richard's side. He'd gone back to his sister and Mr. Rieger, and as she approached, Sir Paul and Lady Brentwood strolled up.

"You must come sit with us, Campion," Sir Paul cajoled. "We've seats saved at our own table."

"Indeed, we have," added Catherine, turning a brittle smile on Evangeline. "Lady Courtenay, do join us."

Evangeline smiled back, teeth gritted behind her lips. "That is very kind of you, my dear, but I'm afraid we are already engaged."

"Perhaps we might join you in an hour," added Richard. He laid his hand over hers, on his arm. "For dessert."

Lady Brentwood softened under his regard. "We will look forward to it, sir."

"Very good," said Sir Paul in approval.

"Until then," Richard replied, and promptly led her away. "I presume her friend was no help?" he murmured as they reached the doorway.

"None." Once clear of the supper rooms, Evangeline turned to face him. "Richard—"

"I know," he said at once. "We must find her."

"Or Burke," she said, leaving unspoken her worst fear: that the pair of them had slipped off alone together, to do God-knew-what. Evangeline wanted no part of explaining *that* to her brother. "I'll check the retiring room."

He nodded. "I will ask the footman in the reception hall if Burke has left."

She picked up her skirts and hurried away, down the corridor and up the stairs to the room set aside for ladies. Several people were within, one getting a button sewn back on her glove and one lying on a chaise looking a bit green. In the middle of the room stood a young lady, sobbing hysterically, as her mother and another girl tried to soothe her; two maids fussed over the torn flounce of her gown, trailing across the floor. No Joan. Evangeline bit her lip and pretended to powder her nose, as the glove-less matron eyed her closely. She walked out as calmly as possible, and began opening doors along the corridor.

A small parlor: empty.

A larger music room: empty.

Another parlor, more feminine: also empty.

Evangeline tried to tell herself to remain calm. There was likely a very reasonable explanation, she repeated over and over in her mind. The Brentwood house was rather large, and if Burke meant to propose or declare himself, he might well have whisked Joan away to a quiet area just as Richard had done. Any moment now she would turn a corner and spot them, Burke on one knee and Joan beaming with happiness.

But she couldn't stop thinking that she shouldn't have let Richard whisk her away. She was meant to be watching her niece, not hearing passionate declarations of love herself —even if it had made her heart flutter in way she hadn't felt in years.

Richard came up the stairs, so rapidly she knew he also had no news. When he turned around the banister and their eyes met, her composure began to crack.

"Where is she?" she whispered as he strode toward her.

"Shh." The retiring room door had opened behind him, and he stepped to the side, shielding Evangeline from view. "Neither has left the house."

"Via the front door," she replied in an urgent whisper. "Where *is* she?" Panic rippled along her nerves.

He glanced over his shoulder. The woman with the repaired glove was slowly going down the stairs, craning her neck to stare at them. Richard led her toward the back of the house. "I also checked the antechamber and morning room. I saw neither on that floor."

And Evangeline had opened all the doors on this floor. That left the upper floors, with the family's private rooms, or the servants' rooms. No matter how fascinated Joan had been by the water heater and new plaster in Burke's Hanover Square home, Evangeline thought it very unlikely she and Burke were studying the Brentwoods' flues and linen closets. Which meant . . .

She swallowed, her throat suddenly tight and dry. She knew very well why a woman would sneak off to a private room with a man; she'd done it herself. But she'd trusted Joan to be more *sensible,* more aware. Surely Marion had raised her daughter to be more conscious of propriety than Evangeline had ever been.

But Joan has already done this, whispered a terrible voice inside her head. Joan let Burke take her ballooning, without a word to Evangeline. And she'd enjoyed it.

She gripped Richard's arm so hard he started. "We have to find her. Now!"

For once he didn't argue. Up the back stairs they went, as rapidly as possible. With Richard reminding her to be as quiet as she could, they opened every door that wasn't locked.

"Joan!" she whispered, trying to keep her voice down but nearing hysteria. "Joan!" The last door opened under her hand and she lurched into the room, only to stop short.

There stood her niece and Lord Burke. His arms were around her, and they might have been admiring themselves in the mirror over the small fireplace, a lovely romantic couple.

But Evangeline's frantic eyes took in Joan's high color and disarranged hair, Burke's sleepy-eyed smile, the wrinkles in both their clothing. Behind her, Richard swore under his breath. He could tell, too.

Her heart seemed to stop, then resume with a ferocious banging that made her vision dim. Oh God. George had trusted her to keep his only daughter safe, and she had failed, distracted by her selfish desires, her lack of sense, and her complete and utter stupidity.

"What the devil are you doing?" Richard snarled at Burke.

The younger man gave him a cocksure glance before giving Joan an intimate look that made the girl blush and smile. "What does it look like?"

If there had been any kind of weapon in her hand, Evangeline would have murdered him on the spot. "Joan—Joan, come with me right now. We have to go!" Before she flew at Burke and gouged out his eyes, before she flung herself off the roof of this house in shame. Now the only thing she could do was get her niece safely out of this nightmare. She couldn't think of anything else.

And Burke, the reprehensible scoundrel, merely kissed Joan's hand and gave her another searing look.

Leaving Richard to deal with him, she seized Joan's wrist and towed her out of the room, down all those stairs, into the hall where she hissed at a servant to fetch their things and summon their carriage. Her hands shook as she practically pushed the girl into it.

Once inside, she took a deep breath to calm her thundering pulse. "I hope," she said carefully, "I shall have nothing dreadful to confess to your parents."

Joan's reply, cautious but still entirely too self-satisfied, made her throat clench. "I'm sure you don't."

Her brother would never speak to her again. Marion would despise her until the end of time—with good reason. She would be banished from her family forever. She tried to hold herself together; Joan was at fault, too, but only because Evangeline had been criminally negligent.

Joan began to apologize, seeming to sense at last how badly she'd erred. Evangeline's hopes that she would disclose good news—namely, a marriage proposal—were crushed, as the girl went silent at that query.

"But I *want* to marry him," Joan added in a small voice.

"I should bloody well hope so!" she snapped. "You may

have no other choice." She couldn't fend off the memory of her father's expression when he'd walked in on her and Court—the contained fury, but also the stony acceptance, as if he weren't surprised at all. *George isn't like that,* she reminded herself frantically—but then, she'd at least been a widow, not a modest, virginal young lady. And while Court had been brazen in his seductions, he'd recoiled from any actual danger. She had no illusions Burke was the same. If George lost his temper and called out Burke, Evangeline had no doubt the viscount would meet him.

Perhaps she could prevail upon Richard to give her his pistols, and she could save her brother the trouble of shooting the viscount, she thought wildly. She would ambush him on his way home. Perhaps she could whisk Joan away to Chelsea and pretend she'd been taken very ill, and not bring her back to London until any scandal had blown over.

And then she stopped thinking at all, as the carriage turned into South Audley Street. A travel chaise stood outside the Bennet home. Janet, Marion's maid, stood on the steps directing the unloading of luggage.

George and Marion were home. And her sins were about to catch up with her.

CHAPTER 31

Richard thought it a marvel of restraint that he didn't break Burke's nose.

The younger man had kissed Miss Bennet's hand and then watched Evangeline pull her from the room without a word. If anything, he looked entirely too calm and pleased with himself. He even smiled a little as he folded his handkerchief back into his pocket.

Never in his life had Richard seen Evangeline as anxious as she'd been while they searched the house. She, who could laugh in a thunderstorm and merely sigh over the tree that fell on her stable roof, had been terrified. He knew she would blame herself for any scandal that accrued to her niece's name . . . from sneaking out of a ball to let a known scoundrel have his way with her.

He pitied his sister, with two sons to raise. How did parents manage not to run mad?

"I trust I need not remind you to say nothing at all to *anyone* about this," Richard said acidly to Burke.

The man looked affronted. "How dare you. I'd never do that."

"Then keep your bloody trousers buttoned, if you don't wish to be shot," he said, and stalked from the room.

He took deep, controlled breaths as he hurried down the stairs, trying to restore his calm. Evangeline and her niece had vanished; he guessed they'd left, due to Miss Bennet's disarray and Evangeline's upset. The memory of the woman on the stairs, though, watching them so avidly, lingered in his mind.

He didn't want to be here, either. He longed to rush after Evangeline and make certain she reached home safely. He would let her scold her niece, then send the girl to her room to contemplate her error, while they worked out what to do. He could use a stiff whisky at the moment, and he imagined Evangeline could, as well.

But he was a guest of honor. People were watching him. They had seen him dancing with Evangeline and walking through the rooms arm in arm with her, and if he and she both disappeared from the ball, people would notice, and wonder.

He squared his shoulders and strode into the supper room. Perhaps he could stave off any rumors before they took root.

"Ah, Campion!" Sir Paul beckoned him. "There you are!"

He joined the man, smiling, bracing himself internally. "Good evening. What a marvelous party you've hosted."

Lady Brentwood beamed and peered past him. "Where

has Lady Courtenay gone? I was looking forward to speaking with her."

"I believe her niece felt unwell," he said vaguely. "She may take the young lady home, as any good chaperone would."

Lady Brentwood's lips pursed and her brows went up, but she accepted it.

Richard allowed himself to be towed around the room like a prized goat, introduced to stuffy lords and flirtatious ladies and even some young bucks, including the Brentwoods' son, who clustered eagerly around him, demanding to know about rumors of diamonds and gold just lying on the ground in remote corners of India.

He answered every question, no matter how trivial or silly, as fulsomely as he could manage. After a while, Gerhard joined him, and Richard cajoled him into singing some of the chants they'd learned in Mongolia. Gerhard had a good voice and was a clever mimic, able to pick up the intonations much better than Richard. His friend gave him a quizzical look, but he obliged. By the end of the evening, they held the better part of the supper room in thrall.

"Goodness, Richard, I've never seen you make such a spectacle of yourself," remarked Clemency when they finally left.

"It seemed appropriate," he said lightly. Appropriate, and apt to distract anyone who might have noticed Evangeline's hasty departure.

"If you wish me to sing again, you must also do so," grumbled Gerhard.

"You have the better voice," Richard told him.

"Oh, you *do* have a marvelous voice," Clemency added warmly, and Gerhard went pink and closed his mouth.

But after depositing Clemency at her home, Richard slumped against the cushions and cursed, long and fluently in three different languages.

"What happened?" Gerhard leaned forward. "It must be serious, to require singing."

Richard sighed. "Evangeline's niece may have been a trifle indiscreet." Not even to Gerhard would he say *how* indiscreet.

His friend tilted his head. "That is why you were searching for her."

He rubbed his hands over his face. God, they had been too open about that. But the seriousness of the situation had crept up on them slowly, until it was too late. "Yes."

Gerhard nodded philosophically. "I hope the young lady was unharmed?"

He thought of the young woman standing in Burke's embrace, her face flushed with pleasure. "No violence was done to her."

"That is good. Who has not been indiscreet once or twice?"

He closed his eyes. If only that were all it was. "One fears what her parents will say."

"Parents often know very well what their child is capable of," Gerhard pointed out. "They are rarely surprised."

"But when they are, it doesn't go well," Richard retorted.

"Ah. That is so."

Richard stared out the window into the dark night. "That is so."

Evangeline knew it would be bad.

Marion, to no one's surprise, had heard tittle-tattle from some friends in London about Joan and the scandalous Lord Burke. Not about the events at the Brentwood ball, of course, but about Burke calling on Joan and dancing with her. Evangeline did her best to put on a pleasant expression and calmly explain, and to her relief, Joan also piped up in her own defense. Marion was still upset, but George sent them all out so he could speak to Joan alone.

Joan caught her eye as Evangeline left the room, and gave her a reassuring nod. *Good,* she thought with a burst of relief. It would be so much better if George and Marion listened to Joan about Burke.

She also hoped Smythe was right about George, but she went upstairs to her room and told Solly to pack her things.

Solly raised her brows. "So suddenly?"

Evangeline sighed. Whatever happened out of this, she was going home soon. "Sir George and Lady Bennet are home. It's been over a month." An endless month. She felt old and tired. She missed her dog. She kept thinking of Richard's words: *I want to take you home with me at the end of every evening, without secrecy or sneaking.* She missed him, too, more than ever at this moment. If he were here, he would listen to her angry raging against Lord Burke, he would pour her a tot of whisky, and then he would do that thing he did, running his fingertips in circles over her back until she relaxed and could think of how to ameliorate this.

But because Marion disapproved, he was not here. She wondered how long it would take the gossips to let Marion know that her wild and wicked sister-in-law had gone right back to her scandalous ways, dancing with that dangerous foreign explorer, as bold as brass at Catherine Brentwood's ball . . .

She gave herself a shake. She was too old to worry about that. She went to help Solly, working out in her mind how to approach things in the morning.

In the end, she decided to fall on her sword. She asked Smythe early the next morning to let her know when Lady Bennet awoke, and as soon as he gave her the nod, she hurried to her sister-in-law's sitting room.

"Please forgive me," she said as soon as she entered the room.

Marion smiled wearily. She had always been petite and slim, but she'd lost weight, and in the bright morning sunlight she looked wan and almost gaunt. "Come in, Evangeline. Will you breakfast with me?" The table was already set for two. Evangeline had expected it would be for her brother, but now she realized he was gone. Marion motioned to the seat across from her. "I hoped to see you. I must also beg your pardon."

She rushed to take Marion's outstretched hand. "If there were anything to forgive, I would grant it at once. But of course you must have been very alarmed, to rush back to town—"

"That was my fault," Marion said quietly. "I received a

letter and urged George . . . No." She shook her head, the light catching every line on her face. "I flew into a state and made him return with all possible speed."

Evangeline bit her lip. "I should have written to you about Lord Burke."

The other woman sighed. "If you had, I only would have railed at George to return sooner." She looked down, plucking at the throw that covered her lap. "And that would not have been good for my health."

Her heart lurched. "Are you—?"

Marion shook her head. "The doctor believes I am out of danger. A lung inflammation, he said, and urged me to remain in the country air longer. But I do feel far better than when we left London." She squeezed Evangeline's hand. "And I have not thanked you for leaping into the breach and dropping everything to come care for my daughter."

"Of course I would."

Marion looked at her, her eyes clear. "I did not take it for granted. I know I have not always been . . . supportive of you in your times of need."

She released Marion's hand and forced a smile to conceal her surprise. "Water under the bridge."

"Please let me apologize. I was wrong."

Evangeline looked at her and nodded. "Thank you."

Marion picked up her tea. "George spoke to Joan last night. I understand I may have been . . . hasty in my assessment of Viscount Burke."

Evangeline took a deep breath and prayed she could find the right words. "I did not entertain him lightly. He said Douglas entreated him to call upon Joan, and Marion, I wish you could have seen her face when he came. I—I think he may have vexed her at first, but she quickly came to delight in his visits. I would have told Smythe to throw him into the street if not."

"And Smythe would have done it, for you," murmured Marion with a knowing look.

Evangeline stifled a grin at the thought of Denny kicking Lord Burke in the seat of his breeches and slamming the door behind him. "I also questioned Burke directly about his intentions," she forged on. "He didn't retreat at all when I warned him about raising expectations. If anything, he seemed to grow more determined. I do believe he cares for her, Marion."

He'd damned well better, after what he did last night, she thought grimly.

"I was persuaded that he was in earnest when he invited us to see his house, currently being repaired and redecorated into an exceedingly modern, handsome home in Hanover Square. Joan was very taken with the house, and when I overheard him asking her opinion of finishing touches like paint colors and plumbing, she answered him very eagerly." She paused. "I cannot imagine how deeply in love I would have had to have been, to enthuse about coal chutes and water closets at her age."

Marion gave a reluctant laugh. "So said George."

"She told him?"

The other woman nodded. "With great enthusiasm, in George's telling." She sighed, turning her head to look out the window. "I want my daughter to find love and happiness.

Of course I do. But I don't want it to be short-lived. If only Burke were a more respectable sort of gentleman . . ."

Evangeline crossed her fingers under the table. "I believe he's not so bad as his reputation suggests. If I had *any* doubt, I would have chased him off with a pitchfork."

She still might, if this rebounded horribly on Joan, but didn't mention that.

"I have known more than my share of rakes and scoundrels, as you know," she went on, choosing each word with care. "Believe me, I learned painful lessons from every one of them. I asked several friends for the most scurrilous gossip they could find on Burke, so that I could know the worst, and all reports came back that he's possibly the most elusive, prized bachelor in London. He's no saint, but his affairs are discreet. He's not in debt, and he has an extremely large fortune. His vices are the usual ones a man of his age and station would have, and he does not pursue them immoderately. And . . . if he willingly calls upon a young lady, and takes tea with her, and dances with her in front of all society, he knows precisely what he is doing, and he is doing it of his own free will because nothing on earth could induce him to do it *against* his will." She tried to smile, despite the hammering of her pulse. "I do believe Douglas would thrash him senseless if he trifled with Joan, and he knows it."

Marion continued to stare out the window. "Perhaps you are right. Douglas . . ." She touched one hand to her brow. "I cannot think about him. My main purpose is to prevent Joan being caught in a scandal." She looked at Evangeline with compassion. "You know well how vicious and unkind that always is to a lady."

She nodded, a hard lump in her throat.

"It is not easy, as a mother, to see your children unhappy," Marion went on. "For years I've hoped and prayed a gentleman would appear who loved Joan for who she is, whom she loved in return. I know she dreams of that, too. Joan has always found it desperately unfair that Douglas is allowed far more freedom and . . . well, more excess. George assures me Douglas knows his bounds and keeps to them, and I take his word for it. But as much as I would like to see Douglas married and settled, it is far more important for Joan. Life is harder for a spinster than a bachelor." She hesitated, glancing at Evangeline. "But I cannot bear the anguish I would feel if either of them should be married in a way that prevented all future happiness."

Evangeline couldn't move. Even her heartbeat felt sluggish. Marion meant Court. If Court hadn't got himself shot, she would still be tied to him for life, still forced to put up with his public affairs, his arrogant selfishness, his complete lack of care for anything about her. She might have remained respectable and been received by every hostess in London . . . but she would have been beyond miserable.

"Could Burke make my daughter happy? I don't know," Marion went on in the same measured tone. "If she loves him, I hope he can. But I am afraid . . . He has been wild his entire life. I don't know that he *knows* how to be a good husband. Douglas, at least, has had George as an excellent example." She seemed to gather herself. "I shall do my best to reserve judgment. If Joan cares for him, it will matter. But in the meantime . . ." She poured more tea. "Do tell me about this dressmaker who creates gowns my daughter likes better than anything in Ackermann's."

By the time Joan peered around the door, Evangeline had begun to breathe easier. Her heart leapt when Marion apologized to her daughter for insulting the gold gown; Evangeline couldn't fathom her own mother openly apologizing for anything. And Joan responded with perfect contrition about causing her mother to worry.

Evangeline drank her tea in relieved silence, saying prayers of gratitude to every deity she could think of. They'd squeaked through, it seemed. Burke remained an open question, but now Joan's parents were on hand to deal with him, and Joan showed every sign of confidence in her choice.

When the post arrived, she seized the chance to excuse herself. Joan followed her to the door. "You're leaving?"

She clasped her niece's hand, fondness filling her heart. "Yes. I miss my Louis, and now your parents are home, you've no more need of me."

Joan looked at her with big eyes. "I'll miss you."

The faintly forlorn note made her eyes grow damp. *And I shall miss you,* she thought. Perhaps she would be able to see Joan more often, especially if she married Lord Burke. She hoped she would. She was still angry at the young man, but not irrevocably.

When Joan asked what she should do, though, she rallied her confidence. "What does your heart tell you to do?" she asked gently.

"It would be easier to answer if I knew what *his* heart felt," her niece muttered.

Make him tell you, she thought. But as she was doing her best to reassure the girl, she spoke encouragingly. "Men don't always blurt it out, you know. Some of them take a fearfully long time to acknowledge that it is love they feel."

It had taken Richard six years—but then, he said he'd been following her lead, and that he had wanted to say it forever. She had promised to think about that. In a fortnight, he would tell her again, and ask her . . . Ask her . . .

And that moment, just as it appeared she and Joan had skirted true disaster and would pull through unscathed, was when it all went wrong.

"You lied to me."

Joan and Evangeline both froze at Marion's voice. Slowly they turned, to see her holding a letter, her eyes wide. *Bloody hell.* Evangeline wasn't sure to whom Marion was speaking, but she had a terrible feeling she knew what was in that letter.

"You disappeared from the Brentwood ball with Lord Burke last night and weren't seen again." Marion gazed, aghast, at her daughter.

Joan's lips parted, but she said nothing, her face pale.

"I made her come home," said Evangeline in a rush. "I felt a headache . . ."

Marion gave her a look that sent a chill to her bones— anger, humiliation, fear. "And you were remarked searching the house for Joan!" She turned to her daughter. "Where did you go, young lady?"

Joan did not share Evangeline's devious, sneaky soul. Instead of putting up her chin and brazening it out, she stammered, she blinked, and her cheeks went from white to scarlet in the blink of an eye, as damning as any confession.

Stricken with guilt, Evangeline lowered her gaze to her hands and listened as Marion recounted every fact that had so alarmed her last night: Burke's disappearance, at the same time as Joan's, after they had danced together—"indecently close!" Marion exclaimed in dismay.

Joan flinched with each word. She looked as if she would cry, even before her mother started talking about sending George to deal with the man. "Oh Joan, what have you done?" she finished in despair.

Evangeline's knuckles were white; her fingers had gone numb. She made herself look up, her throat painfully dry, and Marion sent her a look filled with such betrayal, she simply bowed her head. Marion sent Joan back to her room, then turned on her. She had got to her feet but now swayed unsteadily.

"Evangeline," she said, her voice thick, "did you lie to me?"

She took a deep breath. "No. I . . . I omitted a few things."

Marion gave a little sob, then collapsed into her chair.

"She did go off with him," Evangeline made herself say. "Or perhaps he led her away. I did look for her, but discreetly. I . . . I do not know what happened between them."

Without a word Marion held out the wretched letter. Evangeline would rather read her own death warrant, but she took the paper.

Althea Crocker, read the signature at the bottom. Dimly

Evangeline remembered the woman in the retiring room with a loose button on her glove. The letter was polite, even effusive, but—like Catherine Brentwood's note to Evangeline—that was merely a sugarcoating on malice. She wrote of her delight at seeing Joan in society, even if so surprisingly attired; her astonishment that the elusive Lord Burke danced such marked attendance on Joan; her concern at noting Joan wasn't seen at supper; and how frantically Evangeline had been searching the whole house. She made it sound as if Evangeline had run up and down corridors screaming Joan's name. She ended with concern for how it would look, Joan disappearing with Lord Burke from the ball and neither ever returning. She hoped Joan hadn't suffered a misadventure.

Lady Crocker, of course, had two unmarried daughters of her own. And, now that Evangeline thought about it, the woman was also friends with Lady Ambrose.

"This puts the most spiteful exaggeration on everything," Evangeline said quietly. "She merely saw me glance in the retiring room for Joan."

Marion had leaned back, resting her head on the chaise behind her. Her face looked bloodless, and lines of stress bracketed her mouth. "Althea Crocker is a horrendous gossip. If this is how she's portraying it to me . . ."

It would be even worse when she told others. How well Evangeline knew that.

"I am sorry," she whispered. "Surpassing sorry."

"So am I," said Marion, as a tear leaked down her cheek, quickly followed by another and another. "But I must leave it to George now, and I have no idea what he'll do."

CHAPTER 32

Evangeline left Audley Street before she could be thrown out.

As Smythe opened the door for her for the last time, she paused. "Thank you, Denny," she said softly. "For attempting to guide me."

His eyes softened. "It was a pleasure to see you again, Miss Evie."

She nodded, her throat too tight to speak, and got into her carriage.

The drive home seemed interminable, and yet she was startled to see Wyndham House appear in front of her. Her own home seemed foreign and strange to her, after all this time. She wandered through the house until she reached the conservatory, her favorite room, and stood staring out the tall windows.

All the way home, she'd been telling herself that George was a different sort of father to their own. He loved his daughter, very much. Even if he went to speak to Burke, he would keep Joan's happiness in mind . . .

But he would have to call on Burke, while Marion prayed he wouldn't call the man *out*, because of Evangeline. He had entrusted her with his only daughter. She had promised she would take good care of the girl, and then she had failed. Even now, that harpy Lady Crocker was no doubt gleefully telling everyone that Miss Bennet had been lured away by the scoundrel Lord Burke to debauchery and ruin, which should surprise no one since her so-called chaperone was the wicked and scandalous Lady Courtenay.

Her throat closed as she imagined Joan being burned alive by vicious gossip in all the drawing rooms of London. George browbeating Burke into doing the right thing, perhaps risking his life to protect his daughter and her reputation. Joan walking down the church aisle, cowed into acquiescence by her frantic, worried mother. Joan fighting back tears on her wedding night, knowing she was the property of a man she hadn't chosen, 'til death did them part. Evangeline's stomach churned so hard she thought she would be sick.

She knew exactly what that felt like. She had lived it herself.

But this was worse than when it had happened to her. Then, she had been the victim. This time, she was the *perpetrator*. She had been careless. She trusted Joan, she truly did —but Burke? She did not know him. She had no reason to trust him. He could be another Court, craving only the pursuit, willing to lead an unsuspecting young woman astray if it served his own pleasure. He seemed to care for Joan, and

Evangeline wanted desperately to believe that he did . . . but she could be wrong, as she'd been wrong about Court. She had been fooled by her own wishes and fancies, dreaming arrogantly that she could help her niece find the sort of happy marriage that had eluded Evangeline herself.

Instead of learning from her own mistakes and unhappiness, she had done even worse. Joan wasn't even *her* child. Evangeline had betrayed Joan, and George, and especially Marion, who had been so very right to doubt her.

She barely heard the French window open behind her, and when Louis gave a little bark and jumped on her skirt, she flinched so hard she almost fell.

Richard stepped in. "My gardener spotted your carriage on the road. This little fellow has missed you so desperately, I decided to bring him at once. And, I confess, I was eager to see you myself."

She bent and scooped up her dog, who was leaping around her feet, making happy whining sounds. She cuddled him to her heart and pressed her cheek against his head. His happy licking of her chin made her eyes sting.

"I did not think to see you home so soon," Richard went on when she didn't speak. "Is Miss Bennet well?"

"Her parents came home," she whispered. "They were waiting when we arrived from the Brentwood ball."

"I see," he said. There was a long pause. She could see his reflection from the corner of her eye. He wore country clothing, soft and familiar, the way she usually saw him—not the crisp, elegant evening wear he'd worn when he professed himself in love with her. "Were you expecting them?"

"No." She drew in a shuddering breath. "Someone wrote

to Marion about Joan dancing with Lord Burke, and she was worried."

His footsteps were loud on the flagstone floor. "What happened?" he asked gently, touching her shoulder.

She twisted away. In her arms, Louis struggled, and she put him down. He backed up, looking at her and barking. When she shook her head at him, he ran up the steps and out of the room, yipping for Solly. She didn't blame him; she wanted to be away from herself, too.

"Evie, what is wrong?"

"There was an argument," she said, swiping at her eyes with shaking fingers. "Last night. George and Marion were both deeply alarmed, and I did my best to explain . . . Well, not *all*, of course, I hardly wanted to tell them about the Brentwood debacle . . ."

"They could not have known of that," he said in concern. "Not if they were awaiting your return last night."

She gave a bitter laugh. "They discovered *that* this morning! When that evil Lady Crocker wrote to Marion that Joan allowed Burke to debauch her on the dance floor, and then they slunk off together for more sin, and that I almost tore down the house trying to find her—with the strong suggestion that I must have been off doing something very wicked myself to have allowed Joan to be spirited away to ruination."

"That is hardly what happened," he countered. "Lady Brentwood would surely tell her—"

"It doesn't matter," she said in despair. "Althea Crocker will spread her version far and wide, and enough people will believe it that it doesn't matter."

"Why would she set out to ruin Sir George Bennet's daughter?"

"Because she has two unmarried daughters of her own, either of whom could use a rich viscount for a husband. Never underestimate the ruthless plotting of a society mama." She sighed. "And because her dear friend Cynthia Ambrose will applaud anything that pushes me out of society again."

He was silent for a long moment. "Is there anything I can do? You have only to say the word."

"No. There's nothing anyone can do." Burke, she supposed, could cure most of it by declaring himself madly in love with Joan and begging to marry her. But what if he didn't love her? Images of Court's handsome face flitted through her mind, so charming and smiling when seducing her, so dismissive and cold when not. Perhaps Burke would decide he didn't actually want to marry Joan, now that he'd had her. Perhaps he would despise having his hand forced, and any actual affection he felt would wither away. Perhaps he would never let Joan forget that her father had marched him to the altar under threat of death, and make clear to her that he never would have married her otherwise.

And Joan would be left to hold her head high and try to hide her feelings when people whispered about all the ways she must be disappointing her unwilling husband. That only a scandal could have compelled the viscount to marry her, tall and forward and unfashionably plump. Evangeline's chest felt so tight she could hardly breathe. Joan deserved better.

"That cannot be true," Richard said. "Lady Bennet will have friends of her own, ready to defend her daughter."

"George will go to Burke and—and make demands of him," she whispered. Again she saw her own father's face, stony with disapproval and fury, but not surprise. He'd expected to find her in a scandalous liaison.

"Burke cares for Miss Bennet. I doubt Sir George will have to press him—"

"Does he?" She flung out a hand to stop him. Once her father mentioned pistols at dawn, Court hadn't protested, either. He'd simply shrugged as he buttoned his breeches and said, *As you like.* He'd known he wouldn't be faithful, affectionate, or even kind to her, and he'd known it didn't matter to her father. "Will he still care when he's forced to wed her? Will he still want her after my brother has called him out? Will he still be kind to her in five years, or ten, or whenever he decides Joan is too old for his taste, or her looks don't appeal to him, or he simply wants someone new?"

Richard was quiet again. "Evie," he said at last, "come have a cup of tea."

She almost stopped breathing. That's what her mother had said, both times Evangeline had gone to her to protest her father's edict that she marry first Cunningham, then Court; to plead with her mother for help, for support, for guidance. But her mother, like Marion, had been mortally terrified of anything disreputable. *Your father knows best,* Mama had said anxiously. *Don't make such a fuss, dear, have some tea and you'll see it's all for the best . . .* While Evangeline knew it was her last chance to escape.

Her skin felt turned to stone even as guilt and anguish

howled inside her. Richard meant well. In a remote corner of her mind, she knew he was being sensible and she was being emotional. But she also knew the toll such emotions could take on a person's soul.

It was easy for him to dismiss her concerns. He was a man—moreover, a man who had made himself famous by defying rules and propriety. How easy for him to say Burke would do the right thing, that he cared for Joan, that it would all work out in the end. Things *usually* worked out well in the end, for men. The main impact upon Burke's life would be the added expense of a wife. Nothing would stop him from taking a pretty young widow ballooning, or seducing another woman at another ball, or engaging in shocking behavior that scandalized everyone in London. Nothing would stop him from crushing Joan's lively spirit, from breaking her warm and generous heart, from making the rest of her life a misery.

"No," she said, her voice shaking slightly. "I—I would like to be alone."

He shifted. "Very well," he said, sounding concerned. "I will come back tomorrow."

She shook her head, a tight, sharp movement. "Please don't. It . . . It is over."

Richard frowned in bemusement. She could see it in the glass, hear it in his voice. "Do not lose hope. The young man does care for her—"

Evangeline made herself turn to face him. "I don't mean Joan." She waved her hand toward herself, toward him, then curled her fingers into a fist. "Us."

Richard jerked backward. "What?"

"It is over," she said again, her breath coming faster. God, she wanted him to leave. She wanted to hide from everyone she had disappointed and betrayed. First George and Marion, then Joan, now Richard. Everyone she cared about. The expression on his face would kill her. "We both agreed—it would end when either of us wanted it to end. I am ending it, now."

He looked astonished—and horrified. "What? But—no, you do not mean it!"

"I do!" She lurched backward as he took a step toward her. "I do mean it," she insisted. Her heart was pounding so painfully, she thought she might faint. Her vision was blurry around the edges, and she couldn't stop her hands shaking. If he touched her, she might go mad. "It's over. You agreed! You promised! No reproaches, *you promised me!*"

His face was stark white. "Please," he begged. "Please don't say that now. I will go—leave you time to think. Wait a few days, see how it ends—"

Her laughter was wild with hysteria. "Wait, to see if someone else can repair the damage I caused! Wait, to see if I haven't wrecked an innocent girl's life! No! No, I will not wait, I will take responsibility for what I've done!"

"And this is how you choose to punish yourself?" He advanced on her—foolishly, because she couldn't bear the sight of him at that moment. "And how you will punish me?"

"It was because of you I left her unsupervised," Evangeline lashed out. "I only left the ballroom at your instigation!"

He stopped, stricken. "I love you," he said quietly. "I never wanted to hurt you."

She shook her head as self-loathing and agony roared inside her like a hurricane. She had been selfish, going off with him in total dereliction of her responsibility and in blatant violation of her promise to George. She did not deserve the happiness that Richard offered her; she had been right to wall herself off from that, and because of her momentary weakness, daring to think she might have it after all, she had hurt an innocent girl. *Till death do you part,* intoned the vicar in her memory, the weak sunshine shining on Cunningham's bare pate, almost blinding her. It had felt like a form of death, standing there, feeling herself vanishing into the legal void of matrimony. She had ceased to be a person in her own right. Would Joan feel the same panic? The same sense of despair?

Even Richard didn't know how terrible it had been. Those early months, when Cunningham had directed every aspect of her life, trying to train her into his idea of a wife, trying to snuff out all traces of her rebellious nature. The furious helplessness she had felt, knowing no one would stop him or save her. The rage that had built inside her, until it fermented into bitter scorn for her husband, followed by the reckless disregard for propriety that led her into a miserable marriage with Court, then the disrepute of his unfaithfulness and the blazing scandal of his death, and finally near-banishment from society as she willfully thumbed her nose at society's strictures.

And she hadn't learned one bloody lesson from it. Not when she needed it most.

"You don't," she said numbly. No one could love her. No one should.

His brows lowered, and the color came back into his cheeks. "I know what I feel," he said tersely. "You must not castigate yourself—"

"I deserve it!" she screamed.

The words seemed to expand and ricochet around the room until they pressed in on her, acrid and sour. They scorched her lungs, her throat, her lips until she thought she might choke on the bitter taste.

She had wrecked everything. She had long thought Joan a girl after her own heart, and now she had sentenced Joan to the same terrible fate that had brought her so much misery for so many years.

Richard said nothing. The silence was terrible. But what was there to say?

Evangeline couldn't even see him through the tears in her eyes. "Go," she said thickly. "Please *go*. Good-bye, Richard."

He stared at her for a long, long time, saying nothing. Evangeline turned her back on him, unable to bear that gaze.

And several painful heartbeats later, the door opened, then closed.

He was gone, and with him her stupid, dangerous dreams of happiness.

CHAPTER 33

When Richard was ten and Gerhard nine, they had discovered a cavern in the mountains near their home.

They had never seen such a thing, although they had heard of it, and there was no question but that they would explore it. They collected a lantern, a torch, a sack of food and drink, some rope, and a pickaxe, which Gerhard had stolen from his older brother's climbing kit.

"What if we should discover a vein of gold in there?" he'd said, when Richard asked why they needed it. Which had sounded like a sensible idea at the time.

So they wriggled down the narrow opening into the cavern, lit their lantern and torch, and set out into the bowels of the earth. They used the rope to descend several sharp inclines, but never once thought of unspooling it behind them.

After an hour or more they had reached a flat area, very appealing as a secluded grotto where they might set up a campsite, when a sudden icy draft of wind extinguished both lantern and torch in the blink of an eye. By some instinct, Richard lunged and caught hold of Gerhard's jacket, to avoid being separated. But that still left them marooned deep in a cavern in pitch black darkness, with no idea how to find their way out.

In his memory, it took hours to strike a spark from his flint in that damp, dark cave, with his hands shaking from cold and terror. He'd had to rip off bits of his shirt for additional tinder, and when he finally, *finally* got a spark to catch, Gerhard's face had been ghostly pale and streaked with tear tracks through the dirt that covered him. They'd both burst into tears and clung to each other.

After that, he remembered nothing before stumbling into his home hours after midnight and hearing his mother scream with relief that he was safe. He had no idea how they had made their way out, how they had got home, or what he told his parents. Not a single piece of their assembled gear made it home with them. Gerhard never spoke of it again, and he didn't, either.

Richard had never gone into another cavern. That feeling of utter isolation, of not knowing which way was up, down, left, or right . . . of the serious possibility that he was standing in his own grave . . . had never been forgotten. And it was the nearest thing he could name to how he felt, walking out of Evangeline's house with her parting words echoing in his head.

By the time he reached his home, he was beyond numb; he might have been deaf and blind, oblivious to everything around him. He sent Karl away and just sat. The next day he didn't leave his room. The day after that, Gerhard knocked on the door and demanded to know what was wrong. Richard didn't reply. Gerhard then shouted that he was sending for a doctor. An hour later there was a tumult when the doctor arrived, but Karl went and spoke to the man, and all was quiet again.

The third day, when Clemency—summoned no doubt by Gerhard—knocked and called his name in a pleading whisper, Richard opened the door.

"What is wrong?" she asked anxiously. "Are you ill?"

"No. Why would you think so?" Richard headed for the stairs. Behind him, she gasped, no doubt spying through the open door Karl clearing away the empty brandy bottles and half-smoked cigars, opening the windows for fresh air, and carrying away the rumpled and stained clothes Richard had worn for three straight days.

"What has happened?" she cried, rushing down the stairs behind him.

"Nothing." That was true, reflected Richard. Nothing had happened, certainly not the thing he desired most in the world, and now it never would.

"Have you and Evangeline quarreled?" his sister asked hesitantly.

He stopped at the foot of the stairs. Clemency stopped, too, twisting her hands together, her face creased with concern. "Do not worry about me," he said gently. "Lady Courtenay . . . She and I are no longer seeing each other. That is all."

"That is all!" she exclaimed in astonishment. "Not seeing

each other! When you're so madly in love with her you can't even see straight? What happened?"

In truth he didn't know, as if the trauma of it had burned his memory to ash, destroying all traces of that night. He remembered dancing with Evangeline, holding her close and knowing that he was helplessly in love with her and always would be. How he had drawn her into a quiet room and laid his heart at her feet and asked her to reconsider her vow against marriage. The way her face had turned pink, and her slightly stunned smile, as if she hadn't known. Hadn't even suspected he might be mad for her. And how she had said she would consider it.

It hadn't been a proposal, and there was no engagement. But it had been a step toward one, and Richard was still dumbfounded over how it had fallen apart so disastrously.

He had hoped . . . prayed . . . it would blow over. She had been violently upset, and he acknowledged that he'd been responsible for some of the actions she was currently flaying herself over. For three days he had waited, smoking, drinking, neither sleeping nor eating, always listening for the sound of a rider, a carriage, an arrow shot through his window—anything that might be a message bearing a softer tone. If she had written to him . . .

But there had been no word. No message. It had unsettled him, unnerved him, and finally unmoored him.

He looked away. "Alas, dear sister. The lady is not in love with me, and she has sent me on my way."

Clemency inhaled in understanding. "Oh, no. *Richard* . . ."

"It is her right, of course," he went on, speaking over her.

"She is not my wife. No promises were made, so none were broken. She asked me to leave, and I have left. I cannot force my company upon one who no longer desires it."

"Richard." Clemency laid her hand on his arm. "She must have spoken rashly. It—it happened after the to-do over Miss Bennet and Lord Burke, didn't it? She's upset. Call on her."

The moment either one of us wishes to end it, it will end—calmly, rationally, with no outburst of recrimination or dismay from either. He could still hear her saying it, just as he could still hear his own voice accepting the bargain. He had known all along, but he wasn't prepared for it. He hadn't thought it would happen; he had taken such care to respect her every boundary and right. He hadn't guessed that some random scoundrel of a viscount and a headstrong girl in love would be able to ruin everything.

"No. I promised I would not badger her. She told me to leave."

"Oh, but she couldn't have meant it! She was upset! You must be patient, go back when her temper has cooled . . ."

"And then?" he demanded, his temper finally fraying. "She told me to leave, Clemency. Now I should barge my way in, and say that I did not believe her? That she could not mean what she said? Scold her for being emotional and over-wrought?"

"No," she protested, cowed. "Perhaps . . . persuade her . . ."

Richard pressed his thumb to his forehead, between his brows. Some in the Far East said it relieved stress and encouraged calm. He didn't think it was working today. Nothing was easing the tension that strung his muscles miserably taut. He'd thought of those things—he'd thought of a lot of things, in three long days of silence and solitude. "I cannot do that, either."

"But why not?" his sister cried.

"Because it would make me the sort of man she despises," he said savagely. "Tell her what she ought to think or feel or do!" He shook his head. "Or else it would make me despise myself. Persuade a woman to have me, against her own inclination? Even if she agreed, I would always know it was not her wish to be with me, that she had been browbeaten or beguiled into having me, and I cannot live like that. If she wants me gone, it is better for me to go." He sighed at his sister's stricken face, his anger and despair draining away, and clasped her hand for a moment before easing it away from his sleeve. "Clem . . . I'm giving up this house."

Her eyes went wide. "No! No, do not run away! Richard, she cares for you—I know it! It may have been a bad quarrel, but she *loves* you—"

"She never said so." He stepped away. That was what had tormented him most for three days. She had never said the words—not once. Neither had he, until a few days ago, but he would have sworn on his life that her feelings for him were as potent as his for her. He must have been wrong. "I am not running away. I am removing myself from the place where my heart would be mutilated repeatedly and regularly until I could no longer survive it. Perhaps I will return to Zürich for a while."

"Don't! No, I need you," Clemency pleaded. "The boys need you! Please don't leave, how will I get on without you?"

Richard paused in the act of reaching for his coat. He had given his word not to stir this particular pot, but . . . He also had nothing left to lose. He turned to face his sister and took her hands in his. Tears sparkled in her eyes and she looked utterly woebegone, her face splotched with pink.

"Gerhard will stay," he said gently. The big oaf must be lurking about somewhere, after sending in Clemency to assault him with tears. "He will help you. You have only ever to ask, and Gerhard will always leap to assist you." Her lips quivered, and he threw caution to the wind. "He adores you, Clemency. He has for years."

Her mouth opened in shock. "How dare you say that, Richard. He doesn't . . . no. I am like a sister to him! Don't be cruel."

"Cruel?" He smiled sadly. "It could only be cruel if you cared for him."

Now she was pale, and tried to pull her hands from his. "I— Oh, it's too humiliating— Don't make me say it."

"Say what?"

"That I . . . I . . . That I have come to care for him a great deal!" she hissed, her eyes darting nervously from side to side. "A *great* deal. But he only visits me when you do. He barely speaks to me at other times."

"If you claim to know a woman's heart, allow me to assure you that this is how gentlemen behave when they are besotted beyond reason but too tormented by nerves to profess it."

Her mouth sagged open, and she blinked several times, now fully diverted from her tears.

"Ask him," added Richard. He doubted Gerhard would even try to deny it. "Better yet, tell him you care for him. It may untie his tongue."

She turned scarlet. "Very well. If you will stay, I will tell him. But you—"

He released her to put on his coat and pick up his hat. "I must go, Clem. I cannot bear to be near her and to know—"

That all my hopes and dreams are dead. That the great love of my life is over.

"I have to go," he finished, and was out the door before Clemency could muster another protest.

Had she really been longing after Gerhard for years? While Gerhard pined for *her* in silent longing? God save him from people too stubborn to admit their feelings, he thought —and then reconsidered, remembering how his own profession of love had turned out. At least Gerhard hadn't been foolish enough to get himself banned from Clemency's presence.

If only *he* had said nothing. If only he hadn't enticed her to come away with him for just a few minutes. If only that young ass Burke had been able to keep his bloody breeches fastened for one godforsaken hour. If only Lady Bennet had been just slightly more ill and unable to return to London at the worst moment. If only . . . If only . . .

He stopped walking when he reached the pond. He had taken the house because of this pond, which had brought her into his orbit again. That day the water had glittered like diamonds, as one might imagine the air would shimmer before a goddess appeared—and then one had, rising from the water like the answer to his wildest dreams. It had seemed like a blessing, a sign from heaven.

Today the water was flat and black under the gloomy sky. Nothing stirred the becalmed surface. Perhaps that, too, was a sign. Today it looked more like the River Styx.

He walked back to the house, into his study, and took out a piece of paper to write to the estate agent.

CHAPTER 34

Evangeline felt every one of her fifty-two years in the days following The Debacle. She waited, sleepless with anxiety, for news. She heard nothing from George, let alone from Marion or Joan. Every morning she sent her groom into London with orders to buy every newspaper and gossip rag he could locate, and she read every one of them from front to back. For a few days there was ominous silence, then a small announcement of the wedding of Miss Joan Bennet to Viscount Burke.

That eased her most crippling fear, that she'd been entirely wrong about the viscount, but as the days dragged on and still no letter came from her brother, or his wife, or Joan herself, she realized her other fear had been well-founded.

Joan had been rushed into marriage because of the scandal, and they blamed Evangeline. It was a hard blow, even though she knew it was deserved.

That week, Wyndham House might as well have been a

mausoleum. She couldn't summon the energy or will to go outside, not into the garden where she and Richard had sat so many times together, nor to the bathhouse where he'd made love to her in the steam and heat. It was all she could do to walk from her bed to the table, to the sofa in the drawing room, and back to bed. Deprived of his usual walks, Louis added to the misery by being anxious and troublesome. Evangeline walked in on Solly scolding the little dog, who was replying with sharp, angry barks of his own.

"What's he done?"

Solly held up the shredded remains of a straw bonnet. "He has destroyed it. I left it out to replace the ribbon, and I return to find it so."

Louis darted up to Evangeline's feet and licked her ankle, whimpering.

She sighed, stooping to pet the dog. "My poor pup," she murmured. "I'm making you miserable, too."

Louis licked her hand frantically, dancing back and forth.

"Why don't you take him out?" urged Solly. "Fresh air would do you both good."

Evangeline stood and glanced listlessly at the window. It was a fair day, but she had no desire to feel the sun on her face. "Perhaps."

Solly nodded. "I will bring tea to the garden. And a biscuit for you, Your Majesty," she added to Louis, who had perked up at the word *garden*. He barked and ran from the room. "Do it for him," she said gently to Evangeline. "If you will not go out for yourself."

She sighed. "Very well."

She chose a bench facing the house, not her favorite set by the French doors, where Richard had once walked her home in the rain and agreed to her terms for their affair. She had all but told him then that one day she would end it and send him away. She had forced him to promise that he would accept it, and now he had kept his word and gone. Her throat felt tight and she determinedly faced the other way, trying not to think of those giddy days when they couldn't get enough of each other, when she had suspected, deep in her heart, that she'd found something rare and precious at last.

Solly came out with a tea tray and set it down. "You have a caller. Shall I show her out here?"

"No," said Evangeline. She had avoided Fanny since returning to Chelsea, and wasn't about to stop now. Three times Fanny had sent a note, and three times Evangeline had sent it back unopened.

"It is Lady Burke," said Solly quietly.

Evangeline froze, then lurched to her feet. "Is she—?"

"She looks perfectly well, and she is alone." Solly waited, brows arched.

Heart in her throat, Evangeline stepped past her and started toward the house, her steps growing faster until she was almost running, Louis at her heels.

Joan was standing in the drawing room when Evangeline burst in. "Joan," she said, and then could say no more.

"Aunt Evangeline!" Her face glowing, Joan turned toward her. She looked very elegant, in a rose pelisse that flattered her complexion. "What a lovely home you have! I've always wanted to see it." She bit her lip. "I hope it's not too presumptuous of me to call without asking?"

Evangeline shook her head. "No," she managed to get out. "Of course not." She hesitated. "Won't you sit down?"

Joan took Richard's usual chair. Evangeline's nerves twinged as she perched gingerly on the sofa. "Are you well?" she asked cautiously.

Her niece blushed. "Yes. Very well. Exceedingly well, if I'm to be honest. I—I hoped to see you at my wedding."

She hadn't been invited, and had known better than to ask. "It didn't seem proper," she said with an attempt at a smile.

Joan looked dismayed. "I feared as much," she said to herself, then moved to the edge of her chair. "Now that I am married, I can go where I want and visit whom I like, and tell you anything I please, no matter what my parents think. And I want to tell you, Aunt, that I am very grateful for all your help. I know I behaved badly and caused you grief, and for that I am terribly sorry."

She held up one hand. "I was supposed to keep you safe, and instead you were caught up in a scandal. I should never have allowed that to happen. I am at fault."

Joan shook her head impatiently. "No, Aunt. It was my choice that night to go off with Tristan. I—I knew it was wrong, and could cause trouble, and I did it anyway."

"No, dear," said Evangeline with a despairing laugh. "You couldn't have known what he meant to—to entice you into doing—"

Joan's face went blank, then fiery red. "Oh," she said in a higher-pitched voice. "Oh, you—you mean—? Oh, but,

Aunt Evangeline, I *did* know—" She stopped suddenly, with a guilty glance at the door. "There's a marvelous little book called *50 Ways to Sin,* have you heard of it?" she whispered in a rush, her eyes shining with excitement. "It's all the rage with ladies of the ton, and it is far more educational than anything in Ackermann's! Oh my goodness, and I didn't think it could all be *true,* but now I rather think it might be!"

Evangeline's brows shot up. She'd heard of that naughty little book, but how had *Joan,* an innocent, proper young lady—?

"Well! The important point is that I love Tristan, and I wanted him, and I am not sorry for anything we did," Joan went on in a brisker tone, though her color was still high. "But I took advantage of your trust, and I must apologize to you for that. It was thoughtless and deceitful."

"Joan," she whispered, guilt-stricken once more, but her niece held up a hand.

"You gave me a great gift." Joan's smile trembled. "You taught me to believe in myself and to know my own heart. You helped me to feel almost beautiful—"

"You *are* beautiful!"

"—and you weren't disapproving of Tristan. You were kind to him, and welcoming. He told me that he wished his own aunt had been half so kindly disposed toward him." She paused, chewing her lower lip. "He grew up so unloved and unwanted. He's not a scoundrel at heart, he just had no one he loved and trusted to inspire him. He appreciates your kindness to him and wishes me to express to you his deep regret that he also disappointed you, at the Brentwood ball."

She shook her head. "None of it would have happened if I had not—"

When she stopped, unable to say Richard's name, Joan gave a tentative smile. "Well, I am *not* sorry that I'm married to Tristan. And that is largely due to the confidence and encouragement *you* gave me. I will be forever grateful to you for that."

Evangeline let out her breath. "It delights me beyond words to hear it. I wish you and Burke every happiness, my dear."

Glowing again, Joan nodded. "I think we shall be happy. He does love me. You were right about that. He had the most difficult time admitting it, but once I told him that *I* love *him*, he told me—he said he hadn't much experience at being loved, but that he's absolutely mad for me. Which suits me perfectly, because"—her face was bright pink now as she lowered her voice—"I really am out of my head for him. He showed me things I didn't think a man could—" She stopped abruptly. "Well, we're both very, *very* happy things have turned out this way."

Evangeline's heart gave a hard throb. "That brings me more joy than you can imagine, my dear."

Joan beamed. "Might I ask a favor of you?"

"Of course!" Her lips trembled in a shaky smile. "Anything."

Joan blushed again. "Would you convey our apologies to Sir Richard as well? I don't have the nerve to call upon him myself, and Tristan said he won't go near . . ." She paused. "I believe Sir Richard threatened to shoot him, and he's not inclined to risk it."

And again she could barely breathe. "Alas," she said with a strained smile. "Sir Richard and I are . . . Well, I don't expect to see him again."

Joan's face blanked. "Oh no! Why? Not—not because of us?"

Evangeline flipped one hand and tried to speak lightly. "No, no, don't concern yourself with it."

Dismay filled her niece's expression. "Oh, Aunt. No! You mustn't blame him for my actions!"

"Don't be silly," she tried to reply, but her voice cracked.

Joan jumped up. "It was *my* fault. It's because of the dance, isn't it? I didn't know what Tristan would propose, when I encouraged you to dance with Sir Richard, but I *did* want you to be happy. And Sir Richard had no idea I would be so impulsive and foolish! He is desperately in love with you, and I . . ." She bit her lip, looking as if she might cry. "I only thought you deserved a man who loves you. I still think it—even more so!—after hearing how dreadful Cunningham and Courtenay were. Oh, please don't say that I've ruined your happiness, when you have helped me to find mine!"

She stood and took Joan's hands in hers. "Nonsense. Nothing of the sort." She hesitated. "I know you meant no harm. I truly do. Things are . . . complicated, between Sir Richard and me. Don't blame yourself for my little frets."

Joan's eyes were wet, but she gripped Evangeline's hands fiercely. "It is not a little fret. I shall never forget how certain I was that I would never find someone who loved me, someone I could love with my entire heart and soul."

"But you have." She squeezed Joan's hands and forced a smile. "To my immense joy."

"And so have you," replied Joan, her chin set stubbornly. "I know you have. I saw you with him, and I saw his face when he spoke of you. He *adores* you, Aunt Evangeline."

Evangeline raised her eyes to the ceiling to stop the moisture in her own eyes from becoming tears. She disengaged her hands and turned away, touching her hair to hide her face. "As romantic as it sounds, that isn't always enough to sweep aside every obstacle."

Joan came around to face her again. "But it is significant enough that you shouldn't be so quick to discard it."

"My dear, please don't trouble yourself—"

"*Don't* say I am too young to understand." Joan hesitated. "I stood for years at the side of every ballroom and drawing room, knowing that no man there cared to speak to me or dance with me, let alone marry me. When you asked if we were trying to bring Tristan up to scratch, I denied it because I didn't think it was possible, for me . . . with him. But I *wanted* it to be true, even then. In fact, I—I think that alone made me so rash. It seemed like a dream, when Tristan said he wanted to—" She blushed scarlet. "And he was reckless, too, but he's a man and mistakes don't hurt men as much, even though he also didn't mean to cause trouble. He told me that he meant to ask Papa for my hand in marriage even before we— Well. He didn't know how it would go wrong." She searched Evangeline's face. "Is it possible," she asked hesitantly, "that Sir Richard was the same? You and Mama told me things are different for a woman . . ."

Evangeline held up one hand to stop her. "Yes. It always is."

Her niece's face cleared, misunderstanding. "Then you can forgive him," she said. "If you can forgive *me*, who did far worse, you must see that he deserves forgiveness, too."

Evangeline couldn't speak, but she made herself smile. It felt stiff and unnatural, but it seemed to reassure Joan. She walked with Evangeline to the door. Outside a handsome carriage waited, gleaming black with red wheels. It would be Burke's, of course, not George's. Burke, who had not objected to Joan coming to see the wicked Lady Courtenay. Who made her niece radiant with happiness. Who sent his own apologies.

Joan paused to embrace her one last time. "Give Sir Richard another chance," she whispered. "To make me feel better, if not for yourself, even though I think it will be tremendously good for you, too. Will you?"

Evangeline made herself smile, without nodding. That seemed to be enough for Joan. She gave Evangeline a smile, then hurried to her carriage and was helped in by the waiting footman.

Evangeline lifted her hand in good-bye as the carriage drove off, Joan leaning out the window and waving back, still beaming. Her heart gave a little sigh. She'd thought, several weeks ago, that young Burke had all the hallmarks of a promising husband. It was reassuring that she hadn't been completely wrong about that.

But Richard . . . Oh, Richard. She could hardly bear to think of what she had said to him.

Once again, she had ruined everything.

CHAPTER 35

Despite telling his sister that he was leaving Chelsea, and his claim that he would go immediately, Richard couldn't seem to do it.

He wrote to the estate agent about selling the house, but the completed letter, signed and sealed, lay on his desk for days. Finally he told Gerhard to get it out of his sight. His friend nodded and took it away, but no reply came from the agent. Richard suspected Gerhard—no doubt acting at Clemency's urging—had not delivered it, and might well have burned it.

He didn't ask.

Even without giving up the house, he could still leave. Karl could pack his things and he could be in Calais by the end of the week, in Zürich within the fortnight. Perhaps he should go south, into the Piedmont. There were mountains there. He hadn't climbed a mountain in an age, perhaps that's what he needed . . . to freeze half to death, and possibly plummet all the way to death in an icy crevasse. A very satis-fying ending that would be, he told himself morosely.

But he didn't tell Karl to pack. Instead he walked for hours every day, sometimes with Hercule and sometimes alone. He had no destination, no purpose; the exercise served to mute his tumultuous thoughts, and that was all he wanted. One day he found himself at Hampton Court, some five miles distant, and could hardly understand how he'd got there.

Perhaps he should complete his memoirs. Sluggishly he got out his travel journals and paged through them, trying to find the gripping thread, trying to remember how exhila-rated he'd been to embark on these journeys. He read his own words, written in enthusiasm and wonder and even the aftermath of terror, and thought they all sounded dry and dull, even the very first one, when he'd been barely nineteen years old and had decided to climb a nearby mountain with some friends. He'd been transfixed as a child by stories of the men who climbed Mont Blanc, and was determined to do the same. Those men had made it to the summit, only to barely survive the trip down. But they, young idiots, had survived and thought themselves very dashing and brave heroes. He'd exulted in their good fortune, and had written a heroic epic about their quest.

He sat and stared out the window blindly. It all seemed so insignificant now. No one cared. Certainly not he.

The rattle of carriage wheels punctured the blankness of his mind. For days he'd listened for that sound, and now he flinched from it. Every day so far it had been Clemency, coming to ask anxiously after his health, or to speak far too cheerfully of her sons, or—worst of all—to retreat with Gerhard and whisper about him.

He closed his eyes when the tap came at the door.

"Richard?" his sister inquired softly.

She knew he was in here; she'd brought him a tray of food a few hours ago. It still sat on the end of his desk, untouched. Richard frowned. Oh yes; Clemency had been here since late morning. Who had just arrived?

"Ja," he said.

She peered around the door. "You have a caller."

He looked at her and said nothing.

She pursed her lips. "Shall I show up your visitor?"

It must be the estate agent. He doubted Clemency would admit anyone else. He sighed, strangely reluctant to see the man. "I will come down."

She nodded and left, closing the door behind her. He looked at the tray and sighed again. She would be upset that he hadn't eaten anything. He took a biscuit and ate it, to mollify her and in an attempt to shake off the lethargy that had engulfed him.

He would go to Zürich, he decided. His parents were both gone but he still had friends and other family there, and he was in no state to plan a longer expedition. It had been so long since he'd gone on one. Perhaps his travels would become more of a tour. He could visit the Americas, or Greece. War had always interfered with his plans to see the Mediterranean. He would visit famous sites and art exhibitions like a normal tourist, instead of joining a caravan of camels heading into the desert.

He went down the stairs and opened the door to the

small parlor. Clemency had had it painted blue and the shrubbery outside the windows cut back, but it was still small and always felt dark. It took him a moment to locate the visitor, who stood looking out the window.

She turned at his entrance. He froze, hand still on the door.

"Thank you for seeing me," Evangeline said quietly, when he was incapable of speech. "I feared you might not."

Slowly he closed the door. "I did not expect you."

Her throat worked, and she seemed to shrink a little. "Mrs. Murray didn't tell you it was I."

"No."

She nodded. She looked tired, with shadows under her eyes and anxious grooves bracketing her mouth. The sunlight from the window caught the silver creeping into her hair. Her clothing was somber and dark, and she wore her pelisse buttoned up, as if she didn't expect to stay long. He didn't know if he wanted her to, or if he wanted her to leave now. The sight of her unleashed a searing mixture of yearning and anguish in his chest.

"If you wish me to leave, I will." She hesitated, darting a wary glance at him. He didn't know how to answer, so said nothing. She drew herself up straighter, gripping her hands together. "I have come to apologize for my behavior and words when last we spoke. I was cruel and unjust to you, and I know I hurt you. I am deeply sorry."

She paused, and he tried to think of something to say. "Is there word from Miss Bennet?"

Her eyes flickered. "She married Burke four days ago."

He'd seen it in the newspaper. "I wish them every happiness," he said.

"Thank you." She wrapped the strings of her reticule around one hand, then unwound them. "My niece came to see me yesterday. She . . . She is happy. She tells me Burke is also well satisfied with the marriage." She paused, biting hard on her lower lip. "I believe her. Time will tell, of course, but she is pleased this is how things turned out. She wished me to extend to you her sincere apologies, and Lord Burke's as well, along with her devout hope that you will not actually shoot Burke." She glanced at him uncertainly.

"No," he replied. "I shall not shoot him now. Love makes a fool of any man."

She blanched and looked away from him.

Yes, love did make a man a fool. Even after the last several days of misery, it ripped at his heart anew to see her so wretched. He didn't want her to leave; he could never want that. Now he knew why he hadn't been able to leave Chelsea, even after she'd told him it was over. He'd been waiting for this. "Is that all you came to say to me?"

Gaze fixed out the window, she gave a slight nod. "I will not ask your forgiveness, because what I did should not be forgiven. You did not deserve anything I said to you. Nothing that happened was your fault."

"It appears to me," he said slowly, trying not to misstep, "that what happened was not your fault, either." She swung around, primed to argue, and he held up one hand. "The young lady was elated to be pursued so ardently by the man she loved. The gentleman was so mad for her that he acted rashly. Neither was in their right mind. If not at that ball, they would have found other opportunities to be . . . indiscreet. Any chaperone can be thwarted, where the desire to do so is that powerful."

She shuddered, looking away.

"Why do you blame yourself?" he asked quietly.

Again she stared out the window for a long moment. Then she turned toward him, without meeting his gaze. "Yes, what you say it true. I know it is, because I thwarted my parents' watchful eyes many times." She wrung the reticule in her hands. "That does not change the fact that I was meant to keep her from trouble, and I failed. Perhaps it is even worse because I knew very well that girls in love will do stupid, reckless things, and men in the grip of desire will entice them into every sort of sin. I, of all people, should have been more on guard against it. To my immense relief, it appears Joan shall not pay a terrible price."

"As you did," he murmured.

She looked at him, her face stark and drawn. "You cannot know . . . No man can. To be handed to a man, a stranger, against your will, and be told that you—and everything that you think of as yours, including your own body—belongs to him. To know that he can beat you, starve you, lock you away from the world, and no one will stop him. To be held responsible for actions you are helpless to prevent, and then to be blamed for a man's terrible behavior."

"I'm glad your husbands are dead," he said in a low voice. "They deserved to die."

Her chin quivered. "I love you, Richard. I have loved you for years, more than I ever thought possible. But marriage has never meant anything *good* to me."

Slowly he nodded, finally understanding. "I frightened you."

"No. That is, it wasn't *you* that frightened me—never. It was . . ." She looked at him, as lost as a child.

Richard had never spent much time thinking about Cunningham or Courtenay. They were both dead, and good riddance. Evangeline almost never spoke of them. Today, though, right now, he felt a surge of hatred for those cruel, arrogant men who had hurt this incomparable woman. "I understand."

She took a deep breath. "You asked me to think about it, and I couldn't bear to. Yet after I sent you away, I could think of nothing else. Even when I knew I'd wrecked any chance of it, I thought of what I had thrown away, and despite my fears and worries, I felt a terrible loss." She put out her hand, which trembled. "You are the center of my happiness. If you still want me, the answer to your question is yes."

He felt lightheaded with shock. God, he'd forgotten to breathe. He took her hand and drew her to him, gently, because she looked as if she might break. When he folded his arms gingerly around her, a shiver went through her before she relaxed against him.

"No," he said softly. "I withdraw my request that you consider marriage."

She tensed.

"It was the wrong thing to ask," he went on, stroking her back in light, lazy circles, which always made her soft and relaxed. "As it turns out, it was not actually marriage I wanted. What I wanted was to be with you, openly and proudly. Marriage was only the first means that came to mind. But on reconsideration, I do not think it will do after all."

She hadn't moved a muscle. "What, then?" she asked, her voice muffled against his shoulder.

"Marriage would make you my property, which I do not want. Marriage would give me all that is yours, which I do not want." He shifted, settling her against him better. She fit so perfectly in his arms. "I was thinking of visiting Zürich again. Come with me. I would like to show you my home, where the air is clean and free of ugly gossip. You can be anything you like there."

"You want me to go with you?"

He smiled down at her. "Wherever I go, I want you with me. Yes."

"But without marriage." She sounded shocked.

Richard took a deep breath and exhaled. "You do not wish to be married. I do not wish to do anything that frightens you. We could be married in our hearts, without setting foot in a church, and that would be enough for me."

"But . . . you would have no rights . . ."

He shrugged. "I never wanted any right to control you. I don't want your money, your property . . . certainly not Prince Louis, who would never consent to be mine! All I want is your company and your love, and no priest is necessary to bless that desire."

She stared at him in amazement. "Everyone will know, when they hear my name . . ."

He smiled ruefully. "My darling, men change their names all the time. Generally to commit an intrigue or to escape the consequences of an intrigue, but they do it. Why shouldn't a woman be permitted the same license?" He pulled a face. "You have been Lady Courtenay for too long. I am thoroughly tired of calling you by that faithless swine's name, as if you were still his."

Her mouth dropped open, and then her face slowly brightened. "You're right!" She fell silent, a distant expression on her face. "Evangeline Campion," she murmured at last, as if tasting the words.

Richard pressed his lips to her temple. "A beautiful name for a magnificent woman."

She smiled, then pulled back to look at him, somber again. "You . . . you will never have children, if you remain with me."

"When have I ever wanted children?" he said in surprise. "Rafael and Gabriel are near enough, and thanks be to God in Heaven, I am only their uncle." He cast his eyes upward. "Gabriel especially promises to lead my sister a frantic dance, and I do not envy her."

Evangeline looked at him, her eyes wet. She put her hand on his cheek. "I don't deserve you."

He laughed. "A restless wanderer with no purpose in life? You deserve far better, but I fear one of my failings is a ruthless streak of selfishness, when it comes to you."

She smiled faintly. "A restless wanderer who hasn't left the tame confines of England in six years."

Richard started, then tipped up her face. He felt a bolt of astonishment that she was right. "Do you know," he said slowly, "until you said that, I had not realized it had been so long. Not once has the desire to wander come over me, in the six years with you." He studied her. "Perhaps I wandered in search of you."

"Don't be silly," she tried to say, before he put a finger to her lips.

"No," he murmured. "I believe it is true. I went in search of adventure because I was restless and impatient at home. What is there to keep a young man of good fortune, no profession, and little family fixed in place?"

"You thrilled to the adventure of it."

"I did." He smiled ruefully. "But not as much as I thrill to the delight of having you in my life. Once I achieved that, there was no longer any need to wander. Alone, that is."

"I have never been away from England," she confessed.

"I can change that." He kissed her hand. "Will you come with me?"

She looked at him with love in her eyes. "Always."

_1823_
Zürich

The chiming of the Grossmünster bells woke her. Evangeline rolled over and stretched. Spring had come to the city, and the windows stood open, admitting the crisp mountain air. She was alone, and for a moment she luxuriated in it—the soft linen of the bedclothes, the fresh breeze, the peaceful music of medieval church bells.

She rose and pulled on her dressing gown. Richard always rose early, she had learned in the last several months, and only on the coldest mornings in winter did she wake to find him still abed beside her. But today was sunny and promised to be warm.

She followed the sound of barking down the stairs and out to the small terrace. There sat Richard, a newspaper in one hand and a piece of bacon in the other. Both dogs sat at perfect attention at his feet, eyes fixed on the bacon. He was speaking to them in German, which Evangeline still had not learned beyond a few words, so she had no idea what he told them—until both lay down and put their heads on their paws. Hercule's tail thumped steadily, swishing the flagstones.

Taking his time, Richard tore the bacon in two and laid a piece before each dog. Neither moved, although Evangeline could see that Louis was nearly vibrating with excitement. "Jetzt," said Richard, and in unison, the dogs lurched forward and devoured the bacon, in one bite in Hercule's case. Louis trotted away to chew his piece under the table.

"You are spoiling them again," she said.

He glanced up, the morning sun winking off the gold frames of the spectacles he'd begun wearing to read. "*You* speak of spoiling them, to me? You, who would feed them roasted goose and syllabub from your own plate? You have no foot to stand on."

She laughed, coming to take the chair across from his. "Just because I spoil them doesn't mean no one else does."

He gave a quiet harrumph and opened his newspaper again. "One piece of bacon will not harm them."

"Was it only one piece, then?" she asked in amusement, as Louis emerged from under the table to lick her hand before sniffing around her feet.

Richard didn't look up from his newspaper, but his mouth curved slightly. "No more will two pieces harm them."

Evangeline lifted Louis into her lap, where he sat and

panted happily, his tongue hanging out. Hercule came over to her side, and she obliged him with a good scratch around the ears before he settled himself with a gusty sigh beside her chair. When Richard wasn't looking, she slipped each dog another small piece of bacon.

Hilde, the maid, emerged with a fresh pot of tea. "Guten Morgen, meine Dame," she said brightly. "Toast, ja?"

"Bitte," said Evangeline, smiling as Hilde hurried back for the toast. She poured herself a cup of tea and for several minutes just sat enjoying it as she stroked Louis's fur.

Richard had taken a house in the Lindenhof, not far from the river Limmat. Evangeline had been charmed by the quaint little town, so different to London. They had taken a circuitous and leisurely route from England, winding through the Low Countries and into eastern France before coming within sight of the Alps and following them to Bern and now Zürich. He had teased her about scaling some of the snow-tipped mountains with him, and she had promised to leave him for a Frenchman if he ever suggested such a thing again. He had taken her to see the goldsmith shops his mother's family owned in Bern, and introduced her to his father's family of bankers, who were still in Zürich. They had been here now for four months, and it might be the most beautiful place Evangeline had ever seen.

Hilde brought in the post, just delivered. Evangeline's brows went up as she took out one letter, much creased and marked from its journey. It was from Marion.

She slid it quietly into her lap and waited until Richard was back behind his newspaper to open it. She and Joan had kept in touch, and Evangeline had nearly stopped holding her breath every time one of her niece's letters arrived. But Joan continued to be in love with her husband, and he continued to give every appearance of reforming into a good husband. In her last letters, Joan had said she was expecting a child, which must have been born by now.

Marion wrote:

Dear Sister,

I have only a little time to write now, forgive me—I will write more later. Joan begged me to write to you at once. This morning she was safely delivered of a fine, healthy son. He is tiny but very loud, to his father's great pride. I will confide between us, that Lord Burke insisted on being in the birthing room, and quite a scene he caused—encouraging Joan as if she were a fighter in a boxing match, urging her to punch him if the desire should take her! I tried in vain to make him leave, although he did cause Joan to laugh at times, but she refused to let him go and clung to his hand so tightly he was bruised.

It was all rather raucous, but I am completely persuaded of their true love and affection. You know what a relief that is, to me and to George.

In any event, I am writing to ask your blessing, and Sir Richard's, for the child's name: Colin Richard. Joan said for months she would have a girl and name her Evangeline, but now it is a boy, and they both wish to know if Sir Richard will consent to this use of his name, and even stand as godfather to the child. I have tried to tell her this is something that must be broached in person, but she is adamant, and begs to know your answer as soon as possible.

I enclose a note from Lord Burke to Sir Richard, begging this honor.

Burke says that if Sir Richard does not approve, they will name the child Colin Richmond, which Douglas tells me is in honor of a boxer Burke particularly admires. As a grandmother, I beg you to intercede with Sir Richard and prevent this . . .

Evangeline was smiling as she finished reading Marion's letter. "My niece has had a son," she said.

Richard's newspaper rustled. "That is excellent news. I trust she and the child are well?"

"Yes." Evangeline folded the letter. "They wish to name him after you."

The newspaper came down. He looked at her, brows raised.

"Colin Richard," she explained. "Colin was Lord Burke's father. They would like you to stand as godfather as well, if you are amenable." She handed him the smaller folded note that had been inside Marion's letter.

Looking startled, he took it. A faint smile curved his lips as he read, then he laughed. "Yes, of course I will. Any child of Burke's will need a godfather of calm and steady temper."

"Then we really must visit soon, to meet the child," she said.

"Of course we must," he replied, as if he had been on the brink of suggesting that very thing.

She beamed at him. He was so unflappable, this man of hers, with the kindest heart.

He went back to his newspaper, and she read the rest of

her letters, including one from Fanny. When Evangeline had told her she and Richard were going abroad together, Fanny had sighed in relief and declared that she couldn't think of anything better for Evangeline's battered spirit. "Tell him to show you a real adventure," she had said, and Evangeline had laughed and replied that being a chaperone had been more than enough adventure for her, and she hoped for a quiet, peaceful journey.

"What a lovely day," she remarked when she had put the post aside.

"It is. On just such a day, it is beautiful in the mountains." He inhaled deeply, giving her a wicked look. "Perhaps you have reconsidered mountain climbing?"

She laughed. "No. I have reconsidered something else."

"Oh?" He put aside the newspaper. "What is that?"

Since they left England, she had allowed people to think her Richard's wife. It had begun with neglecting to correct a servant who referred to her as such, then to allowing innkeepers and hoteliers to believe he was her husband. In every way that made a husband appealing, he was.

In becoming, in some slight way, Mrs. Campion, it had struck her that all her life, she had borne the name of one man after another who had hurt her—first her father, then Cunningham, and finally Courtenay. Richard had said he was tired of calling her by "that swine's" name, and she had finally realized she was also tired of hearing it. Just like the shame he had heaped on her with his indifference, his infidelity, and his ignominious death, she was sick of it, and ready to rid herself of the last traces of Court.

Evangeline Campion sounded much better, to her ears.

Richard had glanced at her in surprise the first time she allowed it, but never said a word of protest. She knew he also liked the sound of it.

And that, she finally realized, was what marriage should be like. *Would* be like, with him.

"It strikes me as a fine day to be married," she said lightly, then darted a quick look at him.

His brows went up. "Married! Who should be the fortunate couple?"

"I shouldn't dare to make such a decision for anyone other than myself."

"I see." He paused. "Have you selected a bridegroom?"

She pretended to think. "You, if you are free."

He studied her for a moment. "I have never been proposed to before. I believe I like it."

"I have never proposed to a man before," she replied. "Heavens, I hope I did it correctly!"

Richard laughed. "You did it splendidly. I do accept."

She smiled back at him. "Very good. Will this afternoon suit you?"

"Perfectly."

And that was that. They lingered over breakfast, then took the dogs for a walk along the river. When they returned home, Evangeline went upstairs and changed her dress. She put on the sapphires Richard had given her a few years ago and her best bonnet, and went downstairs.

He wore a fresh coat, with a sprig of small white mountain flowers pinned to his lapel. To her delight, he handed her a bouquet of the same. Then he offered her his arm.

They walked to the Rathaus, where his cousin Johann,

some official of the town, came out to meet them. Too late Evangeline remembered about the restrictions and requirements for marriage, but to her astonishment, Richard handed over a packet and Johann took it with a nod.

"Oh dear. Did we need to have the banns read?" she whispered as Johann paged through the papers.

Richard smiled. "Only a small matter of forms and declarations. Johann will take care of it."

She glanced at him in surprise. "And you have these forms and declarations already prepared?"

He looked at her. "Whenever one sets out on a long journey into new territories, it is crucial to plan for as many possibilities as you can think of. You never know what might confront you on any given day, and you must be prepared for anything. Yes, I had the forms prepared. I also had a license in England, and the necessary papers in France."

Her mouth dropped open.

"When—or rather, *if*—the proper moment ever arrived, I was determined to be prepared to meet it, without hesitation or delay," Richard went on. "Fortunately, I am also a Protestant. It would have been considerably more challenging if I were Catholic."

Words failed her for several heartbeats. "All this time," she murmured, feeling her face grow hot, "I made you wait—"

"No, no." He covered her hand with his. "I told you, this is merely a formality, to please the rest of the world and, I hope, to resolve any fears you may have. You and your love are all I want."

Evangeline looked at him, the most remarkable man she

had ever known. He'd followed her lead from the first moment they met, not from weakness but from deference to her desires—always. "I do believe I love you more than ever," she whispered.

He leaned closer, his blue eyes twinkling. "Then my plan for our journey together has come off perfectly. Being with you is the most exciting adventure I could ever dream of."

Stay in Touch

If you enjoyed this story, please consider leaving a review online to help other readers. Thank you!

Joan's and Tristan's story can be found in Love and Other Scandals, the first book in the Scandals series.

If you would like access to special previews, giveaways, and my very latest news, join my VIP Readers list. New members get a free exclusive short story as a welcome gift.

Also by Caroline Linden

Scandals

Love and Other Scandals

It Takes a Scandal

All's Fair in Love and Scandal

Love in the Time of Scandal

A Study in Scandal

Six Degrees of Scandal

The Secret of My Seduction

How to Get Away with Scandal

Desperately Seeking Duke

About a Rogue

About a Kiss

A Scot to the Heart

How the Scot Was Won

All the Duke I Need

The Ultimate Epilogue

The Wagers of Sin

My Once and Future Duke

An Earl Like You

When the Marquess Was Mine

About the Author

Caroline Linden was born a reader, not a writer. She earned a math degree from Harvard University and wrote computer software before turning to writing fiction. Since then the Boston Red Sox have won the World Series four times, which is not related but still worth mentioning. Her books have been translated into seventeen languages, and have won the NEC Reader's Choice Award, the Daphne du Maurier Award, and RWA's RITA Award. She lives in New England.

Visit CarolineLinden.com to join her newsletter, and get an exclusive free story just for members.